Moonlight
on the
Mississippi

River Romances, Book Two

Books by Stephenia H. McGee

Ironwood Family Saga
The Whistle Walk
Heir of Hope
Missing Mercy

The Accidental Spy Series
*Previously published as The Liberator Series
An Accidental Spy
A Dangerous Performance
A Daring Pursuit

Stand Alone Titles
In His Eyes
Eternity Between Us
The Cedar Key
The Secrets of Emberwild
The Swindler's Daughter

Time Travel
Her Place in Time
(Stand alone, but ties to Rosswood from The Accidental Spy Series)
The Hope of Christmas Past
(Stand alone, but ties to Belmont from In His Eyes)
The Back Inn Time Series
(Stand alone books that can be read in any order)

Novellas
The Heart of Home
The Hope of Christmas Past

Buy direct from the author's online bookshop!
Support the author and find great deals.

https://shop.stepheniamcgee.com

Moonlight on the Mississippi

River Romances Book Two

Stephenia H. McGee

BY THE VINE PRESS

Moonlight on the Mississippi
Published by: By The Vine Press, LLC
www.StepheniaMcGee.com

Printed in the United States of America

Cover design: Roseanna White Designs
Model photography: Period Stock, LLC
Other images used under license.

Library of Congress Cataloging-in-Publication Data
Names: McGee, Stephenia H. (Stephenia H. McGee) 1983 –
Title: Moonlight on the Mississippi / Stephenia H. McGee
Description: By The Vine Press digital eBook edition | By The Vine Press Trade paperback edition | Mississippi: By The Vine Press, 2024
Summary: A lost treasure, a mysterious disappearance, and a deadly family secret—but winning her heart might be the real challenge.
Identifiers: LCCN 2024937526 | ISBN-13: 978-1-63564-094-6 (paperback)
Subjects: Christian Historical Fiction | Novels

But store up for yourselves treasures in heaven,
where neither moth nor rust destroys,
and where thieves don't break in and steal.
For where your treasure is,
there your heart will be also.
Matthew 6:20–21 (CSB)

T his fella had lost his sunbaked mind beneath that striking mop of smoky-brown hair. Camilla Lockhart stifled a smirk as she propped her hip on the *Alma May*'s wheel. "You'll need to explain why you think *this*"—she slapped one of the spokes—"old gal will help you find a boat at the bottom of the Mississippi."

He opened his mouth, then pressed his lips together.

Why the confusion? If he couldn't see the *Alma May* had sputtered ten years past her usable life and was being held together with a handful of prayers and buckets of tar, then she couldn't help him. They did their best, but they could only do so much for a ramshackle packet boat.

And if he thought she would ever get involved with treasure seekers again, then her first estimation of the nature of his wits had been too generous.

The man—not much older than her own twenty-six years if she didn't miss her guess—tipped his hat back in a roguish way that made her heart give a traitorous tremble.

By her boots, her dog, Lula, rumbled a growl. *Exactly. This fella's too handsome for anyone's good.*

1

"You run a scavenger boat, right?" He rubbed a day's worth of dark scruff and then shoved his hands into the pockets of clean but worn britches.

Camilla snorted. "Who told you that?" She'd wallop them for sure for stirring up old rumors better left buried.

"Look, Miss—"

"Captain."

He blinked. To his credit, the surprise vanished quickly. "Captain Lockhart. I promise this will be a venture worth your while."

A sweltering May breeze poked through the windows and attempted to cool the sweat from her brow. What a mess she must look. Though to be fair, she hadn't planned on receiving company when she'd docked in Natchez. Least of all the handsome sort. She ran a hand down her trousers and hoped there weren't any grease stains.

Lula pawed at her knee, waiting to be picked up. When Camilla scooped up her furry companion and settled the black-and-white terrier on her hip, Lula swayed toward the man, sniffing.

The fellow's face softened, and an endearing tip curved his lips.

Handsome *and* turned a kind eye on her pup? Something in her chest pinched. She needed to get this man off her boat before he could cause all sorts of trouble. Like muddling her senses.

She cocked an eyebrow at his near-threadbare shirt and put her mind back on topic. "I don't indulge in fool's errands."

His cheeks tinged pink, and his broad shoulders straightened. "I don't have the money yet, but as soon as we find that treasure—"

"You mean if. *If* we find this supposed treasure." She blew out a breath and gestured toward the exit. Whoever had let this man into her pilothouse deserved three extra shifts mopping the deck where Lula did her personal business. Camilla turned sideways to squeeze past him and escape.

"Please. You're my only hope."

Maybe it was the desperate notes in his voice. Or perhaps it had something to do with the arresting quality of those emerald-green eyes that seemed to hold a century's worth of life. A girl could get lost in eyes like those. Dangerous waters, that.

Whatever the reason, she and Lula paused at the door. "Mr. ..." She twisted her lips. "What did you say your name was?"

"Gray." He thrust out his hand, and she slid her palm against his calloused one. "Daniel Gray."

His gaze latched onto hers. Snakes and saltwater. This man could convince a common field mouse she was a warhorse, and she'd follow him into battle.

Camilla extracted herself from his grip. "Sorry, Mr. Gray. I wish I could help you."

She'd barely made it three steps from the pilothouse, that unnerving fellow on her heels, when a shout came from the deck.

"Trouble ho!"

Great. What else could go wrong today?

She peered over the pilothouse railing. Finn, one of her three crewmen, cupped his palms by his mouth, ready to shout at her again. He nodded to where two other men glared at one another on the portside.

She scrambled down the ladder.

Her engineer, Solomon, stood on the main deck, arms crossed over his barrel chest. Black eyebrows dove toward his nose, and his generous lips tipped toward a snarl. Oh no. She knew that look.

Sidling past a haphazard stack of crates from their latest job, she placed herself between Solomon and the object of his building fury. "Good morning. How may I help you?"

The stout man in a jacket too heavy for the weather snapped a book shut and angled his upturned nose her way. "Where is your captain?"

Spine straightening out of habit, she waited until she was certain he fully acknowledged her. "I am Captain Lockhart."

His forehead crinkled toward a receding hairline, and he opened his book again to scan the contents. "Yes, Lockhart." Beady eyes flashed toward her, then back to the page. "Where is your father?"

"Dead." The word landed between them like an anchor. "I'm captain now. Licensed by the state of Mississippi."

The man grunted. After a breath, he hiked a meaty thumb toward Solomon. "Your n—"

"Wait." Camilla thrust out her palm. "Unless your next words are about to be *nice* engineer, you best rethink them."

"Engineer?" He slapped the book shut again. "A woman captain and a Negro engineer?"

His laughter caused Solomon to take a step closer, eclipsing the short man in his shadow. The intruder's snickering sputtered out. He cleared his throat. "This vessel is past due for the docking fees." He scanned the page with his finger. "Bringing you to ten dollars. Either you pay now, or you pull out."

Ten dollars? She barely had two nickels to rub together. "If I could get an extension until I get payment for this last job, then—"

He shook his head. "No extensions." He sniffed toward Solomon, whose presence loomed closer, and then he took a step back. "I suggest you get your *crew* out of Natchez."

He spat the word like a curse.

Pain twisted in her empty stomach. Why couldn't he have waited until this afternoon to board their boat? That would have given her time to get some funds together and—

"If I may?" A masculine voice poked through her devolving thoughts.

Mr. Gray? He was still here?

The man strode forward, something extended from his hand. Money?

Not a chance. She plucked the bill from his fingers before the greedy dockmaster could snag it. "We don't need charity, thank you."

She waved the money back at Mr. Gray, but he stuffed both hands into his pockets. "Not charity. Consider it an advance payment."

Her stomach flipped, but she did her best to keep her face passive. "I never agreed to take the job."

They engaged in a battle of wills, her with a determined thrust of her chin and him with a frustrating calm until the dockmaster barked an annoyed cough.

"Whatever details you two want to work out isn't my concern. Pay the fee or disembark. Simple as that."

She couldn't leave. Not until she met with Mr. Copeland and collected their fee for this month's haul. She had a crew to pay and mouths to feed. They'd already stayed with her long after they'd all grown hungry. Mr. Copeland had promised her full payout today if she could meet him before he left for Jackson. They couldn't wait until he returned next week.

If only Papa was here. He'd be able to charm the dockmaster into collecting the fee tomorrow. He'd possessed skills with people she'd never mastered. She pulled in a long breath to steady herself against the wave of grief and shored up her resolve. She could only do her best with the circumstances at hand.

"I'll not be in any man's debt, either." She faced Mr. Gray, still ignoring the dockmaster. Best he knew where they stood.

What she assumed he meant to be a reassuring smile graced his lips. "Not a debt, either, Captain. Simply an advance on a job."

She crossed her arms, whatever ground she'd gained in concealing her desperation slipping out from under her feet. "Nonrefundable, even if we don't find what you are looking for."

He thrust out a hand. "Deal."

After only a brief hesitation, she slapped her palm against his, gave one pump, and then released him to whirl back to the dockmaster.

The bullish man had taken three steps away from Solomon and now had his back pressed against a particularly unstable section of railing. She'd better get him off her vessel before he ended up in the water. No doubt the nasty fella would blame her for his own clumsiness.

She thrust Mr. Gray's money his way. "Here. Now we're paid."

The sweaty man puffed his chest in a poor attempt at pretending he wasn't frightened of Solomon. He snatched the bill from her hand, stuffed it in his jacket pocket, and stroked a mark in his book. Then he snapped it closed and marched down the plank without another word.

Her shoulders deflated. "Always something, isn't it?"

Solomon turned out his palms. Then, as though remembering the other intruder in their midst, he flashed a rapid series of hand gestures.

You want me to toss this one overboard?

A rueful shake of her head swished her braid against her back. "No. I reckon he saved our hides for the day. Best let him leave by his own two feet."

Solomon grunted as his steely gaze swept over Mr. Gray.

"He's harmless." She faced Mr. Gray to judge his reaction. Some men recoiled like they were offended, which told her they took pride in violence. Some grinned too quickly, betraying their desire to be underestimated and thus alerting her to their propensity toward deceit.

Mr. Gray's expression held nothing more than openness and maybe a touch of curiosity.

After a moment, Solomon must have come to the same conclusion she had about any nefarious intentions Mr. Gray might harbor and tapped his finger to his mouth with a nod.

Fine. Holler if you need me.

Grateful, she dismissed him and turned back to Mr. Gray. "I don't appreciate being backed into a deal I didn't want to make."

He shifted his feet. "My apologies. I was only trying to help." He scratched the back of his head. "You can repay the ten dollars if you don't want the job. But you should hear me out first."

Her pulse quickened, and she ground her teeth against the traitorous feeling. No. Hadn't she learned better than to hop at the thrill of discovery? It never ended well. All treasure hunting did was drain resources and leave a person empty-handed. Papa's misfortunes were all the evidence she needed in that regard.

"Please. I need to recover the inheritance to save my family."

She withheld a groan. Now he had to play the knight-in-shining-armor angle? As though she wasn't having a hard enough time turning him down. Against all the better judgment she'd thought she'd earned since she'd lost Papa, a question leaked from between her lips. "What inheritance?"

At the crack in her defenses, a charming smile lit his eyes. "How about I buy you lunch and tell you all about the secret clues we discovered hidden in the estate."

Secret clues? A tingle jittered down her spine.

Snakes and saltwater. She was hooked.

D aniel stuffed a nervous hand into his pocket and gestured down the gangplank with the other. The captain's engineer sighted them and stalked over, his hands flying in a series of complicated movements.

This time Captain Lockhart didn't reply out loud. Her hands flashed rapid responses. The engineer frowned, then daggered a glare at Daniel.

Not sure what else to do, he turned out both palms. "She has nothing to fear from me. But you're welcome to join us for lunch if you'd like. I'm sure she'll want to go over my proposition with you before making any commitments anyway."

Both of them stared at him like he'd sprouted gills. Had he said something wrong? Perhaps he'd misjudged the nature of Captain Lockhart and her engineer's relationship. He hadn't meant any offense.

The towering man emphasized another gesture, then thrust his chin toward Daniel.

Captain Lockhart notched her hands on her hips. "Solomon says he likes you. Which doesn't happen often." Before relief could fully take hold, she added, "But he said if anything happens to me, he will..."

She tilted her head to the side, signed something suspiciously like gutting an animal, then lifted her eyebrows.

Solomon bobbed his head.

"He said..." Pink colored her cheeks. "He said if you prove him wrong about you, then he will skin you like a fish." A grimace accompanied the last part.

Daniel had to catch his laugh before they took his relief the wrong way. Instead, he managed a respectful nod. "I'd expect nothing different from a captain's loyal engineer."

That earned a snort, but the big man strode away to motion at a skinny redhead with a gesture easily interpreted as "get back to work."

Captain Lockhart plucked a wristwatch with a broken armband from her pocket and squinted at the time. "I only have an hour before an important meeting, so you best find a fast way to convince me this isn't a harebrained scheme held together with nothing more than vague rumors and assumptions."

As there was indeed an abundance of rumors and no shortage of assumptions, he opted for a hopeful smile and nodded to the gangplank. He'd likely jumped too far ahead of himself. It would have been better to gather more evidence before he attempted to make his case and solicit help. He didn't have the first idea where to start in what he had once considered a ridiculously fanciful endeavor. But the providential sighting of the *Alma May* docked in Natchez on the very day he discovered the Lockhart name secreted away proved too much of an opportunity to waste.

If he couldn't convince her to have mercy on his plight, he'd have to find another way. Just because his father had worked with hers didn't mean she was his only option.

There had to be someone prepared to journey through turbulent waters to unknown locations. Surely some other captain intimately familiar with the dangers of this stretch of river would be willing to risk life, limb, and vessel to help him for only a promise of a cut of the treasure....

If he found it.

Tamping down the newest wave of doubt, Daniel pressed forward. Too much depended on him, so how could he not fight for what they needed with every shred of his being? No matter how foolish it seemed.

Captain Lockhart sauntered down the rickety plank, a braid so deeply brown it bordered on black swinging against a work shirt more suited to a man than a sprightly woman. But then, everything from her cocked newsboy hat to her scuffed boots said she'd intentionally dressed as a man.

Only her thick, shiny locks and the smallest touch of lip rouge suggested any interest in feminine frivolity. That and the clean scent of something floral he'd caught as she'd passed him.

Not that she could hide her appeal, even dressed that way. He'd never seen the like.

She stopped on the dock, head cocked to the side. A sullen breeze attempted to nudge a loose lock of hair by her temple but gave up under the heavy humidity.

He shifted his thoughts to recover whatever words had exited her rosy mouth but had failed to find meaning in his ears. "Beg your pardon. I didn't catch that."

She hiked a dark eyebrow toward the shabby brown cap. "I asked if you had a destination in mind."

Oh. Right. He had invited her to eat. Never mind he'd spent almost everything he'd had in his wallet to keep her in port. "Are you opposed to sandwiches while we discuss business overlooking the water?"

She shrugged and returned her steady pace toward the hill leading to the town proper.

"Wait!" He thumbed the other direction. "I know a place this way."

Her nose wrinkled. "You want to take me to a tavern under the hill?" She glanced toward the boat, clearly waffling over marching up the gangplank again.

"It's not like that. I promise."

Shallow lines formed the corners of her intelligent eyes as she studied him, but then curiosity must have won out because she pivoted in the other direction.

He couldn't blame her. Natchez Under the Hill didn't have a sterling reputation for good reason. But these days, moral folk made an honest living and carved out a pocket of decency in what had traditionally been a hive for undesirables.

Thankfully, the place he had in mind stood on the outskirts. He matched his stride to the woman who only reached his shoulder. "Thank you for your time, Captain Lockhart. I'm sure you are busy, so I appreciate you considering my situation."

The sultry breeze mustered more strength and played with a lock of her hair, sending it skittering over her nose. Deep-brown eyes studied him with an intensity he'd not often encountered. "Lula and Solomon both think you seem decent enough, so that earns you a half hour."

"Lula?"

She checked her watch and then stuffed it back into her pocket. As they walked, the sharp cliff of the riverbank rose higher. "My dog. Named for the Tallulah River. I call her Lula for short."

A chortle rumbled from his chest. "Glad she approves of me."

Captain Lockhart grunted. "I didn't say that. But she didn't take off one of your fingers, so that saved you from Solomon chunking you overboard."

He sobered, unsure if she was joshing or not. "Solomon. He's your engineer."

"And my father's closest friend."

"I'm sorry for your loss."

"Thank you." Only the twitch of her nose gave any indication the grief still stung. She cleared her throat. "Where are we going?"

Daniel followed her gaze to the general store boasting "Moses and Sons Cheap Cash Store" on a rough-hewn sign protruding from a brick building. Several similar edifices huddled along a dirt road snaking along the river's edge, most in need of more tending than the residents could afford.

"It's up ahead." He moved over to allow a cart to pass, the weary gelding's plodding steps stirring up dust.

Boats crowded the landing on the other side of the street, and the scent of silty water, sweaty men, and a variety of goods from tobacco to cotton thickened the air. Men hustled from general goods stores and greeted one another with nods as they loaded supplies into waiting wagons.

"Hmm. Not quite the den of debauchery I was expecting." Captain Lockhart mumbled as Daniel tipped his cap to a boy of about fourteen carrying a fifty-pound sack of flour.

Spices and the smell of fresh bread broke through the river of other scents and tickled his nose. His stomach rumbled in response, and he quickened his pace. "Almost there. Anna makes the best po'boys you'll ever eat."

She stopped. "Poor boys?"

He flashed a grin and hurried forward, leaving her to succumb to curiosity and follow him. A good quality. One desired a healthy dose of curiosity in a person he wanted to decode clues with.

They approached a squat tin-roofed structure wedged between two brick buildings. Some twenty years ago, Anna's father had closed in the alley between a warehouse and a dry-goods store. A resourceful use of the tiny strip of land he'd purchased from both owners for minimal cost.

The boards on the narrow front stoop sagged under Daniel's weight as he pulled open the door, causing a bell to ring overhead. Fried seafood, yeasty bread, and horseradish washed over him, and he savored it before motioning Captain Lockhart inside.

"They bake their own bread every morning and fry up whatever Anna's brothers can bring in, but the crawfish are my favorite. Fried with extra pickles. But she also serves an *étouffée* that'll have you licking your fingers."

Captain Lockhart chuckled and followed him to the counter set behind two narrow rows of two-person tables. Only three were currently occupied, as most patrons took their wrapped sandwiches and headed back to work.

"Danny boy? Is that you?" Anna slapped a kitchen towel over her shoulder and squeezed her girth out from behind the counter. "I ain't seen you in a coon's age! Where you been?"

Coon's age happened to be roughly a week ago. He wrapped the motherly woman in a familiar embrace. "You know. Just taking care of Mabel and the boy and trying to get everyone settled." He extracted himself from her grip. "How are you?"

"Fat and sassy, like always." She winked. "Who's your lady friend?"

Captain Lockhart's lips twitched into a smile as she extended a hand. "Captain Camilla Lockhart."

"Captain?" Anna fanned her face. "Ain't that somethin'? Didn't think we'd had no female captains since Blanche took over the *Natchez*."

The Queen of the Mississippi, famous as the first licensed female steamboat captain.

Captain Lockhart's grin grew. "Yes, ma'am. There's been a couple of us, but Captain Leathers is an inspiration."

"Got you a good one, Danny boy." Anna smacked his shoulder. "Takes a strong woman to do what she does. Best you give her all the respect she deserves."

Daniel spread his hands. "I wouldn't dream of doing anything less."

Captain Lockhart shifted her feet and averted her gaze from Anna's open consideration, but her twitching lips gave away her pleasure.

Anna patted his cheek. "Good boy. Now, what you two want to eat? I got *court bouillon*, and then we got river cats, *crevette*, and chicken livers for the po'boys today."

After Anna shuffled back behind the counter, Captain Lockhart's harsh whisper stopped Daniel's forward progress across the brick floor.

"Cats? Did she say cats?"

Anna burst into laughter, the frayed ends of her yellow hair wrap dancing on her shoulder. "*Pauvre ti bête.*"

At his look, Anna translated. "Means poor little thing."

Captain Lockhart smirked. "Who? The cat or me?"

That earned another round of laughter from Anna. And judging from the twinkle in the younger woman's eyes, that had been her intention. To solidify his suspicion, the fetching riverboat captain winked at him.

Anna dabbed her face and called something in French over her shoulder to one of her brothers working in the kitchen before turning back to her guest. "My family, we are Cajun. Danny boy here knows the basics well enough to eat what he wants."

Taking the cue, he explained the unfamiliar words. "Court bouillon is a spicy tomato-based stew made with fish filets, onions, and mixed vegetables. Crevette means shrimp. So, for the po'boys today she has fried shrimp, catfish, and chicken livers." He darted his gaze back to Anna, who stood smirking at them. "No crawfish today?"

She snorted. "Now you know it's getting too hot for them critters. Shoulda come see me a month or two ago. Had 'em in bucketfuls. As it is now, we was right lucky Mo got them crevette. Came packed in ice kept cold by one of them fancy generators, they did. Big fat ones they brought up from the Pontchartrain this mornin'."

"And what exactly is a 'poor boy'?" Captain Lockhart eyed the man nearest to her seated at one of the ladder-backed chairs, thick hunk of crusty bread in his hand.

"It's a French baguette stuffed with goodness. You'll love it." Daniel tapped the counter, his stomach having grown impatient with all the talk of food. "I'll have the shrimp."

"Extra remoulade sauce and pickles?"

"Of course." He glanced back at Captain Lockhart.

She shrugged. "Make it two."

A handful of minutes and a goodbye hug to Anna later, Daniel tucked the paper sack into the crook of his elbow and held open the door for Captain Lockhart.

They strolled in silence back toward the *Alma May*. She didn't speak as they passed her steamer and made the turn to climb the hill into Natchez. From atop the hill, the scene struck him as it always did.

The water glistened in the sunlight, a highway of vessels taking people on one adventure or another. He led her to a bench overlooking the cliff and took a seat. She settled next to him, delicately crossing her ankles.

He fished a sandwich from the sack and handed it to her, then revealed a special treat he'd whispered to Anna without Captain Lockhart's notice.

"Coca-Cola?" Her eyes lit, sending a strange sensation through his center.

He grinned and notched the cap against the metal arm of the bench. Then he popped the bottom of the glass bottle, snapping the top off with a fizzling hiss. He held the bottle out to her.

"Impressive."

The warm sensation in his center intensified, and heat crawled up his neck. Why should he care if he'd easily impressed such an accomplished woman? "I've had plenty of practice."

He cracked the cap on his bottle and then unwrapped the paper from his sandwich, tearing it so the end in his hand remained wrapped to catch any sauce that might squirt free.

The woman at his side did the same, and he waited to watch her take a bite.

She chewed slowly, then swallowed. "Pretty good. I'll have to see about getting some of these for my crew."

"How long will you be in town?" He sampled a small bite, and a delightful burst of Cajun spices and crispy batter erupted on his tongue.

"Just long enough to get the payment due to my crew. So you better get to talking." She took another bite and focused on the river.

Right. Straight to business. He'd practiced how to approach this request on the way to her boat. How to frame it in the right way so she understood what was at stake. "There are these stories in my family—"

She groaned and shook her head. "Mr. Gray, I'm not about to take my crew on a goose chase based on old family lore."

She hadn't let him finish. Horsefeathers. She'd hardly let him start! He pulled a breath through his nose and let it out, then started again. "These stories have been passed down for generations, and none of us thought much of them. Just tales to entertain children. Until I found proof."

"Proof?" She paused, the already half-eaten sandwich hovering near her lips.

How had she devoured it so quickly? She stared at him, expression less than patient.

He cleared his throat and attempted a curtailed description of recent events. "After my grandfather passed, leaving his estate to me, I discovered certain documentation that leads me to believe these were more than mere stories."

"Written accounts of family lore are no more proof than the tales people tell." She wedged the bread between her teeth and tore off a hunk.

Daniel stifled his irritation. "There's more than that."

She washed down another mouthful with the soda and cast him a sidelong glance. "Like what?"

"I'm not comfortable telling you too many details until—"

"Then I'm not comfortable risking my crew's lives for a bunch of fairy tales."

He clenched his sandwich, and two fried shrimp plopped to his lap, leaving a grease smudge. "No one asked you to risk their lives. You make it sound like taking me downriver to a location of my choosing is akin to signing your crew up for war."

She twisted to face him fully. "Asking my men to work without pay is a risk to their lives. We have to eat." To emphasize the last word, she snatched another hunk from her sandwich.

His gaze traveled along the line of boats near the water. The *Alma May*'s twin stacks stretched toward the sky, weary and worn with age. His father's notes said the boat had been named for Captain Lockhart's great-grandmother and predated the War Between the States.

How much did it cost to maintain such a vessel? She had to make decent money running goods, as a seasoned captain was the only way to traverse the Wicked River safely. A river captain's intimate knowledge of the hidden dangers lurking beneath the dark waters meant the difference between surviving or not.

Apparently, the details of the progression of events he'd encountered weren't going to be the way to convince her. He switched to a more direct tactic. "What's it going to take to hire you to ferry me downriver?"

She crumpled the empty paper in her fist and brushed crumbs from her lips. "Depends on where you want to go."

"Not far." Hopefully. Anything he'd gleaned thus far didn't suggest a long journey, at least.

Her gaze spiked through him, obviously disenchanted by his vagueness.

"And I'll need you to help me decode a few clues." He forced the words from between lips that wanted to bite down on them.

"Me?" Her eyes narrowed. "Why?"

He gripped the edge of the bench. This would be the moment. She'd either dive in with him or send him running. "Because I found your name in a hidden journal inside a secret room at my grandfather's estate."

And your father was the last man to see mine.

Those words he kept to himself. She likely wouldn't be ready for that revelation.

The paper fell from Captain Lockhart's hand. She opened her mouth, but no words came free.

At least he'd secured her full attention.

She'd been right from the start. This fella had lost his sunbaked mind. "My name? You're sure?"

Mr. Gray shrugged. "Your father's, more likely."

Her stomach pitched like she'd run aground at full steam. "Papa?"

Snakes and saltwater. The way her voice squeaked, she sounded like a cabin boy who hadn't yet grown into a man. She cleared her throat. Not that it helped any. Her pipes had closed up right good.

"I believe so, yes." Mr. Gray leaned forward and propped his elbows on his knees. "That name led me to the Natchez docking records where I discovered the, um, unfortunate loss of your father. Imagine my surprise when I happened to see that very vessel docked on the banks on my way home."

Heat combusted in her center, stoked by shards of loss, indignation, and fury. Some words on a page could never encompass the truth of what she'd lost. Or why.

She stood and wiped her hands on her trousers. "Thank you for the meal, Mr. Gray. I'll be on my way now."

He lurched from the bench. "Wait! You haven't heard the rest of my story."

The details hardly mattered. She crossed her arms. "Let me guess. You found some clues about an old family treasure. Probably during the war. Everyone thought it was lost, but wait! You've discovered something no one else has in all these years, and now you are the only one who can uncover the true location."

His lips parted, and his jaw dropped a fraction with each throttled word. "He already told you about it?"

These things were all the same. Every family had a tale like... Wait. What? "Who told me what?"

"Your father. He told you about the Hollis treasure?"

The name punched a hole through her chest, and she slumped back onto the bench. She forced air into her lungs. "You said your name was Gray."

A crease sank between his brows. "I did. But this is the Hollis treasure. You know of it?"

"I know it cost me my father." The swell of heat renewed, and she popped to her feet. "Good day, Mr. Gray."

Politeness dictated she wish him fortune on his hunt, but she couldn't bring herself to force the words from her lips as she started to walk away. Nothing good came from treasure hunting. People lost everything in the hopes of filling their empty pockets. Instead, they left their families with nothing more than shredded ambitions and a gallon of sorrow.

She'd have no part of it.

Despite the clear communication of her intent, Mr. Gray gained her side and increased his pace to match hers as she all but scurried like a frightened mouse back to the safety of home.

"Captain Lockhart, if you'll just listen. There's a lot more—"

"I don't care. My crew is close to starving now. All the thanks they get for sticking with me. I am not going to reward their loyalty by taking them down this current again. I won't."

"But what if I know where it is?"

She planted her feet and jerked to a halt. "Impossible. Every fool always says that, but he has nothing more than hunches. My father said the same thing. And besides, if you already knew the location, you wouldn't need my help decoding clues."

"Your father..." Lines tightened around his eyes, and her stomach dove toward her knees. "Your father and mine were looking together. I think they were close. The problem is I don't think you know what really happened that night."

"And you do?" The words snapped from her lips. Wait. Had he said...? "What are you talking about? My father never worked with a Mr. Gray."

Red snaked up from his shirt collar and painted his ears. "He went by Mr. Dixon."

The name hit her like a volley. Her teeth clenched, and she had to force them open. "Why?"

"Something I intend to discover myself." He thrust his hands into his pockets, but not before she caught their tremble. And his tone left no doubt the revelation had not been welcome.

She resumed her walk back to the boat. Mr. Dixon had lied about his name. Then what else had he fabricated? Had he been using Papa?

Suspicions she'd tried to bury resurfaced, tugging along her nerves and making her fingers twitch.

"Captain, if I may, I understand this is troubling news." Mr. Gray's elbow bumped her in his haste, and he widened the distance between them to a respectable arm's length. "But it's why I came to you. I believe we both want answers about what happened to our fathers."

Her forward momentum stalled, and she stumbled. Thankfully, she caught herself before she went tumbling down the hill. She shouldn't be listening to his rambling. Only trouble waited on the end of that line. But if he really had clues...

What if something he knew might help her understand what had happened to Papa?

21

She swallowed the lump gathering in her throat and studied the man holding out one hand to catch her should she choose this moment to resume her fall.

How could she trust the son of a man who had lied to them? Then once again, her mind caught up with all he'd said.

"Your father is also dead?"

One sharp nod.

"How?"

"I'm hoping to find out."

The tight lines of his shoulders and his stiff posture indicated he spoke truth. She kept her roiling emotions out of her voice. "Mr. Dixon—whoever he was—wasn't with Papa that night. He'd abandoned him."

Mr. Gray winced. "I know. From what I can piece together, Father went missing right before he was to meet Captain Lockhart."

Air rushed from her lungs. That changed everything. If something had happened to Mr. Dixon—no, Gray—then perhaps Mr. Dixon wasn't a murderer after all. But with a false name, it was no wonder she'd never been able to track the man down.

His being dead played a part too.

She set her shoulders and attempted a calm exterior in defiance of the storm pitching around in her stomach. "It seems there are some things you and I need to discuss."

"Yes, Captain. That's what I've been trying to tell you."

She could hardly begrudge him his tinge of annoyance. She had cut him off more than once without hearing him through. She fished Papa's watch from her pocket. Not much time.

"I have to collect my crew's wages. You can wait on *Alma May* if Solomon doesn't mind. If not, come back in about an hour. Then we'll talk."

He parted his lips as though planning a protest, then must've thought better of it, and snapped his mouth closed. Good. If it was important enough to him, he wouldn't mind the wait. And she didn't have a choice.

She escorted him back to the boat and waved up at Solomon, who stayed near the railing. Probably watching for her return.

Is it all right if he waits here with you until I get back? We have more to discuss with this fella.

Solomon's sharp gaze traveled to Mr. Gray, and he nodded. Solomon could hear her just fine, but the language of hand gestures he and his mother had taught her years ago proved a convenient way to speak privately with her engineer.

She gave him the thank-you sign by extending a flat palm from her lips downward and then returned her focus to the man at her side. "He says it's fine for you to wait on the port deck. Don't cause any issues for my crew."

"I'm not a child, Captain Lockhart. I can manage to wait without getting myself into mischief." An amused tilt to one eyebrow accompanied words that came out cool and businesslike.

Heat pulsed in her ears. Right. She smeared her hands on her trousers and stuck her hand out. "Camilla, when you're not addressing me in public, will be acceptable."

The amused tilt shifted to a surprised climb toward his cap. "An honor, Captain. You have my thanks. Please, call me Daniel."

After a single pump, she released his hand and spun on her heel. Well. That had been awkward. What was wrong with her wits? Of all the things to say to the man, why had that been what escaped her mouth?

She scrambled back up the hill to the town proper. She needed to focus on her task, but her thoughts kept drifting back to Mr. Dixon. Too well she remembered the day he'd come to the *Alma May* dressed in a fine linen suit and brandishing stories of lost gold and certain fortune. She spit to the side as though she could clear the bitter taste from her mouth.

A woman in a fashionable calf-length pink skirt gasped and bounced away before anything could land on her black-and-white oxfords. She blinked at Camilla in confusion as they passed one another. Camilla tried to offer the lady an apologetic smile, but the woman only clutched her gloved hand to her pearl necklace and shook her head.

Camilla stuffed her hands in her pockets. There were a few perils to having been reared on a boat with a bunch of men. One did forget the finer details of being a lady from time to time. Still, she wouldn't have changed her life on the river with Papa for anything. She only wished she still had him at her side.

She should have changed into her going-to-town clothes, but Mr. Gray's arrival had spiraled all her plans into an impossible heap. Would Mr. Copeland be affronted if she showed up in trousers instead of a sturdy skirt?

Nothing for it now.

The bustle of Natchez swarmed around her, folks going about their tasks for the day. Checking the post office for parcels and heading to the market. Or whatever else people who stayed in one place all the time did. She hardly knew.

They'd had a house on the water's edge when she'd been a small girl. But after Mama died of tuberculosis, Papa left the house and everything in it. They'd never returned. Sometimes she wondered if she could find that old house again. But the memories were too hazy, and she'd never talked herself into asking Papa.

She brushed old memories aside as she reached her destination. The stoic brick edifice crowded close to the street, hardly leaving room for the hitching post notched at its side. No space for motorcars.

"Copeland Enterprises" painted in bold golden letters swung from a carved sign overhead, the chains silently swaying in the breeze.

The polished brass knob cool against her sweaty palm, she opened the door and stepped inside. They'd been lucky to secure a job from such a fine establishment.

Afternoon sunlight poured through head-high windows and bathed the stone floor in a yellow glow. The flat slabs had been artfully pieced together, the edges connecting almost seamlessly. How did they do that? Cut the edges to make them fit or keep working to find the right stone to match its neighbors?

"May I help you?" A pinched male voice pulled her attention to the receiving desk squatted in the center of the room.

She propped an elbow on the polished wood. "I'm here to see Mr. Copeland."

Droll eyes met hers. "And you are?"

"Captain Lockhart." She put a touch more emphasis on the first word, lest he think her a waif from off the street.

A bushy gray eyebrow twitched. She should have put on the skirt.

He ran a finger down his ledger. "Come to deliver a message in your father or brother's stead?"

Apparently, she'd not put enough emphasis on her title after all. She stretched her lips into a pleasant smile. "No, sir. I speak for myself. My crew and I did a delivery for Mr. Copeland, and he is supposed to relinquish payment today."

He tapped a bony finger on the page. "I see no notation about a recompense or a *lady* coming to collect it."

Her fingers tightened on the desk's edge. "I have a scheduled meeting with Mr. Copeland. So if you please, I'll see myself to his office."

The businessman's domain had to be back there behind this ancient gatekeeper somewhere. She'd knock on every door if she had to.

The elderly man moved with more swiftness than she'd thought possible of one so stooped. She'd scarcely made it past his bastion before his clawed fingers pinched down on her elbow.

"You will do no such thing."

Icy currents rolled over her. "You will release me. Now."

His fingers creaked off her sleeve, and she snatched her arm away. "Mr. Copeland promised payment today, and I aim to retrieve it."

Upper lip curling, the rusty codger stalked ahead of her to a hallway behind his desk. He rapped an enlarged knuckle on the first slab of oak to the left. At the answering call, he cracked the door.

"Sir, a young woman here claims to be a captain in seek of payment. How would you like me to dispatch her?"

Camilla dug her nails into her palms. Of all the condescending—

"Captain Lockhart? Send her right in."

Papa would have said a lady never let pride paint her face, but she couldn't help the satisfied smirk as she sauntered into the room.

The grumpy man closed the door behind her without a word.

Mr. Copeland rose and extended a hand. "Don't mind Mr. Naples. He's a...traditional sort."

She accepted his smooth handshake and settled into the leather chair in front of his desk. "Thank you for seeing me today before your trip, Mr. Copeland. My crew and I are grateful for your accommodation."

Dressed in a tailored black suit with a powder-blue tie, Mr. Copland had the kind of features most women swooned over. A strong jawline and a thick head of sandy hair styled with pleasantly scented pomade. But Papa always said the eyes gave away a man's true nature, and Mr. Copeland appeared as slick as an eel's underbelly.

"Yes, well, about that." He loosened his jacket button and draped his tall frame into the masculine chair with little concern.

Her heartbeat pounded against her rib cage, but somehow, she remained poised on the edge of her plush seat. She even held his gaze without showing the terror his words incited.

Well, except for the way her hands kept twisting together in her lap. But perhaps he didn't notice. She stilled them anyway.

"There was an unexpected problem with your payment." He laced his fingers together on the desk.

"Problem? I don't understand."

He drew out his words as though needing to explain shifting currents to a babe. "You see, I can't pay you until I've been paid. I encountered an unforeseen delay in receiving my remittance from the client. But rest assured, I've been promised we will have the funds next week. Two at the most."

She glued her eyes wide in an attempt to dissuade dreadful tears from springing free.

He reached for a pad of paper. "Shall I wire for a bank transfer once it arrives? That way you won't have to schedule a time to return here."

Keeping her tone even, she measured her words. "As I'm sure you can understand, we need to restock before leaving Natchez. We anticipated using the funds promised today to do so." She pushed steel into her voice. "Surely a company of this size has available funds to cover its scheduled payments for hired work."

His smile soured though his words remained pleasant. "I do wish it worked that way, Miss Lockhart." He rose and buttoned his jacket. "I'll have Mr. Naples make a note to wire the money to your bank as soon as we receive it. Be sure to leave your banking details with him before you go."

The hand gesturing to the door blurred. This couldn't be happening. Her insides squeezed, and she grabbed the armrest. Her pulse thrummed.

Whatever platitudes Mr. Copeland cooed as he helped her to her feet and guided her out of his office fell on deaf ears.

The door clicked with finality behind her, leaving her alone in the hallway decorated with fine oil paintings. Bet one of those would fetch enough to feed her crew for a week. Her fingers itched toward it, and she forced her hand into her pocket.

Lord, what are we going to do now?

The engineer thrust a beefy palm in Daniel's direction and twitched his fingers in a motion universally known as "come here." Obliging, he lengthened his stride and scaled the gangplank. The towering man met him with arms crossed over his barrel chest. Despite his stance meant to intimidate, humor flickered in Solomon's eyes.

Tension loosened from Daniel's shoulders. He rubbed the back of his neck and let his gaze roam over the deck. "Anything I can do to help while I wait?"

Solomon's immediate reaction proved Daniel's suspicion that the man could hear. Did that mean he could also speak but chose not to? Or had some kind of injury prevented speech but not hearing? Not his place to ask.

Solomon regarded him while a shorter, leaner man with a mop of red hair sidled up. This had been the man who called Captain Lockhart when the dockmaster had arrived.

The newcomer thumbed at Daniel. "Captain say he could be here?"

Solomon grunted.

"You want me to keep an eye on him?"

Solomon pointed at Daniel and then put a hand to his chin and extended it forward. Then he bumped one fist on top of the other.

The redhead grinned. "He says he'll work, do he? What's he after? Trying to court our captain?"

The friendliness on Solomon's face shifted to storm clouds. Before he could make any gestures to get Daniel thrown overboard, Daniel thrust out his palm.

"I'm only here to hire the *Alma May*. Captain Lockhart had business to attend, so she asked me to wait on her. Not being a man who cares for idleness, I offered to help while I wait. But if I'll only be in your way, I can find a place to make myself scarce."

The crewmen exchanged a glance, and then the redhead shrugged. He extended a rough palm to Daniel. "I'm Finn Wallace. Kind of a second mate, if you will."

Solomon rolled his eyes.

Finn adjusted the stained collar of a work-worn shirt. "If you got time to waste, then we got work to fill it. That is, if you don't mind getting your hands dirty."

More likely than not, he'd be walking himself into some kind of sport for these crewmen, but Daniel gave a nod all the same.

Finn clapped Solomon on the back. "Look-a-there. Seems I don't got deck duty after all."

The grin splitting Solomon's face sent a shock of cold through Daniel's gut, but he tried not to let it show. Solomon nodded to Finn, and the wiry man slapped his hands together.

"All right. Bucket and mop's this way." He sauntered past the engineer, leaving Daniel to follow.

He'd be mopping the deck? And here he'd anticipated something a bit more laborious. Or at least dirty. Like cleaning the black smoke off the steam engine or shoveling coal or the like. Why did mopping a deck instead of Finn garner such a response?

He had to be missing something.

The steamer's open bottom deck had been swept clean, and rolls of burlap had been piled to one side. Looked as though their last haul might have been tobacco, though he didn't know much about such things to tell. They passed between the support poles holding the weight of the cabins on the deck above and exited to a small open space behind the engine room.

Finn plucked a mop from where it propped against the wall. "The moping part ain't so bad. The worst of it is when you got to scrape what's gotten dried on." He plucked a bucket from the deck and thrust it at Daniel. "Drop this down to get some water. You might want to slosh a few buckets first to soften things up. Good luck."

With a satisfied smirk, the man scurried away.

How odd.

Then Daniel noticed the piles. Was that...?

A burst of rapid-fire barking hit him at the same instant as the revelation. Captain Lockhart's feisty little terrier. The black-and-white dervish slid around the corner, tail curled up over her back and hackles porcupine stiff.

Would the dog bite? He stilled. Her teeth couldn't poke through the thick leather of his boots. She didn't come closer. Instead, she positioned herself about three feet from him and continued her ferocious announcement of his presence, the intensity of which sent her front paws bouncing up and down on the deck.

"Whoa there, little one."

His attempt at friendship fell flat as the creature continued to bounce. Over the ruckus, he could have sworn he heard snickering. Heaving a sigh, he risked stepping past the dog to lower the bucket over the rail. The coarse rope slid through his hand and splashed into the water below. Once it sank beneath the surface, he hauled it back up.

Lula, if he remembered the dog's name correctly, continued her assault on his ears as he skirted around her and heaved the bucket of water across the planks to dislodge the unpleasant debris. Thankfully, the waste sloshed over the edge of the boat. Didn't look like they left it out here to bake for more than a day at a time. Lula didn't care for the remaining liquid heading her way and took a momentary reprieve from her vocalization to reposition her paws.

"Who put you to swabbing Lula's deck?" The feminine bewilderment garnered both man and canine's attention, and Daniel turned to find Captain Lockhart eyeing him with one hand cocked on her hip.

Lula gave a sharp bark and scurried to her mistress. The lady bent at the knees, and the dog ran up her body like a squirrel up a tree. Captain Lockhart settled the critter on her hip in one smooth motion. Lula shot her nose into the air and let out a howl just in case Captain Lockhart hadn't been apprised of Daniel's presence.

"Hush, Lula."

The dog lowered her snout with a whine but fell silent.

Captain Lockhart gestured at the deck. "We all take turns doing this job. Let me guess. Finn talked you into doing his shift? He'll earn double duty for that."

Not wanting to get anyone in the line of fire, Daniel shrugged. "I told them I didn't mind helping out while I waited for you." He lowered the bucket. "Your meeting took less time than I expected."

She huffed a breath that stirred a lock of dark hair clinging to her forehead. "Yes, well. I'm available now." She waved to the deck. "Leave that for Finn."

"Yes, Captain," he replied with only a touch of humor.

She caught it anyway. "Camilla is fine. No sense standing on formality today."

What difference did today make when dealing with a person's proper address? It might be better not to ask. He followed her from the stern and up a set of stairs to the second level.

He didn't know much about steamers, but the layout seemed similar to others he'd boarded for transport. The lower deck consisted of open space suitable for hauling cargo or livestock, while the upper deck housed the living quarters for the crew and any other necessary spaces such as a galley and storerooms.

He followed Camilla down a narrow hall toward the bow and waited while she opened a room on the right. Inside, polished wood paneling covered the floor, walls, and ceiling. A bulky desk he assumed would be bolted to the floor guarded the view of a wide window behind the cracked leather of a hearty chair. Camilla sauntered over and plopped her frame into the contours, then gestured to the stiff wooden seat on the other side. Lula turned a circle and sat in her lap, staring at Daniel with her bat-like ears twitching.

He settled his frame and took in the bookshelves covering the wall to his left. "Do those books fall off a lot?"

"I put them back if they do."

"Do you like to read?"

She laced her fingers together on top of a fat ledger, the only item on the desk. "Yes."

Right. Straight to business. "You should see for yourself what I discovered. It will be easier than trying to relay all the details."

Rather than a regular response, she held up her hand and began counting off questions on each finger.

"What type of excursion are you planning? How long will it take, how many people are you bringing with you, and what is your proposed payment?" She pointed a finger at him. "And if your only plan for payment is a cut of the treasure *if* we find it, then this conversation is over. I can't power my boat and feed my people on promises."

Lula twitched her ears each time the captain's wrist brushed against fur.

Fair enough. "As to the duration, I am unsure. The location should only be within your preferred stretch of the river, between here and Louisiana. Most likely staying close to Natchez. No other people will be accompanying us unless you have need of some type of additional help in areas beyond my experience. As for payment..."

He ran through the numbers in his head. Grandfather hadn't left much by way of available money, though they should be able to sell a few assets. They didn't really need that fancy new automobile, did they? It'd be worth the trade to secure the *Alma May*. Besides, if Mabel wanted one, he could always purchase his sister another once he had the treasure.

"Does five hundred sound fair?"

She leaned forward. "You're asking me?"

"You wanted to know a price. The time, duration, and difficulty of this endeavor may be longer or shorter than I anticipate. A factor neither of us can predict. Therefore, we must agree on one price for the duration of the excursion regardless of what unforeseen circumstances may occur."

She harrumphed, and Lula swiped a pink tongue across her cheek. "I can't agree to that. What if you want to keep me tied up for half a year chasing fantasies?" She shook her head. "One month. If we haven't found your treasure by then, we renegotiate."

"A reasonable request." This couldn't take more than a week, at most. Still, knowing he had a month eased the pressure some. Not that he could wait too long. Especially if it cost him everything up front to secure help.

But he'd never unearth the treasure without a scavenger vessel and a knowledgeable captain, so he'd have to take the risk. The price he would get for the automobile might feed them for a few months, but regaining the family treasure would set wrongs to right again.

She slapped her hand on the table, and despite himself, he jumped. "Very well." She pinned him in her sharp gaze. "Then we are agreed. When can you bring the money so we can re-stock?"

He scratched his cheek. "I'll need a little time to procure the funds." Her lips parted, but before she could shoot out what would surely be a refusal, judging by the way her eyes bulged, he added, "I can bring fifty dollars back today. Will that suffice until I can get the rest?"

"That will do." She settled back into her chair, intelligent eyes churning. "Now, tell me about these clues."

His lips twitched into a curve. "Certainly, Captain. Once we sign the proper documents, of course."

Her eyes narrowed, but her words came out smoothly. "Of course."

Though her lips held annoyance, her eyes glowed with respect. And for some reason, that sent a tingle down through his toes.

S nakes and saltwater. This couldn't be right, could it? Camilla stared up at the stately home overlooking a sheer cliff at the river's edge. Maybe she'd misjudged Mr. Gray. If he'd inherited a mansion like this, then he shouldn't have any trouble getting her the rest of their payment. Based on his suit, she'd had her doubts.

Who knew he had a house larger than the United States postal office with soaring white columns and a second-story balcony wide enough to host her entire crew? Sure, the yard could use a gardener and the paint peeled here and there, but these people had means.

An odd contradiction, that. The sense that this situation dipped ocean-deep with nearly as many hidden dark crevices sloshed around in her head.

Maybe the fifty dollars he'd brought to her yesterday evening wouldn't be all she'd see of his money. She'd passed a few dollars to the men to have fun on land last night. Then she gave the rest to Solomon to cover this morning's load of coal, plus enough supplies from the mercantile to survive until she got her payment from Mr. Copeland. Not a penny remained.

But the fellas' spirits were up, her stomach was full of fried shrimp from Anna's po'boy shop, and it was a fine day to discover the money for their most-needed repairs would soon be available.

"This way, please." Daniel climbed the front steps to a spacious porch and fished for a key in his pocket.

She lingered at the rail, looking toward the water far below. Took an adventurous sort to put a colossal house near a drop-off. 'Course, there were a whole row of these fancy residences, so perhaps the wealthy figured if their homes plunged into the river, they'd buy another.

The faded door creaked open, and a small figure burst out, all knees and elbows and the exuberance only a boy of about seven or eight could muster. He latched his arms around Daniel's knees and beamed up at him.

"You're home!"

Daniel ruffled the boy's hair—the same smoky brown as his own. "Where's your mother?"

Was this his son? Close enough resemblance. Did that mean he had a wife too? Not her place to ask. Though if he was married...

She shook herself. Why the surge of disappointment? She'd barely met the man. Didn't know a thing about him. Except that he liked Lula, showed Solomon respect, and offered to help when no one required it of him.

"Went to town." The boy jabbed a finger at Camilla. "Who's that?"

"Captain Lockhart." Daniel grimaced an apologetic smile as the boy bounded over.

"Captain? What are you a captain of? A ship? Oh, is it one of those pirate ships like in those books Mama sometimes reads to me? Only if it's not the scary ones, of course."

His little lips twitched. "Wait. I thought only men could be captains. Never seen a lady captain before. Is it a whole ship of ladies too? That's interesting. I wonder what Mama would think.

Well, she'd probably say I asked too many questions at once and I should—oh." He smashed his lips together and clasped his hands behind him.

A laugh bubbled out of her chest, and she knelt on planks in need of a good sanding. "Hi, there. I'm Camilla. Yes, I am the captain of a boat, but it's nothing so exciting as a pirate ship. Just a little steamboat that belonged to my papa before he went to heaven."

He blinked bright-blue eyes. Ones quite different from Daniel's. "My father went to heaven too. I bet you miss yours. I miss mine a whole lot. Uncle Danny is my friend and all, but he doesn't know anything about baseball." His lip poked out. "Father was going to take me to New York to see a game someday."

How should she respond?

Before she had to come up with a reply, a melodious voice bounded across the porch. "There you are!"

A woman emerged from the door Daniel had been attempting to pass through and pointed a finger at the boy. "You know you can't run off to play until you've finished your arithmetic."

"Yes, ma'am." His lips curled. "I was only greeting our guest, like Mama says is proper."

"Uh-huh." The thin woman who looked to be in her early thirties tucked a strand of dark hair into a lemony-colored wrap around her head. She turned a sassy expression on Daniel. "Danny boy, this little'un is going to cost me the last of my wits."

Daniel smirked. "Get inside, Lucas. You know you have to finish your schooling."

"Oh, all right." He dug the toe of his shoe into the planks.

The adults waited, but the child still didn't move. The woman with the headscarf rolled her eyes and took his hand. "Come on. Get your numbers finished, and we'll see if Bo is giggin' any frogs. We'll fry us up some for supper."

Frogs?

Camilla didn't ask. Something about the woman seemed familiar, though she couldn't say what.

"Oh. My manners." Daniel gestured to the woman. "Captain Lockhart, this is Stella Breaux. You met her mother yesterday when we had lunch together."

Stella's lips parted. Was she surprised by the title or by Camilla sharing lunch with Daniel?

"Stella, Captain Lockhart will be assisting us on our quest."

"Well, now, ain't that something." Stella released the boy and patted his head. "I best find you sitting at that table writing numbers when I get done talking to the grown folk."

"Yes, ma'am." Lucas gave Camilla a wave and then trotted beyond an oak door long deprived of its polished sheen.

Stella's long yellow skirt swished across the top of her boots as she covered the distance between them. "Pleasure to meet you, Captain."

"Likewise." Camilla tipped her chin. "Your mother is a fabulous cook."

A burst of laughter jostled Stella's shoulders. "Don't let her be fooling you. My uncles are the ones doing all the real cooking. She just likes to throw some seasonings around and chat with the customers." She winked. "Of course, don't tell her I told you so."

"I wouldn't dare." Camilla flourished a bow, which earned another chuckle from the woman and an owlish stare from Daniel.

Once Stella excused herself and stepped inside, Daniel motioned for Camilla to follow. The interior proved as impressive as the exterior promised. The front entry boasted wood floors, high wainscoting, and oil paintings of stiff-looking people from the previous century. She focused on one hanging over a table meant for gloves or some such.

"Who's that?"

Daniel hung his hat on a nearby rack. "Those are my great-great-grandparents, John and Francine Merrill. They built this house in 1847."

Not Gray? Must be on his mother's side of the family. She glanced over the paintings in gilded frames situated on blue-papered walls. None of them had his smoky-brown hair. While Daniel removed his jacket and hung it on the coatrack, she took the liberty of gawking. Towering doors alongside the entry stood open to what appeared to be parlors stuffed with delicate furniture, and a stairway loomed beyond. Couches with blue fabric matching the walls lined the broad hallway, and behind the stairs, another glass-flanked door mirrored the one at the front.

"Nice house. I can't imagine what it must have been like growing up here." She'd have tried sliding down those curving stairs a time or two.

The nonchalant lift of his shoulders didn't release their tension. "We came here a handful of times as children, but we were never close with Grandfather. It surprised me when I discovered Father had been working with him, looking for the treasure. I thought the two never got along, especially after my mother passed."

He'd lost both parents as well. Seemed they had that in common. "Lucas is your nephew?"

"He and my sister live here with me." Daniel trailed a finger along the stair rail. "We all moved in a few weeks ago. The Lord was good to us, especially after Lucas Sr. died in that factory accident. Mabel and little Lucas wouldn't have had anywhere else to go."

They couldn't have lived with Daniel? Didn't he have a home prior to moving here? Not her place to ask, so she nodded. He'd divulge whatever personal information he felt comfortable sharing, and she wouldn't push for more even if curiosity often made her mouth run away with her almost as badly as his young nephew's did.

She followed him around the staircase. When they stepped past another room, Camilla slowed to peek inside. She'd never been in a house this size. What did they do with so many rooms?

This particular one didn't prove to be anything interesting. Just a dining space. Though it did have a mammoth fan hanging over the table people used to keep the flies away. Not a bad invention. Maybe she should figure out how to install that kind of contraption on the boat. They could take turns pulling the cord during the summer months to keep the insects off the cornbread.

"Hello!" a little voice called, and Camilla leaned inside the doorframe. "Remember me? I'm Lucas."

She couldn't help her grin. "Let me see. It's been so very long." She snapped her fingers. "Oh yes. We met about five minutes ago out on the porch."

A sound came from behind him, and his posture stiffened. He spoke with exaggeratedly punctuated words. "Please excuse me. I need to complete my assignment so I can go stick frogs with Uncle Bo."

She retreated. Uncle Bo? Would that be Stella's brother or one of her uncles? Were the two families related?

"Bo is Stella's brother and not Lucas's uncle." Daniel supplied from behind her. "I am his mother's only brother. Trouble is, we have a hard time telling him that." He plucked a stray thread from his cuff. "I figure it doesn't matter."

"Does Stella live here too?"

Daniel approached a door across the hall from the dining room and paused with his hand on the dull silver knob. "House this big has too many rooms and costs a lot to maintain. We take boarders." At her surprised look, he added, "Stella is a governess for Lucas and keeps everything around here running smoothly. A good trade if you ask me."

Interesting. A wealthy family that needed to barter rooms in their mansion. She'd never heard the like.

"I took the liberty of drawing up the document." Daniel motioned toward another door opposite the dining space. "Once you sign it, we'll get started."

Contracts were the standard agreements many business-men preferred, though her papa had said a man's word and handshake ought to be sufficient. She'd found paper to be a better seal on the terms than spit and a hand slap. She should have had Mr. Copeland sign one. Maybe she'd have gotten her payment on time if she had.

They entered a sturdy room not much different from her father's cabin on the boat. Rich wood shelving lined the walls, and a hefty desk squatted in the center. Unlike the boat cabin, however, a stone fireplace dominated one wall. She eased closer. Wouldn't one of these things be nice on a cold night? Two lion-head-shaped andirons covered in forgotten ash huddled inside, their mouths opened in silent roars.

"Take a seat please, Captain." Daniel strode around the desk and slid two sheets of paper from a drawer. He placed them on the smooth surface and pushed them across to her.

She took the pages and squinted at them. Such tiny writing. She stuck them close to her nose, then held them out at arm's length. Why not use more paper and write reasonably sized words?

"Do you, um, what I mean to say is, that, well..."

Camilla peeked over the top of the pages to the stuttering man. "I can read perfectly well, thank you." Guess he hadn't believed her when she admitted she liked the read. She shook the pages. "But for some reason, rather than using a typewriter, someone wrote in miniature script. I have to put it an inch from my face to see it."

He cleared his throat. "My apologies."

She cocked an eyebrow. "For what? Assuming that because I'm the daughter of a riverman I can't read or for writing too small for any normal person to see?"

He sputtered. "I, well, that is to say..." He shook his head. "Both, I suppose."

She waved the pages and laughed. "You wouldn't be the first man to underestimate me, Mr. Gray."

Properly sheepish, he palmed the back of his neck, settled into his chair, and nodded for her to continue reading.

She remained standing as she studied the page. The miniature words covered in detail the nature of their agreement. She would ferry him to a location of his choosing as long as it was on or bordered the Mississippi River between Natchez and Louisiana and did not exceed more than five miles inland or more than twenty miles above Natchez or ten into Louisiana.

She lifted her eyes above the page to find him watching her. "You used a lot of specific language. Are you a lawyer?"

"I am."

Double interesting. A treasure-hunting lawyer possessing a mansion filled with tenants. She read another few paragraphs. "I thought you said this trip would have some unexpected particulars."

"It will."

"Well, it seems to me you tried to think of every possible scenario anyway." She didn't bother to see his reaction and focused on the second page. "What's this line here? 'If Captain Lockhart is deemed especially helpful, going beyond the expected parameters, and her dedication directly leads to discovery, she will be awarded twenty percent of the collective value of all monies and objects recovered.' Didn't we already agree on a price?"

And what did he mean about being especially helpful? Sure, she'd agreed to look at some clues to soothe her curiosity and in hopes of finding answers about her father's death, but she was only being paid to navigate the Mississippi.

He splayed his fingers. "Seemed fair to me. But I can take it out if you want."

A chance at 20 percent of a fictional treasure was still better than nothing. Not that they'd find anything. But what could it hurt to gain a little of the proceeds if they did?

"All right. Where do I sign?"

"No questions about the secrecy clause?"

She dropped the pages on the desk. "Mr. Gray, the secrecy part was the only thing in the entire document I was expecting. I know how this works. Don't tell anyone about the treasure. Don't share important clues with strangers."

With a wry smile, he handed her an ink pen. "So long as we are agreed."

She scrawled her signature at the bottom of the page. He did the same and then placed the pages in the drawer. "I'll take that to the bank once we finish here."

The bank? They kept documents too? Not wanting to sound uneducated, she nodded.

"Now. On to business." An excited glint entered his eye. "A couple of days ago, I was in here looking through my grandfather's books. That's when I discovered something rather, well, unexpected."

The dramatic flair to his words latched onto her curiosity and tightened the line. She trailed him as he ran a finger along a shelf about chest high. When he reached the end of the bookcase near a window blanketed in heavy curtains, he hooked one finger behind the casing about two inches away from the wall.

She waited.

Nothing happened.

"Were you looking for a book or—"

His finger caught another spot, and the bookcase swung out toward her.

A secret room?

Well, catch her sideways and call her a lark. Looked like they might have some clues to a treasure after all.

The excitement on her features shouldn't have sent a thrill through him. But somehow seeing the emotions he kept deeply buried mirrored on another evoked instant camaraderie.

Daniel widened the secret door to let in the light from the study's nearby window, and Camilla leaned close to him to look inside. She smelled of fresh air and something sweet. With the slightest undercurrent of mechanical grease. He almost chuckled. Charming. In a way only Captain Lockhart could be.

"It's empty." Camilla's features fell, and she jabbed him with a questioning look.

As though he had tricked her into signing a contract for nothing.

Defensiveness swelled. He never swindled anyone. Regardless of what the newspapers might have said. "A hidden room isn't nothing. What if the treasure was here? And—"

She pulled away from him, taking her contradictory scent and partnership with her. "This is the only clue you have? How can you think this will lead you to a treasure?"

He gripped the bookcase. "You have a terrible habit of not letting people finish. Do you know that?"

She blinked and then puckered her lips. "I do. I'm sorry."

Her easy apology shocked him out of his annoyance. Most people would have struck back with some excuse or pointed out one of his flaws. Instead, she gave simple honesty. What was he supposed to do with *that*?

Clearing his throat to reset himself, he gestured inside. "When I found this room, it wasn't empty. There were a couple of discarded boxes and evidence there may have been several objects here that hadn't been moved in a long time."

"But how could you know—" She bit off the words, shook her head, then motioned for him to continue.

He withheld a smile. "There was a lot of dust on the shelves. Except in little squares and various other shapes. Which led me to believe those items had been recently moved. Probably right before my grandfather's passing."

Camilla stuck her head back into the closet to examine the shelves. He hadn't changed anything.

Well, almost. "There was only one thing left in there. A ledger."

Her bright eyes found his. "The one with my father's name?"

He stepped away from the opening, and after she did the same, he closed the door. The shelf blended back against the wall. Discovering it had been a miracle. At the desk, he opened the third drawer to his left and hefted a thick volume.

Camilla accepted the proffered tome and ran a finger down the leather cover. "My grandfather had a book like this. He kept detailed notes on the river. It's one of the advantages he passed to my father and on to me."

Her words carried such reverence that he paused. How much importance did captains truly put on such details? He'd heard that, if one wasn't intimately familiar with the Wicked River, they could find themselves lost at the bottom of it within moments. He'd never given much credence to the idea until now.

"At first, the only thing I read in there was business notes like you might expect." He kept on topic, instead of focusing on the way her features softened with memories of her family. "Which

I found odd. Why keep a business-expense ledger hidden in a secret room?"

She flipped open the cover and scanned the contents to verify.

"Then I noticed something different toward the back. Riddles. Puzzles." He rocked back on his heels. "I'm afraid we'd begun to question Grandfather's sanity in his final days. He'd started to forget things, and some days, it seemed he thought he lived in the past. His former cook said she'd hear him wandering the halls in the middle of the night, shouting about Rebels coming to burn the house like he was still a young boy during the war."

Camilla thumbed to the back of the book and frowned at a drawing scribbled in one of the margins. "Did you ever see any of these episodes yourself?"

"A time or two. I think he knew his mind had started to slip. That's when he sent for me. Said he wanted to make sure I transitioned into the family estate before he died. And since my sister had recently lost her husband, I brought her and my nephew with me. He passed a week later." Why had he volunteered all that extra information? It had little to do with the book or what he'd found inside.

"If I may." He reached for the book and flipped to *the* page. The one that had sent him to seek out Captain Lockhart. "I found this. It looks like Grandfather hired an investigator to follow my father. If Father suspected anything, that could explain why he used a different name. There wasn't much love between them, I'm afraid."

"Couldn't have been too terrible if he chose to leave everything to you." She scooted closer, and her sleeve brushed his.

Her nearness sent a tingle along his spine. Most people didn't stand this close to relative strangers without unwelcome intent. Yet Camilla didn't invade his space out of threat or false seduction attempts. Curiosity and excitement drove her actions in a way akin to Lucas. No wonder Solomon showed such fierce protectiveness over this spirited woman.

"I wish sentimentality had something to do with it." He focused on the conversation he'd let lag. "In Natchez, families keep their money close and their names in high regard. One does not sell an estate if he can bequeath it to an heir of any kind. Such things are frowned upon. And my grandfather insisted only a blood heir would inherit, so he cut my father from his will."

He pointed to the place on the page for her to read.

Camilla squinted at the line. "'Harry has hired a boat captain by the name of Lockhart. Captain of the *Alma May*. This man might be the key to finding the *Carolina*. He's close. Too close. Can't let him see what died with the gold. This must end with me.'"

She read the last part again. "What does he mean, died with the gold? And the *Carolina* is a boat. If he thinks the treasure went under the Mississippi, you'll never find it. When boats and people are lost on the river, they are never found again."

"If that's true, then why were our fathers close to a discovery?"

"Gamblers and treasure hunters always think they are on the verge of a win regardless of how many losses they've sustained." She plopped into a chair. "I'm not sure what you want me to do here, Mr. Gray. I can navigate you down the dangerous currents of the river, but I can't help you find anything at the bottom of it. That's impossible. The water is too deep and too full of silt. Even if you could survive the current to get five feet below the surface, you wouldn't be able to see anything."

She shook her head when he opened his mouth to protest. "Even if you managed to anchor down in the exact right location where your boat went under, the wreckage could be miles downriver by now. Or it could be buried under ten feet of shifty silt. No, sir. If your treasure sunk, then it's well and truly lost for good."

The seriousness of her tone left no room for argument. His mind churned. "If we find the information that convinced my father the treasure can be found, then we can pick up where he left off."

"You mean pick up with whatever he was doing right before he died." She crossed her arms and pinned him with a serious look. "Likely as a direct result of looking for this treasure."

He took a moment to close the book and set it down. Then he leaned against the desk and matched her demeanor. "Then the treasure must be real if it got him killed."

If he really is dead.

He shoved the thought aside. Harry Gray was most likely deceased, even if they'd yet to find his body and the law withheld an official declaration of death. If he'd been alive, he'd have returned or sent word by now. No. He'd do well and good not to let such ideas fester.

Camilla flipped her long braid over her shoulder and propped her elbows on her knees in her study of him. "Men only need the *idea* of money to kill for it, Mr. Gray."

"Daniel." And he knew that plenty well enough. He'd seen firsthand what greed could do. His father had apparently sold everything he owned to pursue it.

Her tone softened. "Daniel. I know finding this treasure, whatever it is, means a lot to you. I can see that, even if I don't know why. Something tells me your determination runs deeper than greed."

A sharp pang radiated through his chest. How could she know anything about the real motives driving him to finish what his father started? Everyone could see they needed the money. Most people would have considered that reason enough.

She turned out her palm before he had to come up with a response. "Your reasons are your business. But it would be unfair of me to take you down the river knowing there's no possibility you'll find what you're looking for."

"What if it ran aground and didn't sink?" He grabbed the book and flipped to a new page. "It says here that it disappeared. Not necessarily that it sank."

Camilla tapped a slender finger on the armrest. "I suppose that's possible. But if we are talking about a treasure missing for at least two generations, don't you think someone would have noticed an abandoned boat on the banks by now?"

"I'm given to understand there is a dense network of channels apart from the main river. Places that are not easy to navigate. Is that correct?"

A thought line formed between her dark brows. "Yes, but only a few you'd ever get a large steamer down."

"Didn't the Union army send gunboats up shallow channels during the War Between the States?"

She lifted her shoulders. "I suppose."

If they had taken the boat down one of the many channels, then even if it sank, the shallower water would be easier to search. "So the channels could be a possibility?"

"They could, but you have hundreds of miles of back channels. Not to mention all the oxbow lakes from where the river has changed course since then. That's an impossible amount of territory to search."

"But if we know where to start, we can trace the path the *Carolina* would have taken." He flipped to another page in the book. A tingle ran through him. This had been what it'd been like in the courtroom. Finding evidence, following logic and clues. Garnering information from witnesses to build his case.

"So, we've established the back channels could be a possibility." He pointed to his grandfather's script and avoided her tight expression resembling a witness who'd been deftly walked down the lawyer's line of questioning and suspected they'd been guided there for a reason.

He read his grandfather's words aloud. "'They say she went down, but I know better. Oh, I know better. She crept into the backwaters and birthed her illicit cargo. Bad blood there is. Bad blood. Can't let them know.'"

He withheld a wince. Now that he read the words out loud, they sounded less cryptic and more like the ramblings of a madman. Was he gambling his sister's and nephew's future on delusions?

Camilla pursed her lips. "What makes him think they took a back channel?" Without waiting for him to answer, she snapped her fingers. "Of course. How dull of me not to think of it. I know what we need to do."

"What?"

She popped to her feet and scrambled out the door.

Daniel placed the book back in the drawer, checked to ensure the bookshelf had securely latched, and followed his exuberant companion. Satisfaction simmered. He'd constructed his case and established merit to his father's search. And given Camilla's hasty departure, her idea might wrap this up sooner rather than later.

He hoped.

One month. If he didn't find the money by then, their lives would be forfeit.

But he didn't need to worry about that now. Not when Camilla had a lead.

W hy hadn't she thought of something so simple sooner? Camilla hurried out of the study and into the wide hallway. Where to start such a laborious task hinged on a simple factor and a crucial bit of information.

"Oh!"

The feminine yelp snatched Camilla from her thoughts and her gaze from the floor in time to see a basket fly from a woman's arms as their forms collided. On instinct, she snagged the other woman's elbow and kept her from sprawling on the floor when her feet tangled in her slim dress.

Skirts always were such a hazard. Good thing she'd not encumbered herself with one. She steadied the slight woman.

"Sorry about that. I didn't see you. Lost in my thoughts, I'm afraid." Camilla scooped up the basket, and three oranges rolled out. She plucked them from the floor and tossed them back inside. "Here."

The other woman clutched the lace collar of her sage-green dress. Wide hazel eyes blinked. "Who are you?"

"Easy, Mabel." Daniel appeared at Camilla's side. "This is Captain Camilla Lockhart. She's our guest."

Shoes slapped against the floor, and a second later, Lucas snagged his mother's skirt. "She's a pirate!"

"What?" The fair woman paled further, making the dark circles under her eyes more pronounced.

Camilla hiked a brow. "Now what did I tell you, Lucas? Just because I have a boat doesn't make me a pirate like in one of your stories."

"Daniel?" The lady who must be his sister attempted to tuck her child behind her, but the boy sidestepped her grasp and marched up to Camilla.

"You said you were a lady captain."

"I did. But that doesn't make me a pirate. Pirates steal things, and I would never do that."

His cheeks bunched. "Why not?"

"Because Jesus tells us not to."

The child chewed on that for a second and then looked up at Daniel. "I reckon she's right. Still, I think a lady pirate would be interesting."

"An honest lady riverboat captain is interesting enough." Daniel chuckled. "Now aren't you supposed to be hunting frogs? You didn't give up on your arithmetic again, did you?"

"Frogs?" Mabel waved a gloved hand over her face. "Pirates and frogs. What in the heavens did I miss when I went to pick up supper?"

Camilla glanced at the basket the woman hadn't taken back. They were having oranges for supper? Odd. She didn't see any meat or vegetables. But maybe folks who didn't live on steamboats ate different meals. Or maybe Mabel was going to make a pie. Yes, that made more sense. Women baked fruit pies all the time, didn't they?

Daniel stuffed his hands in his pockets, a gesture it seemed he often did when flustered. The man did get flustered a lot. But then, in the short time she'd been in his acquaintance, there had been a few things to get ruffled over.

"Stella told him if he finished all of his schooling, he could look for frogs with Bo," Daniel said. "I didn't see the harm in that."

Mabel's porcelain skin took on a greenish hue. She waved her hand like she could shoo the idea from the room. "Fine, fine. So long as someone keeps a close eye on him. You know how exuberant he can be."

"What's exuberant?" Lucas bounced on his toes.

"Means you have a lot of energy and sometimes that energy gets you into trouble." Daniel nudged the boy back to the dining room. "How many more problems do you need to figure?"

"Just two."

"Good. Then get them finished so you can go."

Lucas threw up a hand in a childish version of a salute. "Good day, Lady Captain!"

She returned the gesture, and the boy dissolved into giggles before dashing from the room.

Seemed everyone had forgotten about Mabel's basket. Should she try to hand it to the woman again or set it on the floor?

"Do forgive my manners." Mabel drew herself up and tucked a strand of light-brown hair underneath a bowl-shaped hat matching her dress. "I'm Mrs. Mabel Shoemaker."

Maybe she should buy an outfit like that. Just for churchgoings, of course. Not much use for such nice things on a rickety steamboat.

Daniel shifted his feet. "And this is Captain Camilla Lockhart."

Hadn't he already said that? Oh. Right. She'd forgotten her manners. Bless him for the subtle reminder she needed to introduce herself even if others already knew her name. She thrust out her hand. "Pleasure to meet you, Mrs. Shoemaker."

Mabel blinked at Camilla's waiting palm before extending her own. Camilla gave her a couple of pumps like Papa had taught her. Not too limp to be considered a weakling and not too tight to be seen as someone with something to prove.

But Mabel had twisted her hand as though she'd meant to turn her knuckles up instead of to the side, which gave Camilla an odd grip.

Mabel extracted her hand with a questioning look at her brother, who stuffed his hands in his pockets.

"Captain Lockhart is going to help us with our project."

"Oh?" Mabel stepped closer and lowered her voice. Who did she worry might overhear? "When you mentioned a riverboat captain who could help us, I didn't picture a woman. And so young and pretty a one at that."

Should she consider that a compliment or an insult? Camilla offered a friendly smile. "Not the first time I've been mistaken for a man."

Oh dear.

That didn't come out like she'd intended. "Not because of the pants, mind. I do own a dress. Trousers are just more practical on a boat. No tangling around your legs or blowing up to show your drawers."

Mabel's lips parted.

Uh-oh.

Probably shouldn't have said *drawers*. Hadn't she learned ladies could be fickle about words men never seemed to mind? Judging by the bright-red splotches on her cheeks, Mabel was one of those types of ladies.

Camilla blew out a breath. "What I mean to say is there's no word for female captain. No Mr. Captain or Miss Captain, so most folks assume a captain to be a man."

Daniel's lips curved. "Captain Lockhart inherited the scavenger boat from her father but earned her captain's license in her own right. I have every confidence she possesses the skills to navigate the journey."

Her spine straightened a fraction. Bless him for trying to help smooth out her awkwardness. "Thank you. But the *Alma May* is not a scavenger boat. I'm not sure where those rumors started. True, we will haul just about any cargo we are paid to deliver, and sure, once we were hired to clean up after a boiler burst and bits of a steamer went sky-high, littering pieces of a packet boat all over the water. But we weren't scavenging. We were recovering and cleaning."

Mabel fiddled with the lace on her dress again, her gaze darting between Daniel and Camilla.

Had she said something wrong? This lady must be one of those delicate types Papa had told her about. They didn't like discussing anything more than peach cobblers or the weather. Though how a person functioned through the trials of life like that, she had no idea.

"My apologies. Salvage boat was a notion I found in the book. I should have clarified with you." Daniel offered a sheepish shrug, then directed his next words to his sister. "Grandfather noted Father had hired a boat for a salvage operation."

"If the boat you're after sunk, you won't be salvaging anything." Camilla crossed her arms. A point worth repeating since these folks didn't seem to understand the nature of the river. What went under never resurfaced.

Never.

"But the boat may not have sunk at all. Father had been close. I know it." Daniel smacked a fist against his palm. When his sister started, he gentled a tone that had grown excited. "Don't worry. We'll find the rest of the inheritance."

Inheritance? Weren't they looking for a lost treasure? Maybe he considered it all the same.

She glanced around the hallway. Come to think of it, it must cost a lot to maintain a house this big. But then, if they couldn't afford the property, they could always sell it. So what if the Natchez bigwigs frowned on that? A person had to do what was best, not what looked good to others.

"Very well." Mabel stretched a tired smile that didn't touch her eyes. "Could you drive me to Cloverdale in the morning? I left a favorite hatpin in the drawer of my old secretary, and I'd like to retrieve it before the bank comes."

"You want to drive all the way out there for a hatpin?" Daniel's brow furrowed.

This sudden shift in topic sounded like a private affair, so Camilla stepped back to deposit the basket she still clutched onto a low couch. Maybe she could pretend to look at the paintings while they talked.

"I thought I could do without it, but I've changed my mind."

"That's over six miles, Mabel."

Camilla drifted to the staircase and studied a painting of a woman with a sharp nose and a bell-shaped white dress. She wore her hair parted down the middle with curls by her ears.

"I said I changed my mind." Mabel's voice faltered. "Please take me. You can drive the motorcar. Lucas would enjoy the outing."

"I've sold the motorcar. They will come retrieve it in the morning."

His soft sorrow nudged Camilla's heart. He cared for his sister. Papa always said you could tell a lot about a person by how they cared for those closest to them.

"Why? I thought you said we could keep it." Each word pitched higher. "We aren't that close to being destitute, are we? We already let out all the rooms."

Camilla edged around the staircase to give them more privacy. She wasn't eavesdropping. Not truly. She couldn't help but overhear them. And they wouldn't want her poking around their private rooms to give them more space.

"We aren't destitute. I promise, it will be all right."

"Then why did you sell Grandfather's motorcar?"

"I needed the money."

Something cold slithered through Camilla's veins. Uh-oh.

"For what?" Mabel fired out the demand with more spunk than anything Camilla had heard thus far.

"I needed it to secure Captain Lockhart's services, but we can buy another one as soon as—"

"No. No, I won't have it. Tell the man coming that you've changed your mind and you won't be selling. He can keep his money."

"I can't." Daniel's voice lowered, though Camilla had no problem hearing him. Perhaps because she leaned so far in that direction she might topple over. She righted herself and slowed her breathing as he finished. "I already have a contract with Captain Lockhart."

"But why?" No problem at all hearing Mabel's screeched words.

Perhaps Camilla should step outside. It didn't seem right to keep listening in, especially given the argument centered on her. She let herself out the front door as quietly as she could and strode to the porch railing.

The white paint flaked in places, creating scales beneath her palms. She closed her eyes, and the hot breeze dried the sheen of sweat from her brow. Either Daniel would honor their contract, or he wouldn't. Either way, she'd resupplied her boat, and she'd insist that portion of the payment was forfeited as compensation for breaking their deal.

But what about the ten dollars he'd spent on their docking fees? She didn't have the money to pay him back until Mr. Copeland transferred the two hundred dollars he owed her. She leaned her elbows on the rail. She'd have to consider sixty dollars as compensation, then.

Ahead, a squat tug navigated a flat showboat down the water. Giant red letters splayed across the white side—*The River Queen.*

Did anyone go to those things anymore? Papa had taken her once as a small girl. She didn't remember much about the play, but she did remember the juggler and the jaunty whistles of the calliope calling folks to see the show. Papa had bought her popped corn and taffy. It had been soon after Mama died, and he'd thought she didn't notice him wiping his eyes in the dark theater. She'd held his hand and smiled as the music played. That had seemed to make him feel better.

The showboat disappeared around the bend, and she closed her eyes. She'd gotten through hard times before. She could do it again. They didn't need Mr. Gray's money. Probably better if they found a more traditional job anyway.

The front door banged against the house, and small shoes pounded across the planks. Camilla smiled without opening her eyes. Little Lucas must have been loosed from his arithmetic prison and could now embark on frogging adventures.

"Hold on now!" Stella's huffing voice followed.

The boy bounding down the steps ground to a halt with a groan. "But you're so slow, Stella. All the frogs will be gone before I get there!"

"They won't do nothing of the sort." She rolled her eyes and shot Camilla an exasperated smile.

Camilla pushed off the railing. "Mind if I walk to town with you?"

"Don't mind at all." Stella tugged a glove over her slender fingers. "You can help me keep an eye on that young'un."

Camilla fell into step. "Have you lived in Natchez all your life?"

"Sure have." Stella fit a hat over dark hair where the wrap had been tied earlier. "How 'bout you? Haven't seen you in these parts. Not that I stay round the docks much anymore."

"My home is the stretch of water from Vicksburg to Louisiana."

Stella nodded and then mumbled something about boys as wild as foxes before cupping a hand to her mouth and shouting at Lucas. "You get out of my sight, and it's straight back to the table for you!"

The boy slowed his steps, scowled over his shoulder, then kicked a rock.

"Thought you were supposed to be helping Danny with something." Stella waved back toward the house. "He coming to town too?"

"I'm not sure." Camilla tucked her thumbs into her pockets. "He and his sister were having a private discussion, so I slipped out. I don't know if we will be working together or not."

"Do you want to work with him?"

Now why would she ask something like that? Camilla cut a sidelong glance at the other woman, but her dark eyes were focused on the boy wrestling a weed from its roots a bit too close to the cliff's edge.

"He promised a good wage. Something me and my crew need. But if it doesn't work out, we'll find something else. We always do."

Stella patted her arm. "'Course you will. Any woman who is brave enough to captain the Wild River can do anything."

Warmth spread through Camilla's chest. For the first time in a long while, hope mingled with determination and anchored down.

What a fine fiddle. Daniel stalked down the porch steps and into a blistering Mississippi afternoon. Mosquitoes buzzed his face, and he slapped one already feasting on his neck. Sometime during his discussion with his sister, Camilla Lockhart had up and abandoned him.

Depending on how much of the conversation she'd heard, he couldn't say he blamed her. Looked like he'd be swimming in hot water with two women today, and the afternoon's heat alone could boil a man alive.

He turned along the river road and sighted blue fabric up ahead. The orange feather bobbing from the top could belong to no other than Stella Breaux. Mabel had tried her best to convince Stella that blue and orange did not mix. Stella kept wearing it anyway either because she liked the colors or because she found Mabel's huffing amusing.

A secondary female figure, slightly shorter and dressed in trousers, sauntered at Stella's side. He quickened his pace and joined them.

"Where are you going?"

Before Camilla could answer his question, Stella leaned past her and grinned. "Lucas near about has her convinced gigging frogs is a worthwhile endeavor."

A grin toyed with one side of Camilla's lips, but she didn't let it fully form. "I haven't ever tried frog, but then I figured as well as Stella's family cooks they could probably make dirt taste good."

Lucas bounded up and made a sour face like he'd sucked on a green persimmon. "Why would anyone eat dirt? That don't make sense. Mama said we are going to be dirt poor, but I thought that meant we had to sleep on the dirt. Not eat it."

Daniel snagged the boy's sweaty palm and hauled him farther from the cliffside. "That's just an expression. You have a nice bed. You won't be sleeping on the dirt. And no one is eating it, either."

"Oh." Lucas fell into a rare moment of silence, content to walk hand in hand.

They followed the river road until it veered from the cliff and meandered back into the more commercial section of Natchez.

"Since you're in town"—Stella adjusted her hat and snagged Daniel's gaze from where it had once again strayed to Camilla's windswept hair—"would you mind stopping by the shop and hauling home whatever vittles we got fixed? Save me from lugging it back up the hill while wrangling that there slippery boy."

"Of course." The nights they brought home supper from Anna's were his favorite. Before he could think through his next words, they volleyed out of his mouth. "We'll fix an extra helping for Camilla too."

Both women gaped at him. Though he wasn't sure if the expression stemmed from the familiar use of her first name or him assuming she'd join them for supper without asking her.

Or Mabel.

He scratched the base of his throat. Likely a bad idea all around.

"Are you asking me to supper, Mr. Gray?" Camilla widened her stance and crossed her arms, her features an odd mix of amusement and self-assurance.

He doffed his hat. "I am. Please forgive my lack of manners in doing so. I thought we could discuss the matters of our arrangement over the meal."

"Do we still have an arrangement?"

Lucas, having freed himself from Daniel's grip, now pawed at Stella's arm, and she sighed. "If you'll excuse me, I'll see y'all later. Best get this boy to his frogs before he tears my arm off."

Daniel mustered a stern look. "Lucas. You behave like a gentleman, or you won't be going anywhere. There's no call for treating a lady like that. You know better."

Lucas pressed his lips together. "Yes, sir." He leveled big eyes on Stella that always made her melt like lard in a cast iron. "I'm sure sorry, Miss Stella. I didn't mean to be rude. I let my excitement about the frogs take over my good senses."

Daniel had to press his tongue to the roof of his mouth not to laugh. It was difficult to correct a child that precious. Poor boy didn't mean any harm. He merely struggled reining in his energy.

"It's all right, honey. Let's just walk at a normal pace, all right?"

"Yes, ma'am." He waved a little hand and bounded by Stella's side with all the calm he could call to bear as they sauntered along the road leading down the hill.

Camilla laughed. "Like a squirrel caught in a shoebox, that one is. But he sure is adorable."

"That he is." Daniel chuckled. "On both accounts."

A motorcar sounded its horn, and a man on horseback shook his fist and shouted something impolite. Daniel cringed at such words being used in the presence of a lady, but Camilla never flinched. Her gaze wandered over the people going about their tasks and the crowded streets crammed with horses, carts, and automobiles.

She fiddled with the end of her braid. "Sorry to ask, but I figure I do need to know. Did you and your sister decide? I didn't mean to overhear, mind you, but did you really sell one of those fancy motorcars to cover my fee?"

"I did." He tucked his hands in his pockets as the road jam cleared. Dust churned and settled into his nostrils, joining with the scents of horses, sweat, and river water. "It was the easiest asset to unload. My grandfather didn't leave much else other than the house and furnishings, and it would have taken much longer to sell several items of furniture than one motorcar."

Her eyebrows twitched, but she only nodded. "Didn't sound like Mrs. Shoemaker wanted to part with it. Can't say I blame her. Hard to trade something you have in hand for something you hope to find."

They rounded the corner onto another street, and he followed her lead. Didn't seem like they were returning to the docks. "My sister is mourning her former life."

Camilla's eyes swam with sympathy. "It must hurt an awful lot to lose your life mate. I know what the loss did to Papa. He never was the same."

Something in his chest pinched. If only that were true. "I'm sure it is. And in her way, she is also dealing with the pain of his death. But most of her frustrations come with the loss of the lifestyle he provided. One that I cannot."

"She didn't get an inheritance from her husband?" As soon as the words left her mouth, she snapped her teeth together. "Forgive me. That was an inappropriate question. That's none of my business."

He followed her around another corner and to a stone structure with green awnings. "That's all right. Turns out, my brother-in-law invested all his money poorly. After he died in the factory, Mabel found out the bank was coming to take the house and nearly everything else they owned to cover Lucas's debts. She thought she'd spend her days at leisure wrapped in furs and attending parties. Not sharing a makeshift boardinghouse with her brother and strangers."

Once again, more words than he'd intended escaped between his teeth. What about this woman greased his tongue?

"I suppose I can understand. A person gets used to a certain
kind of life, no matter what it is. Sudden and drastic adjust-
ment can be difficult for anyone." She smiled sweetly at a
woman who glared at her pants as they passed.

Perhaps that was why he found it easy to talk to her.
Camilla didn't seem to carry any pretenses and navigated the
world around her with simple honesty and kindness.

She opened the door to the stone building before he could
do it for her, so he followed her into the relative coolness of
the dark interior. Gaslights struggled to hold back the gloom.
"Where are we?"

"Shipping offices. I started thinking about what you said
about that boat taking the back channels. There are a lot of
those, sure. But we can narrow it down by leagues if we know
what kind of vessel we're dealing with. If she's a keelboat
or a flatboat or if we're looking for a packet or side-wheel,
it makes a difference." She lifted slim shoulders. "An empty
towboat will sit shallow enough to make most of the waterways if they are wide enough, but a packet or fueler wouldn't."

"Cleaver, Captain. I would have never considered that."

She flashed him a grin and ambled to a high counter
manned by a fellow in a shirt that must be pinching him too
tightly around the neck, judging by the way his eyes bulged.
"I'd like access to the records, please. Boat by the name of
the *Carolina*. Would have gone missing in...?" She looked to
Daniel for clarification.

"In 1865, I believe."

The man barely glanced up as he flipped through a
tome. "Records room is that way." He pointed behind them.
"Ledgers are labeled alphabetically after the year."

They followed the man's instructions and entered a cavernous
chamber. Flickering gaslight hovered in measured spaces, creating circles of yellow against the shadowed walls. Shelving stood

sentry in neat rows, home to hundreds of volumes like the university law library.

If it had been housed in a dungeon.

Camilla squinted at the lettering on the nearest shelf. "Let's see. This is 1800 to 1810." She leaned past to scan the length of the shelf. "Who knew there'd be so many records?"

He counted six more shelves to his left. "Ours should be down here."

"I wonder when these start?" Her voice trailed away, and he turned to find her long legs carrying her toward the other side of the room.

They weren't on a timetable, but what did it matter when the city began keeping boat records? "Haven't you been in here before?"

She shrugged and dipped into a dark shadow. He lengthened his stride to follow. They reached the end of the room, and she tapped a shelf. "These down here are port and docking records. It looks like the city has information dating back to the establishment of Fort Rosalie. Imagine what we could discover in here."

"You're interested in history?"

"Not exactly." She gave the shelf a thoughtful look and walked toward him. "But if there are this many records, then there could be notes on river patterns in stretches I haven't navigated before. I've been thinking about expanding beyond where Papa made his living and giving my crew new opportunities. Any advantage I can find would be helpful."

They ambled over a brick floor uneven with age. "I knew river captains prided themselves on reading currents and eddies and the like, but I always figured those skills could take you any length of river."

"They can." Camilla hooked her fingers on the 1860–1870 shelf and swung around the corner. "But there's more to it. Hidden sandbars, sudden drop-offs. Things like that. If you're running unfamiliar water, you risk trouble you didn't know was there."

He scanned the book spines. Where most law books had been similar in size and shape, these varied as much as the books in Grandfather's library. He read titles as he passed.

Medical logs, 1860–1861. Engineer logbooks, station logs, steam logs, telegraph logs. "Looks like most of these are kept by the Coast Guard."

"And some are port records from the city." Camilla tugged a book free. "Here. This one is for vessel records."

She opened the book, and he looked over her shoulder. She held it at arm's length with a squint, then snapped it closed. "We need better light."

"Have you considered spectacles? They could help you read better."

Her boots clapped against the brick as she stalked to the end of the shelf. "I can see eddies shift from a hundred feet out. My eyes are fine."

"At distances, yes." He followed her to a table underneath one of the wall sconces. "But sometimes people benefit from lenses that help them read small words up close."

She dropped the book on the table and flipped through the pages. "Not something I do often enough to justify the expense."

But didn't she say she liked to read? Perhaps she did, but her eyesight made it difficult.

She leaned closer to the book and then shot him a sidelong glance when she noticed him watching. "Here. You search."

Daniel reached around her to get the book from the table. This close he could smell the treatment she used in her hair. The inviting scent clung to his nostrils and slowed his mind. He blinked to clear the sensation. He shifted the book closer, but his feet locked in place. She remained against the table and scooted so her arm settled against his chest with him partly looking over her shoulder.

Apparently also aware of the closeness, she stiffened almost imperceptibly. He should move away. But since he hadn't been the one to put such little space between them, he waited.

"Are you going to look, or do you need spectacles too?"

At her teasing tone, he relaxed and flipped through the pages, though concentrating on faded words increased in difficulty when he had to lean even closer to see over her.

"Wait." She grabbed his hand. "Go back a page."

Rather than letting him do so, she flipped the thick page herself. "*Carolina*. There."

He scanned the brief notation. "Three vessels by that name, all belonging to Mr. Edward Williams. All three are listed as packets, like your *Alma May*. This shows the first one wrecked with another steamer and the second he sold for a larger vessel. Used the same name for each boat." He ran his finger over the final line. "The last one reportedly sank after a boiler fire."

"That's something, at least, though not much to go on. When we saw all these books, I'd hoped there would be more information. Maybe logs on where and when these boats went." Her shoulders lifted in a sigh and a strand of hair tickled his nose.

He wiggled it to ease the urge to sneeze. "Those records are probably kept by the boat captains. At least we have a name and a type of vessel, which is a start."

"That's true." She twisted her head to look up at him, and her eyes widened. Her lips parted, their faces only inches apart.

He should step away. It was the proper thing to do. So why couldn't he?

She blinked at him, and then a wry smile crept over her lips. "If Solomon saw you standing here like this looking at me like you are, he'd chunk you in the river."

"Then I'd have to inform him you were the one who positioned yourself this close." The words came out low, teasing.

She arched a brow. "I suppose that's true. I find you to be a very intriguing man, Mr. Gray. I'm not sure what to do about that."

The admission warmed his chest. "And I find you to be rather fascinating as well, Captain."

Silence stretched taut between them, and an unprofessional thought forced its way to the surface.

What would it be like to kiss her?

P apa would say Camilla had steered herself right into dangerous waters. And he'd be right. He and Mr. Gray were both right. She *had* been the one to stand so close to the man. To brush her shoulder against him and ease her body into his broad chest. She'd also been the one to look up into those arrestingly intelligent eyes and let herself float away in them.

He continued to look down at her, his breathing shallow and his gaze intense.

What must he be thinking?

Her experience with men mostly centered on crewmen she treated like uncles, fellas in river towns she avoided on account of obvious lecherousness, and businessmen who saw her as either a threat or an oddity to be dismissed.

Daniel wasn't looking at her in any of those ways now. True to his words, his eyes seemed to hold fascination. Those eyes darkened, seeming to drink her in. She'd been kissed by fellas when Papa hadn't been paying particular attention, but she'd never longed to be kissed. It had just been one of those things that had happened.

Heat swirled through her as her gaze detached from pools of liquid emerald and dipped to the shape of his lips.

The smooth skin of Daniel's jaw meant he'd recently shaven, and there was the tiniest little indent in the center of his chin she hadn't noticed before. Her gaze crept over the sturdy line of his jaw and back to eyes that seemed to contain more mysteries than this records room could hold. What would it be like to explore?

Dangerous undercurrents. The possibility of getting swept away by what you couldn't see coming.

And yet...

"I'd like to kiss you." Daniel's gaze anchored to hers. "Even though it's entirely improper to do so and not within the nature of our agreement."

His matter-of-fact statement delivered in a low whisper held as much contradiction as her churning thoughts. She wanted to see what would happen if they crossed over the line of professionalism too, but such impetuous decisions would tangle the nature of their relationship.

"Improper, yes." Her chin tilted higher. "And I agree, there were no clauses about kissing in your contract."

A ghost of a smile played with the edges of his mouth. "No, there were not."

"It could make working together on this endeavor more complicated." Her pulse quickened, pounding through her chest and nearing full steam. She shifted her shoulders, bringing herself to face him a little more.

He didn't move back, and his arm from where he was still holding the book now wrapped around her side. Slowly, he lifted the other hand and brushed her braid over her shoulder. The movement opened the channel gate between them, and she grazed her fingers over the twill of his jacket.

His lips lowered to hers. She closed her eyes, and something she couldn't identify zipped through her. Daniel's kiss was sweet and gentle. Like velvet. And a bit like that strawberry ice cream

Papa had gotten her at the Sugar Parlor that one time. Except warm and inviting, like a late-night mug of lemon balm tea.

Then it was over.

Emerald-green oceans stared down at her when her eyelids drifted open. Words dipped in subtle confusion drifted to her ears. "I've never met anyone like you."

The statement hit like ice water on hot coals. Not again. Was that why he'd stopped kissing her? "Unladylike, you mean?"

A line formed between his brows. "No. Why would you ask that?"

Because that's what people meant. A burn started in her chest as memories flooded in unbidden. Snickers behind gloved hands. Veiled insults about her outgoing manner that wasn't properly tempered by a lady's charm.

Can you believe he keeps that little girl on a boat with all those men?

Guess her father wanted a son instead.

She'd never had many female friends. They generally found her company unpleasant because she was too loud, too talkative, and too prone to say the wrong thing. Men were another matter. Try to be a lady, and they didn't respect her. Be strong and do business like a man, and any romantic notions sank like a cannonball.

Papa had always wrapped an arm around her shoulder and told her to be proud of who God made her to be. Cleaver, kind, and resourceful. She tried to live up to the way he saw her, but sometimes that was hard to remember. Especially when folks looked at her funny. Perhaps never more so than now, when insecurity insisted Daniel had decided kissing such an unusual woman had been a mistake.

Not that she could get any of those words to exit her lips.

He still stood close, and her hand rested on his chest near his shoulder. Under her palm, she imagined she could feel his heartbeat. He pulled a long breath through his nose. The urge to press her lips against his before they could say anything more

71

to ruin this moment permanently pushed up through her and lifted her onto her toes to close the space between them.

"Excuse me!"

The shrill words caused her to jump, and somehow, her forehead slammed into his nose. He grunted and stepped away, hand to his face. Camilla tried to scurry backward but hit against the table she'd forgotten stood behind her.

Shrouded in dim light and annoyance, a stout woman dressed in a black frock two decades out of fashion tapped a toe on the brick floor. Her posture looked as starched as the slim skirt hugging the top of her laced black boots.

Daniel faced the intruder after blinking moisture from his eyes, and Camilla poked her head around his shoulder.

The woman pointed a finger at them. "The records room is not a place for...for..." She waved a hand at them. "Leave. Now."

Heat crept up Camilla's neck, and she grabbed the book they'd been looking at to hand to the woman. She seemed like a librarian, and those were known for strict rules about reshelving books.

"Leave it. Out. Now." The angry librarian waved toward the door.

Daniel ducked his head and took Camilla's hand, leading her past the woman who'd puffed up like a disgruntled hen. They traipsed into the main chamber, and still, his warm palm rested against hers. It wasn't until they'd exited the front door and both stood blinking against the bright afternoon sun that he released his grip.

She instantly missed his touch. And then chided herself for silliness.

So much for not complicating the nature of their relationship. How did she go back to being an aloof professional captain? Daniel stuffed his hands in his pockets and watched the traffic jostle for position along the road.

She wanted to ask what he'd meant when he'd said he hadn't ever met anyone like her. But awkwardness fogged the air between them, and the words stuck in her throat.

He cleared his throat as though discomfort had stuck there too. "Now we know the name of the vessel, what type it is, and that we believe the treasure was once on board."

"Uh-huh." Maybe a direct dive back into the job he'd hired her for would help. "Add to that your grandfather's secret room and the possibility our fathers were working together."

Information they both already knew, but talking helped her focus on something other than the way his lips had felt on hers and the way her heart had responded.

"Yes." Daniel cleared his throat once again, clearly relieved to steer back to familiar waters. "What about records your father kept? Do you know if he had anything that could help?"

"He might." The weight now settled in her stomach pushed out any lingering flutters.

"Might?" He tipped his hat back. "You haven't looked?"

Her jaw tightened. "What I was looking for after his death was the man who'd killed him over a phantom box of gold."

The words may as well have slapped him. He rocked back on his heels. "You mean my father? You think he murdered yours?"

She wrapped her arms around herself. "I did. At least until you said he disappeared." An unnerving thought dropped a pound of ice into her chest. "Unless, of course, he disappeared because he was a murderer and didn't want to get caught."

She put a step between them. "What if they did find the treasure and Mr. Dixon murdered Papa so he didn't have to share? Then he disappeared with his money and his guilt. That's what I'd thought before. 'Least until you showed up and said Mr. Dixon went missing first. But what if that's not the case? What if he did meet with Papa?"

How could she have let herself be so empty-headed? Didn't she know treasure hunting turned good men into obsessed madmen? Would Daniel's desperation do the same?

He seemed the trustworthy sort, but what did she know?

Daniel rubbed the back of his head before answering. "I don't think my father would have done that. But I can see why you would be suspicious, and you have every right to be. The facts of this case are murky at best, and there's logic in the pieces of the puzzle you're examining."

Huh.

A motorcar passed, sputtering black smoke from the tail end.

"We should always examine every fact as it is." His gaze followed the dissipating smoke. "We can't let our thoughts and opinions color the evidence presented. I assure you, I want to know the truth as much as you do. Regardless of what it turns out to be."

The calm assertion settled some of the walleyes thrashing around in her chest. His relaxed posture and thoughtful tone both displayed sincerity. Maybe he did want to know the truth. Him agreeing to consider all evidence, rather than hammering her with assurances her fears were unfounded, suggested he was a man who valued truth and justice.

A fitting quality for a lawyer.

Hot air stirred as people parted around them on the sidewalk, and he didn't pressure her. After two buggies, a woman with a basket slung over one arm, and a father with a wailing toddler passed, she'd gathered her scattered thoughts to form a reply.

"He kept a private journal in his desk. I went through it after he died, but I haven't looked since." She turned toward the river. "Maybe I missed something."

He strolled an easy pace at her side. After two blocks, he broke the silence. "Thank you."

Two simple words, layered with complicated meaning. From the moment she'd met him, she'd known this man could be trouble. Meddling with her senses and whatnot. He'd done that. But he also somehow served as a calming presence with his directness and steadfast hold on logic.

How could one person cause both calm and storm?

She didn't have an answer. After a few more blocks, they began the steep decline toward the water. The *Alma May* had docked south of the bustling area under the hill, like Papa always preferred. He'd not cared for the rough reputation of Natchez Under the Hill and had kept her as far from it as he could. What would he think of her taking meals there and sharing a kiss with a man in a dark room?

Some of the tension eased from her shoulders as she scaled the familiar planks home. The sway of the deck underneath her, the comforting scents of the river, and the greetings of the only family remaining to her slathered a balm over her heart. In a day of slippery situations, the familiar anchored her.

The strain returned a second later, however, when Solomon stepped into her path, eyes stormy and fingers jabbing out words.

What happened?

Two quick gestures and a simple question. Too bad the answer wasn't as easy.

"Mr. Gray and I are looking for clues in order to begin the job he's hired us for." At Solomon's frown, she added, "He's offered a contract to legally secure our payment. We'll take him to a location of his choosing on the river."

Do you trust him?

This time, she answered with her hands. *Not sure yet, but so far, he seems honorable.*

Solomon grunted. He listed off repairs they needed to make and asked if she'd gotten any more money yet.

She shook her head.

Won't get far if we sink.

She glowered at him. "I know that."

His eyebrows hiked at her snapped words, and she released a long breath before signing again.

Sorry. I'm doing the best I can. Should have more money tomorrow after he sells a motorcar to pay us.

She swiveled to Daniel. "You are still doing that, right?"

"Doing what?" He settled on his heels, gaze darting between her and Solomon.

Oh. Right. Sometimes she forgot others couldn't understand their silent language even though she often purposely used it to keep them unapprised. "Are you still selling the motorcar and honoring our contract? If not, I need to know now before this goes any further. Also, it's only fair you know I've already spent the fifty dollars you provided for supplies and the ten you gave us for docking. If you wish to break the contract, then I'm going to have to insist that money is forfeited as recompense."

Solomon gave an approving nod.

Daniel rested his palm on the railing and regarded her. "A fair request. However, it's unnecessary. I don't sign a contract I don't intend to keep. I will uphold my end of the agreement."

Relief and disappointment melded like brackish water. Impossible to separate the fresh from the salt. On the one hand, it would be easier to forget Mr. Gray and his foolish quest, even if she'd be out a good paying job. On the other, she had to admit, even if only to herself, she wanted to see this through.

She spoke to Solomon. "We'll have payment tomorrow. Then you can—"

"Partial payment," Daniel interjected. "If you remember, the contract stated you would receive half at the start and the other half once we discover the treasure or the time limit expires. Whichever comes first."

No, she didn't remember reading that particular statement. The terms were logical and fair, however, and she could respect his forethought. She could easily take all his money and leave him on the riverbank empty-handed. Not that she would ever do such a thing, of course.

She inclined her head in acquiescence. "We will have half of our payment tomorrow, and then you can get the supplies we need."

Solomon raked an assessing gaze over Daniel, then made another series of gestures.

You sure you are all right? Something smells fishy. Anything I need to know about this man?

Nothing he *needed* to know. Her muddled feelings and their kiss was not knowledge she wanted floating around. Being a female captain, even one with a devoted crew, could be a thin line to walk. She didn't need them gossiping about private matters.

She shook her head.

After making her promise she'd holler if she needed him, Solomon disappeared into the engine room and left her and Daniel alone on the empty cargo deck. The crew had done a fine job cleaning and prepping them for a new haul.

Hmm. She lifted her chin, thinking aloud. "The contract states I am to take you somewhere along the river, correct?"

"Or to the passages, depending on the need, yes." His tone turned cautious. "Why?"

"It says nothing about us hauling other cargo while we do so." Triumph warmed its way through her veins. Looked like she could hit two birds with one rock, no matter what Solomon always quipped.

He chuckled. "I suppose it didn't. You are a clever one, Captain Lockhart. Very well, I concede your argument. So long as this cargo doesn't interfere with our arrangement. That is to take priority."

"Agreed." She thrust out her hand.

As soon as his fingers slid against hers, her fickle heart lurched. Not that she let it show.

She pumped his hand and released him. "Good. Now, let's see what we can find in my father's books."

His smile spoke almost as loudly as his eyes. Her clever resourcefulness had earned his respect. That meant a great deal to men, she'd learned. The earning of an equal's respect.

So of course—her being female and all—the surge of pleasure at having done so herself caught her quite by surprise.

D aniel followed the feisty woman to the stairs. She'd barely made the first step when Lula sniffed her out. She bent to stroke the dog's fur, and the little hound's tail swished wildly.

"How old is your dog?" He'd never seen a person and dog as fond of one another as these two.

She scooped the terrier up and settled the creature on her hip like a mother with a toddler.

He withheld a smile. Eccentric as well as clever, feisty, and nigh on irresistible.

"Next month will be three years I've had her. Got her as a weanling pup. She was a puny little thing. Fit in my palm when Papa brought her home."

She started up the stairs, and the dog fixed black eyes on him over Camilla's shoulder. There'd be no opportunity for more kisses with her canine chaperone.

Not that he should be thinking about that. But the way her soft lips had felt beneath his had stirred something within him. Now he had a hard time putting the sensation and the accompanying complications it caused from his mind.

Lula continued to stare at him as her head bobbed over Camilla's shoulder up the staircase, down the hall, and into the office he'd visited earlier. Had that only been yesterday morning?

Impossible.

Camilla lowered the canine to the floor, and Lula trotted over to sniff his boots. After completing a thorough investigation of both shoes, she retreated to a round pillow on the floor by the bookshelf, turned three circles, and then curled into a ball. But her wary eyes never left him.

The captain opened a desk drawer and extracted a journal. Reverent fingers traced an embossed design on the cover he couldn't quite make out.

Her gaze held his. "These are his personal thoughts and prayers. It still feels like an invasion of his privacy for me to read."

Understandable. "You don't have to."

That seemed to be the right answer because an appreciative curve graced her lips before she flipped to the last third of the book.

While she read, he examined the room to give her privacy. He moved toward a document encased in a glass frame nailed to the wall.

From the desk of Capt. Seeley of the United States Steamboat Inspection Service:

A skilled pilot of steam vessels who can be trusted to perform duties and safe navigation in the waters of the Mississippi River. Having passed examination and inspection, Camilla Lockhart is hereby licensed to act as a second-class pilot on steam vessels not exceeding thirty gross tons for the term of five years.

Dated February 22, 1924

She'd only been a licensed pilot for a few months. He didn't know much about the differences between a captain and a pilot except that one seemed to be a position and the other an occupation, though they melded together as far as he could tell. He did know being licensed was a major accomplishment. And for her to earn it at such a young age from men who were likely hesitant to let a woman into their ranks only elevated his estimation of her higher.

"Here's something." Camilla's voice towed him from the document, and he took the opportunity to watch her face while she read. "This entry denotes Papa's meeting with Mr. Dixon, which I now know is the elder Mr. Gray."

She met his gaze before beginning to read. "'Met with Mr. Dixon who has compelling evidence about the location of the Hollis fortune. Supposedly, there's a stash of hundreds if not thousands of gold coins. The worth of that sort of find is nearly incalculable.'"

Her voice thickened. "'I could buy my Camilla a proper house and give her an opportunity to live a normal life as a girl ought. Pay for lady classes and the like. Maybe find her a good suitor. Can't expect her to miss her marrying years taking care of me on this rickety old boat. Not if I hope to have grandsons someday.'"

She paused to compose herself, and he resisted the urge to reach out and comfort her.

After a few breaths, she continued. "'Mr. Dixon claims to have documentation he discovered in his father-in-law's attic that suggests the treasure might not be where they've believed in family lore. If that's true, then there might be more to this than merely old rumors. He's promised ten percent of the findings. Even that percentage would be enough to make a better life for my dear daughter. I have to try.'"

Moisture glistened in her eyes even as she unsuccessfully attempted to blink it away. "There's only one other notation. A short passage he wrote two months later, three days before he died." Camilla turned to another page.

Daniel rested his palms on the desk between them. Lula popped her head up and emanated a low growl. He smirked at the hairy guardian.

Ignoring the dog, Camilla read the final entry. "'Mr. Dixon has discovered the location! Tomorrow, we will begin the search. I must be careful. I overheard Mr. Dixon speaking to a man whose face I could not see. They were talking about someone following him. If others know he is close to discovery, they may attempt to take it from us.'" She closed the book. "That's all I have."

She replaced the book inside the drawer and lowered herself into the chair, the weight of sharing her father's final recorded words sinking her deep into the cracked leather. When Lula scuttled over and pawed at her leg, Camilla scooted back to allow the dog to jump up and sit in her lap.

Daniel took the seat opposite. "The journal mentions Mr. Dixon making a discovery in his father-in-law's attic. I hadn't thought to search there."

She stroked the fur between Lula's pointy ears. "I suppose we can look after we eat supper tonight. Assuming I'm still invited?"

"Of course." He laced his fingers together. "My invitations, like my contracts, are always made in the utmost sincerity."

The quip earned him a ghost of a smile.

They sat in silence before he broached the topic bouncing around between his ears and demanding his attention. "I'd like to discuss what happened in the records room."

"You mean when you kissed me?" Her steady gaze held his. "Or what you meant when you called me unusual?"

Her directness settled his nerves. He always fared better with clear conversations than ones with skirted topics and veiled meanings. "Both. I enjoyed kissing you. Perhaps more than I should have, which is why I couldn't continue even though I longed to do so. Secondly, my statement that you are an unusual woman is true. It is not, however, an insult as you seemed to take it, but rather a declaration of fact that, in my estimation, was a compliment."

She leaned back in her chair. "You talk like a lawyer."

"I am one."

Camilla laughed, a pleasingly robust sound. "And you certainly talk like one. But thank you for the clarification."

When she said nothing more on the matter, he returned to business. "Shall we go fetch Lucas and see what Anna's family cooked for this evening?"

She tugged her watch from her pocket, checked the time, then replaced it. "I also found the kiss pleasing. Will that be an issue with our deal?"

The twists in the conversation left him off-kilter. He jabbed a hand through his hair and dislodged his hat, making it drop to the floor. "I suppose we can postpone any romantic inclinations until after we have concluded the search. That way we can keep things less muddied."

He retrieved his hat and dusted it off before settling the fedora over his forehead.

"So..." Camilla drummed her fingers on the desk. "You're saying you'd like to pursue a romantic relationship with me if we find your treasure? Why?"

How did he answer that? "Even if we do not find the treasure, I'd like to continue to get to know you in a more personal way. It's already clear the hope of discovering something deeper than friendship exists." He splayed his fingers. "At least on my account."

"I like you, Mr. Gray." She sat forward, and the dog spun a circle and settled in her lap, finally no longer glaring at him. "You remind me of Papa. I never had to guess what he was thinking. I appreciate that about a person."

"So do I."

They stared at one another until she broke the strange feeling building between them by thrusting herself backward in the chair and scooting away from the desk.

She scooped up her dog, stood, then turned to place the creature on the chair. "Let's go find your nephew and his frogs. Then we can search the attic. Of course, sooner or later, we are going to need to finish the boat repairs and take to the water."

"Got to know where to start looking first."

"Fair point." She winked as she passed him, dog at her heels. Seemed the terrier had no intention of staying behind.

Like another enchanted puppy, he tagged along after them.

Camilla stopped short at the door, nearly causing him to trip over the dog who had also come to a sudden halt. He caught himself before his big feet could do any damage to tiny paws. Lula looked up at him and yipped.

He held up both hands.

"Oh, hush, girl." Camilla scooped her up. "She's being especially protective today. I'll need to lock her in here so she doesn't attempt to follow me off the boat."

"Why not let her come? Lucas would enjoy it." At her owlish expression, he added, "Unless she doesn't care for children, of course. My nephew can be rambunctious, but I don't believe he'd cause her harm."

She settled the dog on her hip, and the two of them regarded him. "Never had a fella invite me and Lula to supper." She spoke to the dog. "Imagine that. What would Papa think of this one?"

Did she expect the dog to answer?

As though reading his thoughts, she shot him a look, almost daring him to ask her. Instead, he thrust his hands into his pockets and let his previous statement stand.

"Very well. We accept." She waltzed out the door, and he could have sworn he heard her chuckle under her breath.

Had she done that just to set him off-balance? If so, she'd succeeded.

During a prolonged discussion of hand signals with Solomon on the main deck, Camilla gestured for Daniel to go ahead and disembark. Did she need the engineer's permission to go with him to supper, or were they discussing boat business?

He grabbed the gangplank railing to leave as another man mounted the other end. He locked gazes with the grumpy dockmaster from yesterday. Daniel stepped back. He'd wait and see what problems ensued.

The paunchy man climbed the gangplank with obvious effort and placed his hands on his hips upon arriving on the deck. Solomon noticed him and gestured to Camilla.

She stiffened. "May I help you?"

"You've been requested to disembark on account of housing a lawless crew." He sneered at Solomon.

"What? We've been docking here for more than two decades. And what's this about a lawless crew?"

Lula growled.

Without making eye contact, Camilla held the dog out in Daniel's direction. The little thing hung from where Camilla hooked her hands under the creature's front legs, belly stretched out long and rear legs dangling.

Should he...? Before he could talk himself out of it, he accepted the proffered canine and awkwardly held her away from his body. The dog stared at him. At least she didn't look like she might bite. She did seem uncomfortable, though. He twisted her so the length of her belly rested along his forearm, and he secured her chest in his palm. Then he settled her against his side. Her ears twitched as she focused on her mistress.

"We have a report of a criminal on board," the red-faced man announced, punctuating each word with his finger. "Either you depart, or you turn the miscreant over."

Finn and another man Daniel hadn't seen before joined them. Dark-skinned and in his midfifties with close-cut hair.

Camilla tapped her toe on the deck. "You have no right to—"

"There's the criminal there." The dockmaster stabbed a finger toward the older newcomer. "He was recognized in town."

Solomon made a series of gestures Daniel couldn't decipher. Looked like something with eating and a throwing-his-hands-up motion to indicate exasperation.

The red-faced man scowled. "What's he saying with all that voodoo talk? Putting a curse on me?"

Camilla blinked. "Excuse me?" She drew in a long breath, looked to the heavens, then started again in a calm tone. "Mr.—What did you say your name was?"

"Liles."

"Mr. Liles. Every man on this vessel is a Christian. We don't do voodoo or witchcraft or any other such nonsense. My engineer suffered an injury that causes difficulty with speech, so he communicates with hand signals. There's nothing illegal about that. And as for Buck, he's already served his time."

"So you admit to harboring a criminal." Mr. Liles snorted. "That's all I needed to know."

"No, sir. I said he'd served his time." Camilla refused to be cowed, and as Daniel nodded his approval, she drew herself to her full height. "Which means he is no longer a criminal but a reformed man."

Mr. Liles gestured her closer, and she moved near with a frown. Daniel had no trouble hearing the whispered words.

"Miss, I don't want to see you get hurt. That boy there was accused of beating a man and leaving him for dead." He hissed the next words. "A white man!"

Camilla crossed her arms and leaned away from him. "I know that. And while he served the deserved sentence for that crime, he met a chaplain—a chaplain who introduced him to Jesus. Buck spent the next fifteen years turning into one of the finest Christian men I know. He's no trouble to this town or anyone else."

"You trust the word of a n—" He cleared his throat as Solomon's already impressive stature seemed to expand. "A colored man?"

"I trust the fruit I've seen in his life and the power of the Holy Spirit to transform us all. So yes, sir, I do trust my brother in the Lord, no matter who he was in his previous life."

Daniel couldn't help but grin. Heaven help any man who thought to go against Captain Camilla Lockhart's convictions.

Buck stepped forward, hat in his scarred hands. "Won't go to shore again if it makes folks uncomfortable, sir."

Mr. Liles glared at him, then addressed Camilla. "Any more complaints, and I will be forced to send the law this direction."

"Understood."

They all watched in tense silence until the man stepped foot on shore. Once he disappeared around the bend, tension drained from the air. Daniel ran a hand down the dog's soft back. The fur beneath his skin felt surprisingly nice. How long had it been since he'd stroked a pet? Not since boyhood.

"Well, how do you like that." Camilla rubbed her forehead, shoulders deflating. "I'm sorry about that, Buck."

"It's all right, Captain. I know how it is in the free world." The man's dark eyes held sorrow. "I don't want to cause you no trouble. This is why I don't often come out of the kitchen. But I didn't think anyone would recognize me here."

"It's not your fault." She sighed and leveled a look at Daniel. "Got any questions for me?"

The words sounded like a challenge. Did she think he'd agreed with Mr. Liles?

He gave the first answer that came to mind. "'Therefore if any man be in Christ, he is a new creature: old things are passed away; behold, all things are become new.' So said Paul in Second Corinthians. I forget the exact verse." His fingers made another pass down Lula's back. "Besides, I don't see how your crew or their past is any of my business, so I'm not sure what question you are expecting me to ask."

Solomon made another series of quick gestures, and Buck grinned. Finn tipped a respectful nod. Apparently, he'd passed muster. The idea tugged on the corner of his mouth, but he withheld his pleased grin lest they mistake it for him joshing with them.

The redheaded crewman scooted forward.

"Solomon says you would fit in here with our little brother-hood." Finn's gaze darted to Camilla. "Plus one sister. We here is all reformed men her pa gave a second chance. Seems you might be the type to understand."

Another surge of respect for this bold woman surfaced, and Daniel held her gaze even though he spoke to Finn. "A fine captain you have here, gentlemen."

The men hooted their agreement, and her cheeks colored a pleasing pink.

"All right now. Enough of that." Camilla waved their laughter away. "Mr. Gray has asked Lula and me to have supper with his family. Any of you fellas take issue with that?"

Even Solomon shook his head in the negative.

"Well, then." She brushed her hands down her gray trousers. "Best we be off."

The dog still cradled in his arms, he followed her swaying form off the boat. They'd promised to wait to explore any romantic notions until after they'd completed their treasure hunt.

But he suspected it wasn't going to be a promise he could keep.

Smoke curled from the cigarette in Smuggie's fingers, the nub almost close enough to burn. Too bad he didn't have another. Or a drink. Something to numb the headache pounding behind his eyes from lack of sleep and problems that shouldn't be his to think about. From the shadow of an alley, he watched the lawyer and the lady captain disembark her steamer before he took another draw. The last of the paper burned away, and he scorched his thumb. He dropped the rest in the dirt.

Durkin seemed to think these two would lead him to the rest of the lost bank haul some slick fella from St. Louis had swindled him out of last summer. Doubtful the mess with Mickey's gang had anything to do with this patsy and his dame. They were after a sunken treasure. Same nonsense got the elder Mr. Gray bumped off. Happened occasionally to random goofs who stick their noses where they don't belong.

Smuggie waited alongside the mercantile building and jerked his cap low over his eyes. The two approached, their conversation growing louder as they neared.

"Lucas will probably want to keep a frog as a pet instead of letting Bo fry it," the man was saying.

That earned a laugh from the woman, who carried a small dog on her hip. She was pleasant looking with big eyes, a pert nose, and rosy lips. The trousers she wore clung to her curves, and the top button of a man's shirt hung open to expose the hollow of her throat. Little wonder Gray had picked the girl over some greasy bloke to treasure hunt with.

They passed by him without glancing his way and continued to the old buildings crouching along the riverbank. Funny how his world looked different in the daylight. Rather than the warm glow of welcoming bars and the pleasant cool of darkness, harsh light exposed every dusty detail and neglected roof sag. He didn't like to rise for a day's work until the sun started to sink below the trees.

He fiddled with the pistol in his jacket pocket to calm the trembling in his fingers while he gave the two a head start, but he still itched for another cigarette.

This assignment was simple, if annoying. Shadow Gray and see where he went and what he discovered. Any indication he was sniffing too close or any hint he knew where Scissors hid that stash, and Smuggie had been ordered to run straight to the big boss. He didn't often deal with Durkin directly. The shyster and this skirt must have gotten under the boss's skin.

After flipping up his collar and settling his brim as close to his eyes as possible, he stepped out of the alley to follow.

The bright light seared his eyes even from underneath his wide hat, and he had to blink away the sting. Usually, there were other blokes for this kind of business, but most of the higher-ups were busy with what was going on down in those caves. Leaving men who normally did the job of hiding cargo on unsuspecting vessels to take up spying instead.

Didn't sit right.

His long legs closed the distance too quickly, but it didn't matter. They were too busy chatting to pay him any heed. Simple people like them didn't worry about rivals sneaking up from behind to off them, so they tended not to notice their surroundings like they should.

They stopped after a bend in the road, and he had to draw up short or hazard getting too close. He cursed under his breath and acted like he'd been looking in a shop window. His insides churned. Didn't need them being able to identify him to any coppers.

They started walking again, but when he turned to follow, the miniature mutt the woman carried poked its head out from behind her shoulder.

It growled.

Smuggie hesitated, but the chattering couple didn't notice. The woman bounced the dog to shush it. They wove through a gathering crowd on the sidewalk, making it easier for him to blend in.

The dog's eyes locked on him, and it growled again. This time, the woman paused and looked behind her. He sidestepped into the shadow of a nearby alley.

Better to risk losing them than lose one of his fingers because of a dog. Durkin had made the penalty for being discovered all too clear, and a smuggler needed all his fingers. Besides, he knew where they were heading. They'd gone to that same eating hole twice already.

He could wait.

The spicy scent of fried food and the sounds of child-ish laughter along with spirited puppy yipping warmed something in Camilla's heart she hadn't realized had grown cold. Stella set the table in Daniel's mansion with the help of two young women while Lucas played with Lula on the dining room floor.

Camilla didn't know what to do with her hands, so she locked them behind her and let the homey scene wash over her. She'd been content to spend her days adventuring on the waters with Papa. But something about this mismatched land-bound family drew her as well. Two different worlds, yet similar in many ways. She knew a thing or two about creating families out of bonds other than blood.

What would her crew think of this bunch? She should have asked if she could bring her fellas to eat with them. Presumptuous of her, but she might ask for tomorrow anyway. Maybe if she offered to bring some food it wouldn't be so rude.

She'd promised to go with Solomon and visit his mother while they were in town, but they could squeeze in a meal here as well.

Besides, they'd just gotten a barrel of salted pork. They could spare a few slabs to share with these people.

"Can I keep her?" Lucas tugged on Camilla's shirtsleeve and snatched her from calculating the difference between how much other women and a boy might eat in comparison to the portions assigned to her men.

He cradled Lula in his arms, and two sets of wide eyes gleamed up at her.

"Keep Lula? No, you can't do that." Her chest seized when his lips puckered. Maybe she shouldn't have brought Lula after all.

"But we go together so well. *Lu*–cus and *Lu*–la. My father would have called that fate."

Camilla extended her hands, and Lula squirmed, ready to go back to her mistress. "That is a fine similarity, but I wouldn't call it destiny."

Lucas twisted his body and held the dog away. "But I like her. She's a good friend."

"Boy howdy, do I know it." Her heart pinched, and she lowered to one knee. "Lula here's my best friend if you can believe that. A dog for a friend."

"'Course, I can believe it." He snuggled Lula, and the dog stared at Camilla with big eyes that seemed to ask if Camilla was really contemplating giving her away.

Not that she could ever do that. She kept her words gentle, knowing that often the heart needed the unfettered kindness and affection only a dog could provide. "My papa got her for me."

"Oh." His face scrunched, but he still clutched her to his little chest.

"She was the tiniest thing in the litter. Papa knew I'd been pretty lonely as the only girl on our boat for so long. So, he got me a furry little girl to play with. He's gone now, but I still have Lula. She's named for the Tallulah River, where my papa was born."

Lucas sighed and, with an air of great nobility, stretched his arms toward Camilla. Lula took the opportunity to leap and slammed into Camilla's chest, her clawed feet hanging onto Camilla's shoulder. She patted the dog's back and smiled at Lucas.

He tucked his hands in his pockets and rocked back on his heels. "Don't want to separate a friendship like that, then." His eyes brightened. "Could you take me to the Tallulah River and get me one too?"

"I'd have to ask your mama about that."

He groaned. "Then I won't ever get one of my own." He reached out to pat Lula's head. "Can I keep playing with her until you leave, at least?"

"Of course. She especially likes to tug on a length of rope if you have one. Just be sure you're easy about it." She winked. "You're much stronger than she is."

"Don't worry. I won't hurt her." He beamed and dashed off, presumably to raid the house for a length of rope.

Camilla peeled the dog from her shoulder and placed her on the floor. Lula positioned herself between Camilla's feet and sat down. Poor girl. Sometimes new people and situations could be a bit much for her. Must be hard being so small.

She was about to ask if there was anything she could do to help Stella and the others when Daniel's sister Mabel swept into the room in a rustle of shimmering rose fabric. A chain of pearls dripped down the front of the low-waisted gown, and white gloves stretched to her elbows. A headband of sparkling beadwork draped across the dark hair at her temples, two pink feathers sticking out from the side.

She must be going out somewhere. Surely no one dressed like that for a meal at home.

"Fried things again?" Mabel shook her head, sending the feathers dancing. "Stella, didn't I tell you all that grease is terrible for our figures?"

Stella and the two young boarders paused in setting silverware on the table. Camilla had been introduced to both. One's name was Daisy and the other's was Violet, but she'd already forgotten which name belonged to which woman. She'd always been better at remembering faces than names.

One of the two, the shorter girl with bobbed blond hair and a milky complexion, rolled her eyes. The other, a slim girl who didn't look a day over sixteen with thick black curls and a warm brown complexion a shade or two darker than Stella's, ducked her chin.

Lula yipped from between Camilla's feet as though she had something to say about the matter. But then she darted away, and Camilla saw the boy under the table wiggling a rope. No, that was a tasseled curtain tieback someone would likely be displeased with being used as a toy. She took a half step forward, then paused. Too late. Lula latched onto the other end with a growl and snatched her head from side to side. Lucas laughed and held on.

Mabel's cool gaze landed on Camilla. This time, her eyes didn't have the dark circles underneath, and they looked much sharper than before. "Welcome back, Miss Lockhart. I see you've decided to join us for dinner."

She raked a look down Camilla's attire and opened her mouth as though to say something, but then her attention shifted to the ruckus under the table. "Lucas! Come out from under there. We don't play under the table."

The boy dropped the rope, and Lula trotted out with it hanging triumphantly from her jowls.

Mabel pursed her lips. "You brought a dog inside the house?"

"Lula always stays inside. Sleeps in the bed with me too." As horror widened Mabel's eyes and rounded out her mouth, Camilla hurried to add, "Daniel invited us both. He thought Lucas might enjoy playing with her."

The sharp glint in Mabel's eyes softened as her son laughed. She fingered the pearls on her throat. "Please, just don't set it on the table."

Did she mean Lula? "Oh no. Lula doesn't sit on the table. I usually feed her from a bowl on the floor."

For some reason, Mabel looked surprised, but she gave a grateful nod and looked at a doorway at the rear of the room. "Have you seen my brother?"

Stella wiped her hands on a towel and set a platter of fried things on the table. "He went to get something for me from the cellar. Said he'd be right back."

Mabel toyed with her necklace. "What did he go to get?"

"Vinegar, I think," Camilla answered. Something to do with "helping out Daisy's beans," but she left that part off.

One of the girls, maybe Violet, added what must be the bowl of green beans in question to the table. The other one brought over a tray of steaming corncobs from a narrow table anchored against the opposite wall. Then they both stepped back from the table and waited. Were serving duties part of their rent? Stella pulled out a chair and seated herself.

Mabel cocked a slim eyebrow. "We'll wait for my brother to begin the meal. Proper etiquette is to wait until *all* are present before commencing." She peered over Stella's head at the other two and took on an instructional tone. "Along with dressing your best, a hostess is responsible for making sure everyone is properly attended at her dinner party. These are things you will need to know if you hope to marry well and be able to move out of my house."

Both girls ducked their chins in acknowledgment.

Seeming satisfied, Mabel turned to Lucas. "Time to take the dog to its own dinner and tuck it away for now, darling. You can get it out and play with it after we've finished our meal. And be sure to wash your hands extra well."

Lucas let the curtain tieback go and stood. "Yes, ma'am."

95

Wait. What did she mean about tucking Lula away? "Lula can stay with me. She won't be any trouble."

Whatever Mabel meant by "tucking it away" didn't sound like something one should do to living creatures.

"I thought you said the dog didn't sit at the table." Mabel's poppy-red lips drooped at the corners.

"She doesn't." Defensiveness rose where it likely shouldn't, and Camilla evened out her tone. "She usually sits under the table between my feet. She won't bother anyone."

Mabel put a hand to her throat and opened her mouth.

"She gets nervous if I leave her alone in unfamiliar places," Camilla interjected before the woman could try to do something mad like stuff Lula in a hatbox. "She'll bark all night if you put her in a different room, and if she gets too upset, she might start chewing on something."

Mabel pinched the bridge of her nose. "Fine. It's not like I don't already live in a nuthouse. Why not add dogs at the table to everything else?"

Daniel entered with Lucas at his side before Camilla had to come up with an answer. Fastest handwashing she'd ever seen. She withheld a chuckle. The boy hadn't had time to get his hands wet. Not that she'd rat him out.

They took their places around the table with Daniel at the head, Lucas and then Mabel to his right. Stella sat on the left and the two girls settled beside her. That only left a spot for Camilla to sit by Mabel.

Well, she could sit on the other side of Violet. Or was that Daisy? Two girls with flower names ought not to live in the same house. Either way, she got the feeling sitting over there would be rude. Putting four folks on one side of the table and only two on the other would probably break another dinner etiquette rule.

She sat next to Mabel and crossed her ankles under the table like she'd seen nice ladies do. Lula started digging her claws on Camilla's knee, and she remembered why she never sat like that anyway. She uncrossed her feet, and the dog settled into her usual place.

Poor girl. Lula was probably hungry. Maybe she could sneak a piece of meat onto one of those little bread plates and lower it to Lula when Mabel wasn't looking.

Daniel folded his hands and waited for the others to do the same. Then he closed his eyes for the prayer. "Father, we thank you for another day and the blessings you have bestowed upon us. We thank you for this food and the hands that have prepared it. Please bless it to the nourishment of our bodies and guide us in your service."

They echoed their amens, and Camilla kept her hands on her lap. They were fancier here, so they likely didn't reach for the nearest plate like she and the crew did on the boat. Best wait and see what others did first.

The dark-haired girl across from her caught Camilla's eye and slowly picked up her napkin. Camilla caught on and followed. They spread the napkins in their laps. Then the girl looked at Daniel with a tip of her head.

He picked up the platter of fried things, placed a few on his plate with a pair of tongs, and then held the platter out for Lucas. The boy grabbed a half dozen frog legs and reached for a second helping, but Daniel whispered for him to eat what he had on his plate first.

Lucas nodded, folded his hands, and wiggled as Daniel handed the food to Mabel. While Mabel picked one tiny leg from the platter, Daniel grabbed the green beans and started the process again.

Camilla waited her turn with the platter of fried legs. The spicy scent tickled her nostrils, and her stomach responded with a low growl she hoped no one noticed. She selected four fried frog legs and then reached the platter to the kind flower girl across the table. The system continued until everyone had a portion of everything on their plate. Only then did anyone pick up a fork.

Much different from the boat. They said grace and then grabbed themselves a helping from whatever Buck had scrounged up that day. She'd have to tell him about frogs' legs if these were any good. What a wonder he didn't already think of that himself. He'd made them eat turtle before. Why not frog? They could probably gather up plenty of the slimy little hoppers. Might make another free option to go along with walleye and crawfish.

Next to her, Mabel stabbed her fork into the fatter end of the length of meat and sawed off a sliver with her knife. She sampled it, then set the knife aside, and selected a single green bean. No wonder the lady was so thin.

Stella stuck a frog leg between her teeth and deftly separated the meat from the bone. Then she returned the remainder to her plate. That seemed much easier than Mabel's way.

Camilla plucked one from her plate and lifted it toward her mouth. It smelled as good as the fried shrimp she'd had earlier. Her mouth watered.

"Daniel tells me you will be taking a trip along the river," Mabel said. She dabbed her red lips with her napkin, leaving a little pink smear on the creamy fabric. "To where, exactly?"

Camilla reluctantly lowered her bite back to her plate. "I don't know yet." She gestured to Daniel. "That depends on him."

How much did the others know about the treasure? Hadn't he put all those secrecy clauses in their contract for a reason?

Daniel opened his mouth to answer, but Lula barked underneath the table, followed by a low growl. Camilla glanced around the room. Strange. Lula only did that when she felt threatened.

Mabel frowned and Lucas laughed. So much for the dog not disturbing anyone.

Lula scratched her paws against Camilla's knee, the signal she wanted to be picked up. Camilla tilted to look at the dog under the table. Lula increased her digging.

"Not while I'm eating," she whispered.

Lula barked.

What had gotten into her?

"Perhaps you should take the dog outside. We certainly don't want it doing its, uh, business under the table." Mabel's cheeks reddened.

The blond-headed flower girl snickered. She covered her mouth with her napkin, however, when Mabel's eyes flashed her way.

"Would you like me to escort you?" Daniel flattened his hands on the table to push back his chair.

Camilla scooted back, and as soon as there was enough room, Lula sprung into her lap. Mabel mumbled something about flying fur as Camilla tried to stand and keep hold of Lula at the same time. She finally got the squirming dog settled and straightened herself.

"If you'll please excuse me." That sounded plenty proper-like. She nestled Lula to her side and headed to the door.

She hadn't even gotten the chance to taste one of the frog legs.

D aniel followed Camilla onto the front porch, even though she hadn't agreed to his company, and searched for a lamp to dispel the thickening twilight while she took the dog to the grass. Maybe someday that fancy new Mississippi Power and Light Company would stretch their lines out here to Natchez.

The night air carried earthy scents and heavy humidity, tinged with an acidic aroma somewhat like cigarettes. The wind shifted, and the unusual smell dissipated, replaced by sweet azaleas, which had overgrown their beds.

He located a long match in a box by the door and lit the wick on a chimney lamp. He held it up for Camilla, but she'd already disappeared down the stairs and into the yard. Lula had her nose to the ground, sniffing. Camilla's shoulders hunched as she watched the dog in the dim light.

He joined them on the patch of overgrown grass between the porch and the cliff's edge. "My sister means well. I apologize for her behavior."

Her gaze found his, something unreadable in her dark eyes. "She didn't do anything wrong. I should have known bringing Lula might cause trouble. She's..."

Lula's hackles rose, and she rumbled with a growl. Deep and throaty and more menacing than he'd expected from such a small creature. Lula pressed her snout to the ground, sniffing frantically.

"Wonder what she found?" He thrust the light higher as the dog snuffled in a straight line down the front of the house.

"Whatever it is, she doesn't like it." Camilla shadowed Lula along one side of the porch and back in the other direction. Then the dog followed an invisible trail up the front steps and to one of the windows, her growling increasing.

Daniel's stomach knotted. They'd had a few issues with stray dogs. Maybe one had been searching for food. But with his father's disappearance, the dangers of the treasure, and now the hint of something smoky in the air... Had someone been lurking around the house? He strained to see deeper into the encroaching darkness, but no human forms manifested beyond his circle of light.

Lula thrust her snout in the air. Her bark almost instantly turned to a howl. Nose still tilted heavenward, she took off down the steps and into the yard.

Camilla yelped and dashed after her, yelling for the dog.

The bluffs loomed straight ahead.

He lengthened his stride and reached for Camilla's arm. "Stop! The cliff."

Guessing his intention to grab her, she pivoted away from him and made a sharp turn. Lula continued to bay like a hunting dog, short legs churning down the narrow walk between the row of houses and the ravine.

"Lula! Halt!" Camilla's command went unheeded as they continued to chase the dog in the dark, dangerously close to the sheer drop-off to his right. If she took a wrong step...

He dashed past her and gained ground on the dog. Lula looked back at Camilla behind him, let out another bay as though they were doing the right thing in following her, and sprinted faster.

Blasted dog.

She slowed to sniff the air, and he grabbed for her. But she tucked her tail and shot off again. He stumbled, nearly losing the lantern.

He regained his feet as Camilla neared.

"Tallulah! Bad dog!"

Lula's howling stopped and she slowed. Daniel's light encircled the canine's rigid form. She held one paw aloft, and her nose twitched in the direction they'd been going. Camilla stomped up to her. The dog whined and faced the direction she'd been running but didn't take off again. Camilla scooped her from the ground and held her close against her heaving chest.

"I'm sorry," Camilla puffed out. "I don't know what got into her."

Daniel lofted the lantern to examine boot prints in the soft dirt. He had no skill in such things, but one large set of prints appeared to have walked toward the house and, judging by the distance between the prints facing the other direction, ran away from it.

The hairs along his arms rose.

He put a hand on Camilla's arm and turned her toward home. "Let's get back to the house. Next time, we might need to put Lula on a lead rope."

Camilla cradled the trembling dog. "She doesn't usually do that. She must have gotten wind of a coyote or a stray cat that tickled her nostrils and got her in a tizzy."

He didn't mention the boot prints that couldn't have belonged to anyone in his house. Likely, it was nothing worth fretting over. Probably a neighbor.

He hoped.

"Lula was only doing her job." He rubbed between the dog's pointy ears as they walked. "She was protecting her mistress."

Caution rose in Camilla's tone. "Protecting me from what?"

So much for not alarming her. He mentally smacked his forehead. "I can't be sure, but with the way she was sniffing the porch, I'm not sure it was a coyote's scent she caught."

Even in the murky light, he had no trouble reading the dip in her eyebrows. "You think someone was sneaking about?"

"I didn't say that. We've had a few stray dogs around. Could have been a cat."

"But you don't think so."

How did she read him so easily? "She's also unfamiliar with the people around here, so it could be nothing. Probably a neighbor. Or one of Stella's brothers with some strange scent on his boots."

Though none of them smoked tobacco that he was aware of. Something to do with Anna's instance on the only smoke in her residence coming from cook fires.

"Hmm." Camilla glanced behind them. "Who else did you tell about your treasure?"

"Only Mabel. Well, and Stella knows. But that's because she walked in when I discovered the hidden room and my excitement got the better of me." The muscles in his neck tightened. The humid air pulled slowly into his nostrils, too thick to offer much refreshment.

Camilla hesitated as they neared the first house on the bluff row. "Do you think one of them told someone else? Someone who's interested in stealing it from you?"

A possibility he'd rather not consider. "I don't think any of Stella's family would be a problem."

"And if the other girls found out?"

He couldn't blame her tone. He'd been the one with both a secrecy clause and loose lips.

"Daisy doesn't have any family and mostly keeps to herself. Violet is much more social, but even if she did overhear anything, I don't think she knows enough about the stories or the clues to share anything significant."

Her silence said plenty about her trust in those around him.

They ambled down the walk, the lights glowing through the windows of his neighbor's homes. Mosquitoes buzzed around them, and a frog called for his companions.

The uncomfortable weight in his stomach grew. Had someone in his household betrayed his trust? Were strangers with ill intent sneaking around on their porch?

"Which is which?" Camilla slowed as they turned back to the narrow front yard. "The girls, I mean. They both have flower names, and I forgot which flower belonged to who almost immediately after I was introduced."

A smile wiped some of the worry from his thoughts. "Violet is the one with the fashionable bob hairstyle. A trend Mabel despises."

He gestured her ahead of him up the stairs.

"Ah. So that makes the helpful one Daisy. Thank you."

After putting out the light, he left the lantern by the door and made sure to lock it behind him. When they returned to the dining room, only Stella and Lucas remained at the table.

"I'm afraid it's gotten cold." Stella nodded to their plates.

He held out the chair for Camilla, which earned him a pleased expression that warmed his chest.

Before she could sit, however, Lucas scurried from his spot and reached for Lula. "Can I take Lula to play?"

Camilla pursed her lips. "I think she's probably hungry." She lowered her voice. "Is there something she can eat and maybe a bowl she can use? I don't mind washing it."

Stella stood and replaced her chair under the table. "Send her with me. I've got a couple of leftover ham hocks in the kitchen I'm sure she'd enjoy and a pie tin none of us will ever tell Miss Mabel she drank from."

"Thank you." Camilla handed Lula over to Lucas and gave Stella a grateful smile.

When they'd exited, Daniel waited for her to sit and then helped her scoot the chair closer to the table. Then he grabbed his plate and moved to the seat across from her.

She took a bite of a frog leg, a thoughtful line creasing her forehead. Then she ate two more in reserved silence.

"They are better warm," he offered by way of apology.

Camilla shrugged. "They fill the belly, and that's all that matters."

They ate mostly in silence, commenting only occasionally about mundane topics such as how hot it had been this spring and if there might be rain soon. He appreciated how she didn't seem to be the type who needed to fill every space with words. And how she didn't bring up the disturbing subject of being watched. He needed to process that information, and if someone here had loose lips, then he'd need to mind his mouth.

Once she'd cleaned her plate, Daniel rose and took them both. "I'll drop these in the kitchen and then meet you at the stairs. We'll go up to the attic together and see what we can find."

She stood, both hands braced on the table, her movements slow. She met his gaze, then shifted her feet. "It's getting late. I hadn't thought through being out this long and walking back to the boat at night."

He hadn't either. Though at the time, things like being followed for possibly nefarious reasons hadn't occurred to him. "I'll escort you, of course. I wouldn't expect you to go back on your own."

From the way her shoulders relaxed, she'd expected that very thing. Odd, given the protective nature of her crew.

"Usually I wouldn't mind, but Lula's behavior put me on edge." She fiddled with the end of her braid. "Perhaps searching through an old attic in the daylight would be more prudent."

She was right. Even if disappointment at losing her company sooner than expected stung. It had already been an eventful day, and he'd think better after some space and rest. Spending time alone with her at night in a dark attic might not be the best idea anyway.

"Then once Lula has finished her supper, I'll walk you home." He dipped a slight bow.

Her features relaxed. "Thank you."

She followed him through the dining room's rear entrance and down a short hall to a kitchen once detached from the house. Stella's laughter greeted them.

Lula stood on her hind legs on the brick floor, front paws tucked in by her sides. Daniel paused, unable to contain a chuckle. The dog looked for all the world like a featherless chicken.

Her chest poked out, and she stretched her nose forward, jabbing at the air to see what Lucas held in his palm. Must be something that smelled good.

"Good girl!" Lucas pinched off a small piece of meat and tossed it to Lula.

She caught it midair, then settled on her haunches to chew.

Camilla crossed her arms and leaned against the doorframe. "Making you work for your supper, are they, girl?"

Stella waved a kitchen towel in her direction. "Nonsense. That little thing already ate a whole ham hock. Nothing but slick bone left."

The boy and dog repeated the trick. He hadn't seen his nephew smile this much in weeks. Perhaps he could talk Mabel into a puppy come Christmas.

"All right." He rubbed Lucas's head after a third round. "The captain and Lula need to head on home."

"Can I go?" Big eyes pleaded, and Lucas's hopeful expression wiggled into Daniel's heart.

Which was why the boy had grown so adept at wielding it.

"Not this time in the dark." He patted the boy's shoulder to ward off the disappointment. "But they'll be back tomorrow."

Camilla shifted. "Are you sure it's all right for Lula to come back? I can fashion her a rope and harness so she doesn't run away again." She snapped her fingers. "And I'll bring her water bowl too."

"Lucas would be sorely disappointed if you didn't bring her." He ruffled the boy's hair, which yielded a toothy grin.

"Thanks, Uncle Danny. I knew Mama was wrong when she said you wouldn't ever let us do anything we want to do."

What did he mean by that?

Not the time or place to ask.

"And if it wouldn't be too much trouble..." Camilla's eyes looked almost as big around as Lucas's could. "We'd bring more to help, of course, so there's that. But I understand if you wouldn't want to have all the extra folks."

He tried to follow the trail but came up lost.

"I think she wants to bring the men on her boat to eat with us," Stella supplied.

"Oh yes." Camilla straightened. "That."

"Of course." Daniel rocked back on his heels. "I'm sure we can arrange that for one evening. Assuming *all the men* on your boat want to leave, each one is more than welcome here."

Good. He emphasized the words enough for her to catch his meaning.

"Thank you." A sweet smile warmed her lips. "I will tell them *all* you said so."

They said their goodbyes, and at the front door, he paused to light the lantern again and ensure Camilla held Lula securely in her arms.

Lula growled.

This time, cigarette smoke hung in a cloud around the door. His insides tightened. Someone had been lingering on the porch. Did they know about the treasure, or did this have something to do with whatever had gotten his father killed?

It had been nigh on a month since they'd moved into this house and two since his grandfather had passed. Nothing nefarious had happened in that time.

Until he'd discovered the hidden door. And went to find Captain Lockhart, who just happened to be in port. A chill slithered through him.

"Have you noticed any odd occurrences lately?" Daniel tried to keep the question light as they ambled along the bluff for the fourth time this evening.

She rolled her lips before answering. "I'm not sure what you mean. It was uncommon for someone like you to come aboard and start us on this quest. It wasn't so unusual to deal with Mr. Liles or the way he acted. Either time. We're used to that sort of thing. The records room...well, that part was a unique experience for me."

Heat gathered in his chest and pushed its way to his ears. Memories derailed his thoughts—the way she'd felt in his arms, the press of her lips on his, and the sweet scent of her hair. He drew in a long breath.

The light bobbed between them, and he slowed his steps, keeping an eye on their surroundings in case he spotted anything odd. But since Lula snuggled contently in Camilla's arms, he doubted anyone crept close. The tiny hound turned out to be a great alarm.

He cleared his throat and attempted to redirect his thoughts. "I meant more like strange people hanging around who shouldn't be." Additional words he didn't expect to leave his brain popped out of his mouth. "But good to know you don't generally kiss men in record rooms."

"Other than you?"

Wait. Did she mean kissing or strange people hanging around? Was he both?

He paused and lifted the lantern to see her better. This woman had an uncanny way of throwing him off-balance. The twinkle in her eyes said she enjoyed teasing him.

Then, as though she hadn't been unraveling his thoughts, she continued in a professional tone. "There hasn't been anyone suspicious hanging around." She flipped her braid over her shoulder. "Why?"

Rocks crunched under the heel of his boots as they reached the main part of Natchez on Top of the Hill. People dressed in evening wear dipped in and out of the streetlamps, many women with paste gems and sparkling fringe catching the light.

"I think someone was on our porch tonight." He paused as an enclosed carriage veered too closely to the sidewalk. "I'm not sure if they are following you or me."

She spun around. "We're being followed?"

"Perhaps not at this moment." He glanced behind them anyway. The smoky scent had disappeared, and he'd not spotted any more footprints. Lula appeared to be sleeping.

The cigarette person seemed to be gone, though he had little training in spotting the criminal types outside of a courtroom.

He edged as much concern out of his voice as he could. "I can't know for certain, but I think someone's been watching us. Which didn't happen until after I came to you to start the search for the treasure."

She shot him a side-glance and pressed her lips into a line.

At least she didn't raise her defenses. He'd stated nothing but fact, though he could see how the statement could be taken as an offense. Would she dismiss him if she thought he implied her crew had been up to no good? Or would she address the situation and analyze the facts presented?

They passed a sleek motorcar containing a well-dressed couple in the open back seat. The driver wore a cap and a bored expression. The woman's raucous laughter grated as her gloved hands waved a feathered boa above her head.

Daniel let the lantern swing at his side, the light no longer needed along the brighter streets abuzz with people. Must be one of those speakeasy parties going on nearby. He'd heard many of the younger members of the old money families threw them fairly often, but he'd never been invited. Those not born in Natchez were not considered true society members.

Besides, he'd sampled that life and decided it wasn't for him.

"In the months since I lost Papa," Camilla spoke again, resuming the conversation he'd let collapse, "I've done little more than grieve and work to keep my crew fed. We've traveled the river delivering everything from corn to tobacco and once even a shipment of cattle, which I'll never do again. The crew hates washing Lula's deck. Imagine what they thought of cleaning up after four hundred cows packed nose to tail from aft to stern."

He wasn't sure how to respond. Her tone carried sorrow, determination, and strength when she talked about her father but faded into humor seeming to come naturally to her. He'd never met a woman her equal.

"So as far as your question about any odd occurrences and the underlying question about if me or mine has anything to do with us now being followed..." She stopped at an intersection by a bakery, the windows dark for the evening. "My answer is no. To both. Though to be honest, if anyone's been tracking us up and down the river, I can't say I noticed."

They waited as a carriage pulled by four white horses passed and then continued their trek through the town. Night brought cooler air and an abundance of mosquitoes.

He slapped one of the bloodsuckers from his neck. "It could be nothing. But we should pay close attention all the same. Better to go to the police with a little information than wait until something happens and it's too late."

Something he'd learned from more than one case. If people had only been more cautious, they wouldn't have wound up dead.

He made the turn at the end of the road to take the steep decline to the riverbank.

"I'll let my crew know." She eased closer to him. "Do you think we're in danger? Papa has a pistol in his bedchamber, but I've never shot it. He offered to teach me more than once, but I never liked the thing. I know a few ways to disarm a man if I must, but I'm not keen on having to carry a gun."

"I don't think it would come to that." Too bad he didn't feel as confident as he sounded. Perhaps he should consider carrying a weapon for the both of them.

She quickened her pace as they descended the hill. "I'll come in the morning after breakfast to look through the attic with you. But then I'll need to spend the rest of the day trying to procure a delivery. How long until you think you'll have a destination in mind? I'll need to know if I'm going upriver or down."

He should have had more information before securing a boat captain in the first place. She might have to wait to secure cargo. "Soon, I hope."

Answer enough for the moment. They traversed the rest of the decline in silence. When they reached the *Alma May*, Solomon stood by the deck rail, arms folded over his chest and eyes skimming the road. He relaxed as Daniel and Camilla neared. The engineer lifted a hand in greeting. How long would he have stood there waiting for Camilla before coming to search?

Knowing she had good people looking out for her made Daniel more comfortable leaving her. He tried to shake the thought away. Camilla Lockhart had been fine before meeting him. Surely she would be so now.

But the strange sensation that danger tagged along on his heels refused to be dismissed.

D ust tickled Camilla's nose and aggravated her throat. Thus far, she'd managed to keep herself to one ladylike sneeze mostly contained against her sleeve.

She eyed the old furniture, boxes, crates, trunks, and who knew what else in Daniel's attic. "How are we ever going to find anything up here? This place is stuffed with more things than *Alma May* could haul."

Daniel straightened from digging in a trunk. "I doubt it's that much." He shifted through papers. "Besides, we already know we aren't interested in the furniture. That dismisses most of it."

If he'd needed money, he could have kept his motorcar and made space in the attic at the same time. Who needed this much stuff? And did people simply pass their forgotten items to the next generation without ever bothering to sell, restore, or dispose of useless junk? Some of these things had to have been up here before the War Between the States.

She cocked her hands on her hips. An hour in and this quest had already grown tedious. "Very well. I suppose if I wanted to find a long-lost family treasure, this might be the place to do it.

No one's been here in half a century. Maybe your family simply forgot their fortune up here with everything else."

She was only half joshing.

"According to your father's book, my father was up here fairly recently." Daniel tossed the old letters back into the trunk and moved to the next one.

The man focused on an ancient book, her teasing clearly lost on him.

Maybe she should tell him to keep looking and she'd come back tonight to see if he'd found anything. When she'd signed the contract, she hadn't figured on digging through dusty attics. She shuffled around a precarious stack of dining room chairs leaning toward the muted light trying to penetrate the dirty window.

"Hey, look at this." Daniel flung a sheet to the ground, revealing a much newer-looking steam trunk in the far corner. "Not much dust on this."

"Because it was covered." The toe of her shoe caught on a lampstand, and she had to steady it before it toppled over.

"Not much dust on that sheet, either." He popped the lid.

She scooted past two other trunks and peered around him. How strange.

Pretty little boxes, all heaped on top of one another. A couple the size of a good hatbox, but most were like the jewelry box her mother had owned. Daniel selected one with angled sides shaped like an octagon.

"I think this was in the hidden room. I recognize this shape in the dust pattern."

She pressed against his arm to see better. "Well then, open it."

He tilted it toward the light and cracked the lid.

Nothing inside but a black-velvet lining. He set it aside and opened another. Then two more.

All empty.

"Whatever he'd had in there, it's gone now. But why hide the boxes?" Camilla put her fingers under her nose to stifle another sneeze.

"I don't know." Daniel tried all the other boxes to be sure. "None of this makes much sense."

Exactly.

There were more questions than answers, and these pieces didn't fit. They might as well be hurtling downstream after a flood with no engine. On a rickety flatboat. This had all happened so quickly, and they'd jumped in without a plan. Had it really only been a few days?

First her wits had been caught up in Daniel's sudden appearance and her adamant opposition to treasure hunting on account of what happened to Papa. Then there had been the disgruntled dockmaster, Mr. Copeland not paying her, and of course, Daniel's insistence on muddling her senses. Throw in the unexpected kiss, and she'd been completely discombobulated. She hadn't slowed down enough to think and ask pertinent questions.

"Let's go back to the beginning. What made you come look for me?"

He frowned. "I told you. I found the name Lockhart in the ledger. The same one that talked about the treasure."

"Yes, I know. But *why?*" She waved her hand through dust motes. "You saw a mention of an old treasure your family lore talked about in bedtime stories. And then you saw the name of a boat and its captain. Fine. But why did that make you choose now to hunt a treasure no one has ever found? Especially when you don't have extra means to do so, and you don't know where to start looking?"

His shoulders hunched, and he stared into the trunk of empty boxes. "If I don't figure out a way to get a lot of money in a short amount of time, my sister and Lucas will be in danger."

A tingle scurried down her back like a stowaway rat. "What do you mean 'danger'?"

He pressed his lips and then drew a deep breath. "I made some other discoveries as well. Ones not as pleasant."

After several breaths of silence, she prompted, "Such as...?"

"I don't think Lucas Sr. died in a factory accident. After he passed, I started going through his office. I was paying the bills for Mabel." The words tumbled from his lips like rats trying to scramble past one another.

Light tickled the top of his hatless hair, creating whorls of highlights. He brushed his fingers through it, mussing the pomade he'd applied. She liked the way the thick locks settled across his brow. One that currently tilled deep furrows in lines of contemplation.

Camilla lowered herself atop a trunk behind her. This had the feel of a tragic beginning. Best settle in for whatever came next.

"I started finding evidence my brother-in-law might have been involved in illegal activities. Records of shipments, notations of money for a business he didn't own, and the like." Daniel began as though tasting each word and finding it bitter. "I'd wondered about how he afforded the lifestyle he led with the money he made managing a glassware factory, but I never asked. Figured he could have had old family money. And my sister seemed happy."

He raked a hand through his dark hair again, and another lock joined its fellow in rippling over the grooves above his hunched eyebrows. "After he died, some men came to Mabel's house. Thankfully, Mabel and little Lucas weren't there. They'd gone out to enjoy time in the park while I dealt with her accounts for her. Those men had a look about them. You know what I mean?"

"I'm sure I can guess. Big, scarred, and knife-wielding?" She tilted her head. That's what thieves on the river looked like.

Daniel paused to blink at her. "What? No. They were in suits. But there was this undercurrent of danger."

"Oh, right. Slick like an eel's underbelly. I've seen that type too." She fiddled with the end of her braid and waited for him to continue.

"Anyway, they asked a lot of questions. Next thing I know, I'm being accused of some... illegal dealings. As you can imagine, that didn't go well for my law practice. About three weeks later, the bank came saying they were calling in a bunch of Lucas's high-dollar loans. They are going to take the house next week because he defaulted on his payments."

"Wait. You were accused of something illegal, and the bank came calling because of your brother-in-law's loans. What does that have to do with the eel-belly fellas?"

"They claimed Lucas owed them as well. Said if I didn't repay, then Mabel would have to. They left it at that, but I understood the danger implied. I'm assuming Lucas Sr. procured loans outside of the banks as well, and those people won't be as nice about recouping their assets."

He sat cross-legged on the floor and put his head in his hands as though the confession had drained him. At length, his gaze found hers again. "The accusations against me were false, in case you're wondering. But a smeared reputation, no matter if it's untrue, ruins a man's practice."

"I figured."

The affirmation drained some tension from his taut jaw, and he gave her a grateful nod.

Camilla sifted through the information. Lucas Sr. and perhaps Mabel—one never could tell—had been deeply in debt and possibly involved in illegal activity that got Lucas Sr. killed. Somehow, that connected to Daniel being accused as well, which led to the loss of his practice.

Which explained why he and his sister both moved into this house.

Problem was, what did any of that have to do with the lost Hollis treasure? What had the elder Mr. Gray gotten into, and why had he hired Papa to help?

Cold seeped through her veins. "What if our fathers weren't after the old Hollis treasure?"

He met her gaze. "What do you mean?"

"Well, you said your brother-in-law was doing something illegal. Your father was also involved in a quest that got him and Papa killed. What if they weren't looking for a treasure after all?"

Surprise should have brightened in those green depths, but instead, something dimmed them—resignation?

"But you've already thought of that." She speared him with her best reprimanding glare. "Not that you bothered mentioning our fathers might not have been after an old treasure after all. Maybe he got Papa involved in some scheme instead."

Daniel splayed his fingers. "I don't know that for sure. These could be two very different situations. What I do know is my father searched for the Hollis treasure and my grandfather's ledger mentions the same. In my line of work, we deal with the facts we know, not speculations."

"Right now, we have no facts and an abundance of theory and speculation."

He huffed a resigned chuckle. "I suppose you're right."

Good. At least he agreed. "So, who were these people Lucas Sr. was working with? And how do they connect to our fathers and your grandfather?"

"We don't have any evidence they are connected to my grandfather."

"People don't create secret rooms for family-lore treasure, Daniel."

"I don't know. I guess I hoped..." He grunted. "It sounds ridiculous now."

"Hoped what?" She toyed with the frayed hem of her trouser leg and gave him the comfort of not maintaining eye contact.

"I hoped I'd discovered the key to finding the treasure my family always told stories about. I'd hop on a boat to a place downriver where we could dive under the water and come up with crates of gold coins. I could pay off our family's debts and provide for my sister and nephew. Maybe start a new practice here in Natchez. All our problems would be solved." He squeezed his fingers into a fist. "Fanciful is unlike me. I should have known better."

Before she could respond, he gathered his feet beneath him and rose. "I shouldn't have asked you to join me in this harebrained nonsense."

She remained seated. "I never said it was nonsense. Only that finding treasure that sank to the bottom of the Mississippi would be impossible to dredge up."

"Exactly. Harebrained. You told me so the first time I mentioned a salvage expedition."

"I said my boat isn't a salvage operation, no matter what rumors flew around after my father had the same idea about easy money and a quick way to a better life." The words carried more sting than she intended. "I'm sorry. That came out harsh."

"No, you're right. And truthfully, if there's more going on than following a map to lost treasure, then it could be dangerous."

"It's always been dangerous." She tried for an encouraging smile, but it fell flat. Some wounds still festered too much for jesting. She pushed the feeling of loss aside to deal with later. "For now, let's focus on what we know about the treasure and assume your brother-in-law's activities are a different matter."

Daniel plucked one of the boxes from the trunk behind him and turned it over in his palm. "I don't know if there ever was a real treasure."

He was probably right. Prudence would say to leave this treacherous current and seek the safety of calmer waters. Find a few decent cargo jobs and forget all about Daniel and his family secrets.

But then what?

Could she return to a life hollowed out without Papa? How long did she want to navigate the waters without him? She was proud of her pilot's license and the accomplishments it represented, but did she want to spend the rest of her life hauling cargo and wondering what happened to her father? Yet, treasure seeking was dangerous at best and deadly at worst and left people empty-hearted and empty-handed.

But it might also lead them to the truth. Truth might settle her heart. And her future.

"Why don't you tell me the story?" Even as she chided herself to let the past go and move on with her life, more words gained steam and poured from her mouth. "We'll see what parts of the tale we can match with what we already know and maybe figure out where to start looking."

Daniel regarded her, intelligent eyes churning with indecipherable thoughts. Maybe he'd given up on the matter.

He drew a deep breath and began.

"During the States' War, Dorothy Hollis Merrill stole her husband's wealth while he was off fighting for the Union. She was a Confederate at heart, but her father wanted her to marry into the money in Natchez. Rumors of war and discontent swirled in those days, and Mr. Hollis knew tying his family to Northern wealth would prove resourceful if Lincoln's new income tax laws came to pass. So right before the war began, he negotiated a marriage between his sixteen-year-old daughter and the widowed forty-year-old Mr. Oliver Merrill."

Camilla opened her mouth to give her opinion but closed it so as not to interrupt. Her father would never have done such a thing, but even if he'd tried, she would have never agreed. Poor Dorothy likely didn't have a choice. Women then didn't have the same rights they gained in the 1900s.

"Most of the big plantation owners in Natchez were Northern men," Daniel continued. "That's why the governor quickly surrendered the city, and they were never under any Union fire. Anyway, those wealthy men and their families went back to their other homes deep in the safety of Union territory."

He settled back on the floor across from her, his face dipped in shadows that caressed his smooth jaw.

"Oliver decided to join the army in the fall of 1863. He left his wife in the safety of a Union-occupied town and went to war. According to the story, Dorothy's father fought for the Confederacy, and she used her position as a Union officer's wife to spy for the Rebels. Some stories even say she secreted supplies to their army."

"I'm sure that would cause strife in her marriage if she ever got caught." Camilla propped herself on the heel of her hands. "Did she steal the treasure too?"

Daniel shook his head. "It's called the Hollis treasure because most of Oliver's wealth came from Dorothy's dowry. Turned out, he made a good show of living the lifestyle, but he needed Mr. Hollis's money to keep his businesses going."

"Oh. Makes sense. I was wondering about that." She waved a hand. "I'm sorry for interrupting. What happened after she was a spy?"

"When it became clear to her the South wouldn't win, Dorothy arranged a deal to get their wealth in gold coins. She didn't trust the Confederate or Union dollar. And gold would still spend in Europe. She took all her husband's assets and buried the gold along the Mississippi banks."

That would be easier to find than sunken crates. "Then what, she never dug it back up? She must have, or we'd be looking to dig and not find the *Carolina*."

He arched a brow. "Would you like to hear the rest of the story?"

Oh. Snakes and saltwater. She'd let her mouth run away again and jump ahead. She pinched her lips together and, with a sheepish nod, gestured for him to continue.

"At some point while working as a spy, Dorothy took a Rebel lover. The two of them were going to use the money to escape to Europe or South America and start a new life as soon as the war ended. Or her lover would desert the army and come for her. But then Oliver got himself shot and returned home much sooner than she expected. Dorothy told him marauding soldiers had taken everything. Suffering from the loss of his leg and battling with infection, Oliver believed her."

"Oh my." Camilla leaned forward. No wonder the family shared this story for so many years.

"A couple of months later, the war ended. Dorothy and her lover dug up the gold and loaded it onto a steamer headed to New Orleans. He planned to go ahead of her and secure their passage to Europe under false names. She would leave her husband with a nurse and disappear in the night a few days behind him. But the steamer sank in the Mississippi after a broiler fire."

Camilla gasped. "Did the lover die?"

"According to the reports, there weren't but two survivors. Both women, so the lover must have died. The owner attempted to salvage the boat, but no reports indicate the gold was ever found."

How tragic. For many reasons. "So, what happened to Dorothy?"

"Oliver suffered an illness and died." Daniel's voice carried a layer of conspiracy, and he leaned closer to her in the dusty light.

Her breath caught. "Do you think she killed him?"

"I don't know." He sat back. "But it seems plausible."

Camilla smeared dust from her palms down her trousers. "So that's it, then? The gold was lost, so she murdered her husband and lived her life without him or the money?"

"So the story goes."

So much for anything getting them closer to finding the treasure. Papa would say something about folks reaping what they chose to sow. She opened her mouth to tell Daniel this tale seemed inappropriate to tell children when he pointed a finger in the air with more dramatic flair than she'd seen out of him thus far.

"Until she gave her daughter a deathbed confession."

"I knew it couldn't be over yet." Camilla rubbed her hands together. "What kind of confession?"

"Dorothy eventually married another wealthy Union man. They only had one child before he also died and left Dorothy with enough money to live comfortably for the rest of her life.

Eventually, she got the consumption, and her daughter, Mary, took care of her. One night after the sickness had taken most of her strength, Dorothy told Mary about a lover who had betrayed her. But she'd swindled him in return."

"Oh my." Camilla tapped a finger on her knee. "Maybe the gold never made it onto the steamer after all."

"Well, after that—"

Camilla threw up her hands. "It doesn't matter. The story doesn't lead us anywhere. Either the gold sank to the bottom of the river or Dorothy's lover stole it from her and it was lost. He could have taken the gold anywhere." Tingles shot down her spine. "Oh! Unless you think he loaded it on the *Carolina*, which might have gone down somewhere else."

Daniel chuckled.

"I interrupted again." Camilla massaged her temples. "I really must work on the virtue of patience. Words have a hard time staying confined once they've formed. Please, continue."

"All these years, the tragic story was passed down of the woman who swindled her husband and was swindled in return. Mothers used it as a tale of morals for their children." Daniel rolled his shirtsleeves, drawing her eye to muscular forearms. "Speculations and theories became topics of family gatherings following Mary's death. Mary believed her mother had fever-induced dreams. She didn't believe there had been any gold, but if there had, it had been lost along with everything else during the war."

Made sense. A lost treasure made for good conversation around the table and an interesting way to pass the time, but story without substance didn't lead to real clues. Not that she'd interrupt again to say so.

Daniel continued when she stubbornly remained silent.

"Then something my father found made him believe the gold was loaded on the *Carolina* and maybe it could be found, so he hired your father."

"But your grandfather didn't want them searching for it." Ideas swirled in eddies through her mind and insisted on flowing free. "He said something about no one finding 'what died with that gold.' He hired an investigator to have your father followed. But your grandfather's sickness got worse. Your father went missing, and then your grandfather passed soon after."

"Yes, I believe that's the whole of it." Daniel turned out his palms.

"Maybe somehow the men connected with your broth-er-in-law had something to do with whatever our fathers and your grandfather were doing and none of this has anything to do with Dorothy's gold." She sighed and took Daniel's hand, holding it in the space between where they sat. "Either way, I don't think you have enough information to find the Hollis treasure. Sounds like Dorothy's lover took your gold over fifty years ago. Even if it did go on another boat and not the one that sank, it was likely spent a long time ago."

His shoulders drooped. "You're probably right."

Something inside her wanted to say anything to ease the bitter disappointment from his face. She almost wanted to promise him they could keep looking. Maybe they'd discover something no one else had.

But that thinking had already led to death. Finding the an-swers as to why wasn't worth risking sharing the same fate.

The sensible words lodged in her throat. Those eyes of his burned, arresting all logic. Pools of emerald swirled with eddies of hope, sparks of desperation floating like lost lifeboats in an unrelenting current.

Her fingers trailed over his calloused palms. Strange how a lawyer had the hands of a boatman. The thought drifted away as the current in his gaze shifted, darkening while his pupils widened.

Electricity jolted along her skin when his other hand grazed a trail up her forearm. "Thank you for helping me." His voice lowered. "For believing me."

She could only nod. How did one find words when captivated by such eyes? Something within her strained forward, wanting to draw closer to the light and lose herself in the admiration shining there.

Heaven help her, but she'd already cut anchor. Now she was helplessly floating free and losing all sense of direction.

M usic carried on the liquor-laden air and settled in Smuggie's ears where he hunched in a back corner. Usually, he enjoyed the wee hours when the women had softened their hard edges and the men loosened their pockets.

Not today.

He cast another glance at the door stashed behind the bar. Any time now.

The ice in his glass had melted three songs ago, but he gulped the watered-down hooch anyway. Good thing he'd saved himself a crate of that good Irish whiskey. These homemade brews coming from up North kept getting worse. Blast those temperance folk and their insistence all crime stemmed from alcohol.

They'd see the error of their thinking soon enough. Men didn't need to lube their morals with drink to slip between the shadows. Of course, he'd admit it did help.

He tapped the empty glass on the tabletop and watched a girl in a fringed flapper dress tug a fellow's tie toward a dark corner. She swayed with a few loosened morals herself. Maybe those stiff shirts weren't entirely wrong.

The door behind the bar cracked open, and Smuggie's insides quivered. The big boss stepped out, and someone else clicked the door closed behind him, concealing how many others remained inside.

The meeting had gone on longer than expected. At least, longer than he'd thought it would. He didn't concern himself with the parts of the business that didn't involve his particular skills.

Usually.

Tall and refined, "Dimples" Durkin slid his hand inside the lapel of his finely crafted suit and observed the clientele who kept his pockets lined. For a man well into his fifties, he still struck a fine figure that drew the skirts flittering to his side. Must be the dimples. Whatever name the man had been christened with at birth had been stashed away with his previous life. No one knew anything more about him than he came from Chicago.

People said it was cold in Chicago and the wind never stopped biting your nose. Smuggie'd never been farther north than Memphis. Didn't need to. Everything he needed lived right here under the hill.

Durkin's gaze slid over the dancing couples, laughing men, and crooning singer at the front of the stage shrouded in cigar smoke. Pearl wasn't as good as Bella. Bella had a voice like an angel. Smuggie chuckled to himself. If her rejection of his advancements gave any indication, she kept her skirt straight like one too.

Not that he claimed to know much about angels or proper-like women. He couldn't say why, but the girl with the dusky complexion and luminous eyes that looked straight into the dark corners of his soul had gotten under his skin.

Too bad Bella wasn't here tonight. Might make him feel better, knowing a good heart tossed him a kind smile every so often. That or pity. He couldn't tell.

Durkin's gaze hit him before he could let himself wander down that useless path of contemplation, and he jerked his chin in a single nod.

It was time.

The big boss made his rounds, in no hurry to hear Smuggie's news. All the better. He slipped from his seat and sidled to the edge of the bar. Tom glanced his way and then poured a double portion of whatever watered-down concoction they'd stocked this week. Smuggie caught the fresh glass slid down to him and left the empty in its place.

He made it back to his table before the big boss finished a conversation with a bloke who flaunted a woman far too young for him on his arm.

Durkin propped his forearm on Smuggie's table. "What news?"

Straight to business. He'd always appreciated that about the big boss. "Nothing's happened yet. Boat's still docked, and them that's on it stay there. Excepting, of course, the lady captain, who goes back and forth to the gentleman's house."

"And what are they doing at his house?"

"Nothing interesting, I reckon." He shrugged. "They never leave with anything. Maybe they've given up on treasure hunting and became lovers."

Durkin tapped the bottom of his ring on the tabletop. "They're still searching. The old man got spooked after his son-in-law died. Probably hid everything we need. Might take them some time to find it, but I'm a patient man."

If so, how come fingers of ice slid down Smuggie's spine? "Yes, sir. I'll keep watching. Got Elroy keeping an eye out for Scissors too. Like you said."

"Good. That rat shows his face, and you know what to do."

"Yes, sir."

The conversation finished, yet Durkin didn't move away from the high-top. Smuggie smashed his trembling fingers into a fist under the table. Was he waiting for—more information? He scoured his brain for every detail from each time he'd followed the treasure hunters in the past days, but nothing new surfaced.

"Did I ever tell you about a man they called Nice Eyes Nick?"

Smuggie slurped another sip of watery whiskey. "No, sir. Haven't heard of that bloke."

The boss's gaze roamed the room, not looking his way. Funny how that had such an effect on the stiffness between his shoulders.

"They called him Nice Eyes because he was the friendliest-looking man you'd ever seen. Old ladies trusted him. Men shook his hand and never hesitated to make a deal. One look at him and you'd believe he'd been vouched for by Saint Peter himself." Durkin slid a ring from his pinkie and rolled it between his forefinger and thumb.

Smuggie knew better than to interrupt, so he waited while the big boss watched the room.

Dressed in the best kind of gray suit money could buy, the type with a white pinstripe so thin you could barely see it, Dimples Durkin could pass as the same sort of fellow. Cleanly shaven without a single scar on his firm jaw, he looked the respectable type. Ladies loved his thick honey-wheat hair and wide shoulders. Usually a pretty dame, sometimes two, dripped off his arm.

"Nick came up from New Orleans thinking he could find work here in my city. Now, you know me. I'm the amiable sort, willing to give a new man a chance. Let him work for me. He did real nice the first months. The people didn't mind handing over their protection fees so much when Nick asked. He had that way about him." Durkin plucked a cigar from the inside of his coat and tossed Smuggie a gold lighter.

He caught it and adjusted it in his hand. The letters NBN were engraved on one side. He flipped the lid and held out the flame for Durkin.

The big boss snipped the end of the cigar and lit the tip in the flame. After a couple of puffs, he leaned back from the table. "You can keep that."

Smuggie fingered the lighter and tucked it in his pocket. "Thanks, Boss."

"One day, Nick got the idea he could outsmart me. Started his own business on the side. Nothing big, mind. Just skimming here and there. Keeping items for himself. That kind of thing."

A block of ice formed in his stomach, but he kept his face impassive.

After another few puffs, Durkin continued. "I think he figured no one would miss what little he took. Harmless, you know?"

Smuggie swallowed. "Not too smart of him."

Cold blue eyes shot through Smuggie's defenses with the ease of a Gatling gun. "No, not smart of him at all. See, stealing from me, no matter how small, is never a smart choice."

The back of Smuggie's neck itched, but he ignored it.

"What..." He cleared his throat. He didn't want to ask. But Durkin would keep staring at him, growing more impatient until he did. "What happened to Nick?"

"He didn't have much need for those nice eyes anymore once I'd found out what he'd done. They went into the Devil's Punchbowl first. We let him live in the cave a while after that, to think about what he'd done."

Smuggie curled his stiff fingers into his palms.

Durkin took another puff. "No need to worry about your fingers tonight. Not unless you have something to tell me?"

What could he say? He floundered for anything at all. "They got a man on that boat I heard the dockmaster say was a criminal. Might be someone we can turn. Move things along faster."

"Hmm." Durkin eyed him. "Look into it. Any news on our other business?"

Smuggie tried to swallow, but the sandy feeling in his throat wouldn't let him. "No, sir. Nothing's come down from Chicago other than what we've got there behind the bar. I was hoping for some good Irish whiskey, the real stuff. Didn't want to tell you about it until I knew for sure I could bring it down the river. Not wanting to disappoint and all, you know."

Durkin clapped him on the shoulder. "Good to know. But next time, you tell me everything first." His fingers tightened. "I'm not the kind of man who enjoys surprises."

"Yes, sir."

The claws in his shoulders receded. "Good man. I reward men who can keep up their regular duties even while filling in for special assignments. Finish this thing with Gray and the girl, and I'll see to it a crate of real Irish whiskey finds its way to your door. My gift."

Air leaked out of his lungs. "Yes, sir. Thank you, sir."

As soon as the big boss left the table, Smuggie downed the rest of his double and stared at the bottom of the glass. He placed it on the table and then lifted the golden lighter.

NBN

The etched letters seemed to glow, catching on the gaslight like lines of fire.

He tucked the reminder into his pocket and then strode past dancing couples toward the door.

If he was lucky, he still had time to catch the *Sugarland* and save all his fingers.

And probably his eyes.

Warm air tickled the sweat beading on Camilla's neck, and she wiped it away. Her turn to clean Lula's deck, the men's least favorite chore. In truth, it didn't bother her much. A small price to pay for her furry companion.

And the work might help take her mind off what had nearly happened in the attic. She'd almost up and kissed Daniel like some wanton flapper. She hadn't, of course. Had made some silly excuse about needing to get on with finding a new haul and hightailed it out of there. She'd even scooped Lula right out from a game of tug with Daniel's nephew.

They all probably thought she'd lost her mind.

Maybe she had.

She'd needed time and distance to sort out her feelings and the information she'd learned. So far, two days away from Daniel and his sense-muddling presence hadn't helped.

Nor had deck duty.

Her mind insisted on turning over every word and phrase. Analyzing each detail. There were so many questions. Could she even be sure she could trust him? Logic screamed there was more to the tale than he'd let on. But maybe he held back to keep her safe. No matter what she tried to tell herself about using caution, her instincts insisted Daniel wouldn't purposely cause her harm.

It was in the eyes like Papa always said. And she'd found nothing in Daniel's eyes but sincerity, fascination, and hope. Well, and a toe-tingling kind of attraction as well.

Which looped her right back to thinking about that morning in the attic.

"Snakes and saltwater." She pushed the mop across the already clean floor.

Lula yipped as the ends of the mop's yarn slid her way.

"Sorry, girl."

Lula's ears pricked, and she shot off around the edge of the engine room.

A voice sounded a second later. "I found something!"

Her heart skipped. Daniel. She'd started to wonder if he'd taken her instructions to come find her when he had something to start this job too much to heart. At least the advanced payment of the first half of their fee had compensated her crew and kept them busy making the necessary repairs so they'd be able to safely take to the water as soon as Daniel was ready.

She dropped the mop and strode to the port deck with all the calm she could muster. The man had already muddled her enough. He didn't need to see her eagerly bounding to his call like an overzealous spotted pup who clearly had no problem letting people see she'd developed a fondness for him.

Wind toyed with the edges of Daniel's hair under his newsboy cap. He waved a hand in greeting as his gaze found hers. Lula stood at the rail, tail wagging.

Camilla joined her furry companion, hoping she didn't look equally eager to see him. "And here I thought we were about to give up on this venture."

The words shot out on their own accord. So much for not sounding eager.

After days of waiting to see if further searching turned up anything of use, she'd planned on breaking the news to him tomorrow that they'd have to go ahead and make a delivery run while they waited.

Partly because her nerves couldn't take the idleness.

Daniel bounded up the ramp. He'd left his jacket, wearing only a linen shirt, sleeves rolled up to reveal his forearms, and suspenders hooked onto a pair of sturdy gray trousers. He flapped a slim book as he stepped onto the freshly washed port deck.

"Tell the crew to get ready to pull out."

"Now?" She shook her head. "Doesn't work like that. We have to make preparations."

"Yes." He motioned to Solomon, holding his hands apart and mimicking steering. Then he pointed to the water. Then his watch. "Start that now."

Camilla signed to Solomon to wait while she figured out what had the man in a tizzy. "How about we talk in Papa's office about what you found? Then we can decide on a course of action."

The muscle in Daniel's jaw twitched, but he nodded. He attempted another series of gestures to Solomon that could be a greeting. He waved, then patted his own back.

What was that supposed to mean?

"You know he can hear you, right?" She started toward the stairs.

Daniel shrugged. "I was trying for camaraderie, but if my efforts are interpreted as disrespectful, I'll stop."

He wanted to foster fellowship with her crew? "Why?"

They mounted the stairs to the upper level. "Why what? Why do I want to try to make friends with Solomon, or why am I attempting a language of hand signals I know nothing about?"

A laugh bubbled. How did the man manage to sound solemn and humorous at the same time? "Both, I suppose."

"There's rarely a reason to not seek friendship with those around us, especially if we know they are brothers in the Lord.

And I've heard attempting to relate to people helps with such endeavors."

"That so?" She opened the door to Papa's office and ushered him inside. "Then how are you attempting to relate to me?"

Lula clattered in behind them and angled toward her pillow. She clamped it between her jaws and trotted to a strip of sunshine streaming through the rear window. She circled twice, then curled in the sun for her customary afternoon nap.

"Oh." The most adorable shade of pink crept into his ears.

Camilla settled into Papa's chair and propped her feet on the desk. Gracious. Did that left shoe have a hole in the toe already? She tucked her legs underneath.

"We already have a connection, so I haven't searched for another." Daniel scratched the back of his head.

"You mean the treasure?" She leaned forward, studying him. "Or something else?"

Daniel's nervous laughter resulted in Lula's perked ears, but she rejected the notion of stirring from her spot. "You are rather forward for a woman. Do you know that?"

Now heat seared her ears. She'd been told. More than a few times. She declined to answer with anything more than narrowed eyes.

"Don't take offense." Daniel hooked his fingers over the chair's worn arms. "I like that about you. Makes you much easier to talk to than most people." He shifted and rested his forearms on his knees. "The connection I feel between us draws me to you in a way I believe God designed one soul to be drawn to another."

Snakes and saltwater. What did he mean by *that*? Her stomach flipped over itself like a mullet caught in a net.

They stared at one another, her heart beating furiously. Papa might say this was one of those moments that turned the rudder and sent you onto a new course. One she wasn't sure she was prepared to navigate.

"What's in the book?" Why did her words come out all breathy? She cleared her throat and tried again. "You found a clue?"

Better she steer back to safer waters. She still didn't know what to do with these new feelings swimming around inside her.

Daniel looked down at the leather-bound volume like he'd forgotten he still held it. "Yes." He smacked it against his palm. "These might be the notes from the private investigator my grandfather hired. They tell us where my father went that night."

She lurched up from her chair. "Why didn't you say that sooner?" She extended her hand. "Let me see."

He relinquished the book. "They went eight miles upriver."

The words fell between them, and she lifted her gaze from a blocky script to meet his.

"With Papa?" She shook her head. "No, I would have known if he'd taken the *Alma May*. I was visiting someone in town, but the steamer stayed docked."

Memories of that night pressed in on the edges of her vision and stole her breath. If they'd taken a smaller boat into the back channels, then why had Mr. Dixon needed a riverboat captain?

"You never told me what happened." Though gentle, Daniel's words still knifed through her heart.

She closed her eyes and willed her breathing to steady. He should know the details. Whatever had happened between their fathers didn't have anything to do with them.

Right?

"I don't have many friends." Maybe if she started a little farther back, she could ease into troubled waters.

Daniel settled against his chair and waited while she gathered her thoughts.

"We are usually on the river and don't stay in one place long." She picked at the ragged edge of her thumbnail. "That doesn't mean folks haven't made their way into our lives over the years. One of those people is Solomon's mother. She used to keep me when I was small and my mother took a trip with Papa on the water. Whenever we dock in Natchez, I spend a day or two with her if I can."

If she closed her eyes, she could still smell Hattie's warm yeast rolls. The cozy home nestled in the woods almost felt like something from a storybook. Painful memories had kept her away, but had that ended up hurting more than helping?

"I was at Hattie's house that day." She swallowed the tightness in her throat. "When Solomon came for me, he'd said Papa had gone with Mr. Dixon. They'd been searching for the treasure for a while by then. Of course, I'd thought it was all nonsense. But Papa had come more alive seeking the clues than I'd seen him in a long time, so I didn't say anything. I figured he'd give up eventually."

Daniel leaned forward and plucked one of her hands from Papa's desk. He brushed his thumb over the back of her knuckles. A small touch. Yet it infused her with strength.

"Solomon came home and told me that..." She swallowed the lump insistent on rising again in her throat. "That they'd found Papa's body face down on the riverbank, not half a mile from our boat. Mr. Dixon was missing."

"What happened to your father?" Daniel rubbed another pass over her knuckles.

"We don't know. He'd been shot, but the police didn't think he'd been killed where he'd been found. They investigated, but never found anything."

Daniel's fingers stopped their gentle path. "I remember hearing about that. I wasn't in Natchez at the time. We received word from my grandfather that Father had gone missing. They said they thought he fell off a riverboat and drowned in the river. We tried searching for him, but we never found him."

He released her hand, and she withdrew them under the desk.

Had his father shot hers? Had Papa done something to Daniel's father in turn? Could she really trust this man she hardly knew just because he had a way of making her insides flutter?

"What did the book say?" She looked at the thin volume, strangely unable to thumb through its pages.

Lula whined, breaking the thickening silence. Her claws clicked across the floor as she trotted over to Daniel and sniffed his shoes. He glanced down at her, and a hint of a smile lifted his cheeks.

The dog lowered her haunches and sprang into his lap. She turned three full circles while he stared at her, lips slightly parted, and then curled into a ball.

Daniel met Camilla's gaze.

"Looks like you made a friend." Her pup didn't take to new people easily. Warmth melted the ice that had gripped her heart. Maybe the approval of a dog shouldn't make her feel better, but it did anyway.

He ran a gentle hand down Lula's back, stroking the soft fur. She'd never once seen the terrier choose a lap other than hers. High canine praise indeed.

"Those are notes from my grandfather's investigation." When Daniel spoke again, his tone remained businesslike even though he didn't look up from the dog. "Looks like we were right about the inlets."

If they'd gone into the backwaters, made sense they'd taken a smaller boat. "They were looking for the *Carolina*?"

"It doesn't say." His emerald gaze locked on hers. "It says the investigator—I don't know his name—followed my father from Grandfather's house the afternoon of September sixth. He met with Captain Lockhart at a pub under the hill. From there, the two of them took a tug out of port. The investigator followed on horseback along the river's edge eight miles north."

Camilla leaned forward. That was more information than the police had been able to find. "Then what?"

"They took shallow channels, and the investigator lost them in the dark. The marsh became too difficult for the horse, and he had to turn back."

She let out a long breath. "That doesn't give us much to go on."

He flipped open the book and pointed to a page. Lula rumbled from his lap, unhappy with being squished as he leaned forward. He scooted the open book toward Camilla and sat back.

Her stomach flipped as she recognized the markings on the page. "It's a map."

At least he still had all his fingers. And both eyes. Smuggie wrested his hat low on his brow and silently cursed the searing light edging its way into the alley he'd tucked into. He'd had to sleep through Bella's performance last night. Spending too long stalking around in the daylight was getting to him.

Aside from the pressing boredom and opposite waking hours, snooping and watching wasn't so bad a job.

Somewhere to his left, a donkey brayed, and a man shouted. Another thing he didn't care for in the daytime. Too many people angry about the work they had to accomplish before they could kick up their heels and enjoy the finer parts of life. After all, all the good things came after sunset.

Usually.

The dark could also give a man too much confidence. Make him forget where he came from and who held his leash. Maybe all this sunlight was what he needed to snap him out of the overconfidence the shadows provided. He'd let himself pretend to be the king of his little world, forgetting the emperor who ruled over them all.

By now, he should know every friend had itching ears and every woman who warmed his bed whispered to Durkin in the dark. No one made a move unobserved, no matter how small.

Boss might not know he'd moved that crate of whiskey and put it back on the packet with the new cargo from St. Louis. But he doubted it. More likely, he'd been given the opportunity to correct a mistake before he finished making it. And he'd been given the chance to prove his unwavering loyalty.

A tingle jittered down his spine. Durkin wasn't known for second chances or soft spots. Smuggie flexed his intact fingers. Which meant he tolerated the almost-mistake because he wanted something.

He watched the boat across the street. Better find something useful from the lawyer and his dame soon. He curled his fingers, and the scar between his thumb and forefinger stretched. Insurance, so to speak.

Carts rolled past, stirring up dust. Men laughed, and deckmen called out to one another as they loaded their cargo.

Smuggie tapped his pocket for a cigarette but came up empty. Too bad he hadn't had time to refill his case.

He edged closer to the light and propped his shoulder against the bricks. Across the street from his hiding place, the lady captain's steamer bobbed in the shallows. Men bustled around the deck not doing anything in particular. One massive dark-skinned man toted a mop and bucket.

He didn't see the other one. The older bloke with a criminal reputation.

That had been a dead end. The man never left the boat, so Smuggie hadn't had the opportunity to put any pressure on him. And then after three days of nothing from the lawyer, he'd grown anxious.

Thankfully, now he had a lead.

He poked his head out of the alley as a dish in a tight-fitting skirt swept past.

Good thing he'd gotten better at hanging around that house unseen. The bush near the cliff wasn't the most comfortable place to spend the day. Three times, he'd been certain the neighbor lady had spotted him, but his diligence paid off.

About an hour ago, Gray had scrambled out of his house without a proper hat and coat. For that kind of fella, lack of formal attire indicated either desperation or excitement. Either would be beneficial.

After following at a safe distance, Smuggie'd been rewarded with the sight of the lawyer waving around a book before climbing on that steamer.

The blond in the pink skirt slid behind a motorcar, and he eased out farther to track her progress. He'd have to ask around about her. Fresh faces didn't often poke around here. At least not the feminine kind.

He sucked teeth that vaguely tasted of whiskey and focused on the steamer again.

That book Gray had been waving around might be something useful at last. He still had no idea how the lawyer's treasure hunt tied to that double-crosser Scissors who'd duped both Durkin and Mickey's crew out of that St. Louis bank haul. But Smuggie wasn't getting paid to know things. He kept all his body parts by doing what he was told and relaying information.

"Whatcha doin', mister?"

The small voice nearly sent Smuggie out of his skin. He jerked his head back into the protective shadows so quickly he slammed against the brick. Pain scurried up the base of his skull and throbbed through his temple. A growl came from his chest. He'd grown too complacent in his thoughts and had failed to look for danger in the light.

He blinked to adjust his eyes to the boy bathed in sunshine at the alley's opening.

"Breeze off, lad." Smuggie shooed the skinny child of about eight.

The boy didn't move, apparently not having enough sense to recognize the man he stared at wasn't the friendly sort.

"Are you hungry?" The lad took a step closer, peering into the dark. "I'm going to get some po'boys. You want one too?"

What? Why would this boy offer a stranger food? Especially one clearly uninterested in pleasant conversation and juvenile company.

"Don't want no mudbug sandwiches." He waved a hand at the kid. "Move along."

"But what are you doing? Are you lost?" The boy came closer, peering into the darkness. "Do you need help?"

A chuckle ruptured through a closed-off place deep inside, and he nearly choked on it. "You want to help *me*?"

"Sure, mister. Being lost and hungry isn't a reason to hide." The kid rocked back on his heels and grinned. "Those are both things we can fix up fast."

A slimy feeling curled in Smuggie's gut. Why did this boy look familiar?

"Lucas! What're you doing?" A woman's sharp voice made the kid swivel.

Smuggie pulled deeper into the alley, far back enough not to be seen but not so far as to miss what they said. A cat growled somewhere behind him.

"But, Stella," the boy said over the yowling cat. "A man in there needs help."

"What man?" The woman's tone held more suspicion than concern.

Good. At least the boy had someone sensible in his life.

"Come on. Mama's waiting on us." The woman's form moved into the halo of light, oversized hat bobbing. "Bo's got some traps ready."

A shuffling came from their silhouette figures as the woman yanked on the boy's hand, and he planted his feet.

"But the hungry man needs our help."

The woman sighed. After grumbling something Smuggie couldn't hear, she called out to the darkness.

"Go to Anna's in the alley. Tell her Stella sent you with a wooden penny. You can get something to fill your stomach."

She pulled the boy again, and they moved out of the mouth of the alley. Curious, Smuggie eased past a discarded crate and returned to the opening.

"What's a wooden penny?" The boy looked over his shoulder and caught Smuggie's eye.

For some reason, he didn't pull back into the shadows as they ambled down the street, voices mingling with complaining donkeys and shouting workmen.

"Means Mama will give him a free meal," the woman said louder than necessary.

The boy's response faded to incoherent jabbering, and a cart loaded with flour sacks lumbered between them and Smuggie.

He scratched the back of his neck. Someone better keep a close eye on that kid. Boy could find himself with a life he wasn't looking for if he talked to strangers. Or wandered off to places he shouldn't have gone.

He shrugged off the odd feeling settling in his gut and returned his focus to the boat.

The lady captain emerged. Dressed in a pair of high-waisted trousers with wide legs, she looked more feminine than she had before in men's overalls or straight slacks. The blue blouse had sleeves and a functional collar. Her small dog trotted on her heels, followed by the lawyer.

Lockhart made hand signals and called out to her crew, and they began scurrying around.

Finally.

Smuggie stepped out into the offending light.

Time to tell Durkin they were on the move.

T he river wind pushed through the pilothouse's open windows and scurried along Daniel's damp forehead. Camilla pulled a length of rope, and a deep whistle pierced the air. Dog settled on one hip, she gripped the wheel spokes with her other hand and moved the *Alma May* into the current.

Had he ever seen a woman more capable?

As though sensing his study, she cast a look over her shoulder, eyes shining bright. They were finally on their way, and she reigned over her watery domain with confidence.

Lula watched the open windows, gaze following a hawk on its path across a cloudless sky. How did Camilla function with one arm encumbered by a childlike canine?

"You want me to hold her?"

"You can if she'll let you. She insists on looking out the window when we first take to the river. She'll eventually settle onto her own feet, but not until we are well underway."

He reached out for the dog, but she turned her head away and dug claws into Camilla's arm. "I'll take that as a no."

A warm chuckle bubbled from her throat. "She likes you better than most, which is saying something."

A passing steamer belched black smoke into the sky, its rumbling engines chugging up muddy waters. He fingered the map in his pocket. Hope refused to give way to logic, even though sense told him someone would have gathered up lost gold a long time ago—if there'd been anything to find.

"Are you going to tell me the truth now?" Camilla's question snaked along his spine, leaving tingles.

How much was safe? "What do you mean?"

She cocked an eyebrow.

He opened the map and scanned the hand-drawn lines for the markers indicated. "Truth is I doubt we are going to find anything, but I can't live with myself if I don't try."

"Hmm." She tilted the wheel and studied the water ahead. "I was referring to that bit about Mabel and Lucas being in danger if you didn't come up with a lot of money fast. We were so busy talking about how all these puzzle pieces fit—you never expanded on that particular one."

He shouldn't have brought it up. "Remember the men I told you about?"

"The slippery ones, yes."

Her focus never left the water, which helped to loosen words from his lips. He rubbed the back of his neck. "I received a threatening letter about Mabel's debts."

"From the bank?"

"No. The bank is coming for the house, which is all fair and legal as they defaulted on their loans. This is something else."

"And did Mabel have a part in whatever happened with these men? Or were the schemes only of her husband's making?"

The question landed in his gut. He hadn't wanted to consider Mabel having anything to do with the activities that deposited Lucas Sr. in a heap of trouble. "I don't know."

"So what do you know?"

As if to emphasize Camilla's words, Lula turned to stare at him, her dark eyes probing. Heaven help him. The guilt must be getting to him if he was seeing accusation in a dog.

He cleared his throat. "If I don't give them what they want soon, then they said Mabel will pay. They didn't say how, but I doubt I'd want to know."

"And this was in a letter? Why not come in person like they did before?"

A good question. "I have no idea."

"And what does any of this have to do with what happened to your law practice? And why do you have calluses on your hands? I've been wondering that. Businessmen generally have palms as smooth as a lady's. Well, ladies other than me, mind. I'm not the glove sort. But you know what I mean." Lips curving, she shot a single glance at him before returning her focus to the river's currents.

He tried to follow the detour of the topic. "I have calluses on my hands from woodworking."

That gained another glance. "And your law practice and home?"

And they were back on the original course. No conversation was ever boring with this woman. "That had nothing to do with my calluses."

"Ha!" She shifted Lula's weight. "You are a humorous man, Mr. Gray."

Not an accusation ever leveled on him before. He couldn't help a smile before her next words almost instantly dissolved it.

"I suppose not. But something drastic must have happened if it cost you not only your business but your house as well."

She had a right to know the grim details. If there was to be any chance of a relationship between them, he had to be honest. "I was accused of embezzling money from one of my clients."

"And did you?"

How he hated she had to ask. "Of course not."

"Then what evidence did they have?"

"The fabricated kind. Not that it helped with my reputation. I lost all my clients but one and had to close my practice. Then my father went missing, and not long after, my grandfather passed.

I sold my townhome in Jackson and moved south to start over. The last few months have been...difficult. Just trying to keep our heads above water."

Her tone softened. "Papa always said the trials mold a man. He can be shaped into something stronger or something harder."

"What's the difference?"

"Strong endures. It shelters others." She adjusted the wheel a fraction. "A hard man forgets everything but the pain and builds walls to keep others out."

He leaned against the small ledge underneath the front windows. The words struck deep and buried within him. "Your papa was a wise man."

"That he was." She nodded ahead. "We are almost out of Natchez. Eight miles north, and then we should find your marker."

He checked the map and tapped a finger on the picture of stacked stones. "Have you ever seen this before?"

"No, but I wasn't looking for a particular pile of rocks, either."

She didn't ask anything more, and he didn't elaborate. What would he do if men came looking for Mabel? Or Lucas? Maybe he should move them out of Natchez. Settle down somewhere far out West where they wouldn't be found.

The two settled into comfortable silence as she navigated the churning waters and they watched the riverbanks slowly slide by as the old steamer paddled against the currents.

Did it really matter if he sold his grandfather's house? What did a legacy of longstanding wealth amount to anyway? Was that what truly mattered? He'd clung to his good name and reputation. His status in the community. And that had been pulled from under him. He'd made his identity out of the fabric of his education and prestige, only to end up with shredded rags.

What other kind of legacy did he want to leave to his children and grandchildren someday, should God bless him with progeny? If he wanted to be known as a man who'd pursued justice, lived by his faith, and acted honorably, then perhaps he should stop avoiding troubles and face them head-on.

Lest he become hard rather than strong.

After roughly two hours of wrestling with emotions he didn't usually stop to examine, Camilla rescued him.

"I see something." She jerked on a line that disappeared through the hull and snatched Daniel from his thoughts. A moment later, the engines slowed.

She must be using the bells to communicate with Solomon in the engine room.

Camilla steered the vessel toward the water's edge. He scanned the bank but saw nothing more than trees.

"Let me see that map again."

He held it up. After a glance, she pulled on a different rope, and the boat shuddered as it stopped in the current.

"We'll anchor here. Up ahead, a shallow bar could cause us trouble. It's safer if we disembark here."

She pulled the line controlling the deep whistle and then gave two tugs on one of the ropes connected to the bells in the engine room. How strange that she could only steer the boat but needed Solomon to control their speed. One worked blind, and the other worked with only half control.

No wonder they needed to trust one another.

After the boat anchored down and they lowered the walkway, Camilla handed Lula over to Solomon when he joined them on the deck. Then Daniel and Camilla descended the ramp to the riverbank.

Thick mud stuck to the bottom of his shoes and made a sucking noise against her boots. He shielded his eyes from the glaring light.

"Did you see the marker?"

"Just ahead." She strode down the bank and skirted a knobby pine.

About five feet into the shadows of the pine branches, a stack of smooth river stones stood waist-high.

Camilla brushed her fingers over the top one. "In the old days, rivermen would leave markers to guide others to safe waters or to points of harbor. This one must have indicated a branch in the river that's no longer here."

"I'm amazed you saw this at all from the steamboat."

"I've a keenly developed sense of finding what I'm looking for on the river." Humor rumbling through her tone.

"Lucky for us, then." He fished the map from his pocket again and pointed to the drawing matching where they stood. "Looks like we head into the woods from here."

Camilla shook her head. "Not here." She pointed to an indent in the riverbank ahead. "My guess would be over there. See how the bank curves in?"

Not particularly. "Sure."

"It might depict an oxbow or old tributary."

"I yield to your expertise."

That earned a smirk, and she led him to the place. Overhead, a whippoorwill called a lonesome cry while a mockingbird squawked. Insects buzzed, their numbers growing as he and the captain delved deeper into the shadows.

Roughly a quarter mile later, they emerged into a clearing. One glistening with shimmering water.

"We found it!" Excitement edged into his voice despite his attempt to remain passive.

Camilla notched her faded cap. "We found a waterway, not the treasure. A waterway which I'm sure we are not the first to stumble upon."

Leaves crunched under his boots as they ambled deeper into the woods, following the edge of the oxbow. "What do you think brought our fathers here?"

"Not sure, maybe—" She held up a hand and then dropped her voice to a whisper. "Did you hear that?"

He paused to listen. Nothing other than the buzz of insects and the call of birds. The chatter of a squirrel.

"I thought I heard people."

He spread his palms. "Maybe someone lives back here."

Her tented eyebrows suggested she doubted it, though he wasn't sure why. People lived along waterways. Maybe the house here had been built before the river changed course.

All the same, they remained quiet as they picked their way deeper into the woods.

A sound snagged in his ears. He heard it too. Voices.

He edged in front of her and took the lead. They snaked through the high grasses, keeping to the shadows.

"Done told you what the boss said." A masculine baritone disrupted the squirrels' chatter. That didn't sound like friendly neighbor folk.

Camilla looped her hand through his elbow and peered around him. Daniel nodded to a live oak up ahead where they could remain hidden underneath the low branches. They scooted forward, careful of where they placed their boots.

"No one is coming." Another male voice rose in challenge to the first.

"It's been three days. I say we move the cargo tonight."

They ducked under a limb dripping with airy moss and crouched near the damp ground.

"And I told you what the big boss done told Smuggie," the first voice snapped. "We do what Durkin says or pay the price. You know that."

"Yeah, yeah. I know. Quit your bellyaching. I heard Smuggie same as you. But unless you got another boat lined up, then I don't know what to tell ya."

Camilla leaned close to his ear. "They sound like bootleggers."

Her warm breath tickled along his neck. He tightened his grip on the rough bark. "How are we going to search with them here?"

A soft snort brushed his cheek. "We don't. Men like that are dangerous."

"Maybe we can go around them."

Her fingers tightened on his arm. "We wait until they are gone. Then bring Solomon with us and try again tomorrow."

She didn't think he could protect her? A pang knifed through him. He lacked the other man's physical stature and had spent the majority of his adult life at a desk, but he would fight for her if needed.

She slid away from him and out from behind the tree. Withholding a groan, he followed her away from the voices.

He ground his teeth. At best, the smugglers had cost them another delay. And at worst, they'd already taken off with his family's gold.

C amilla forced her thudding heart to quiet. There was more to this plot than lost family treasure. Much more. Bootleggers and river gangsters weren't supposed to be part of this. But then, neither were sinister threats against Daniel's family.

Unless he had a plan much better than sneaking around looking for a lost steamer they would likely never find through bootlegger-infested oxbows, this mission teetered on the brink of failure. Creeping through the vegetation-choked woods without drawing the bootleggers' suspicion throttled her nerves as briars snagged her trousers.

"Let's get back to the *Alma May*," she whispered. "Then we can regroup and come up with a plan."

"I think we can keep looking." Daniel cast a glance back at the woods. "As long as we stay out of their way, they might not notice us."

Was he serious? "It's too dangerous. We don't even know who's mixed up in this."

His emerald gaze searched hers. Resignation, desperation, and worry mingled in a brackish mire.

She swallowed, her heart lurching into a gallop. This kind of thing had gotten their fathers killed. He knew that. No treasure was worth their lives.

He stuffed his hands into his pockets, resignation winning the battle in the emerald depths. "You're right. I just wanted to—"

A gunshot cracked through the air, scattering the birds. Daniel wrapped his arm around her waist and yanked her to the ground, covering her body with his own. Her cheek pressed into the damp earth as her pulse drummed in her ears.

Where had the shot come from?

She expected another shot. Shouts. Or the sound of men crashing through the woods, intent on causing them harm. Only eerie silence tickled through her ears.

"Maybe the bootleggers are shooting at each other." Daniel's warm breath scurried across her neck. "Let's go before anyone comes this way."

He shifted his weight from her back and crouched low, scanning the area around them. Then he grasped her elbow and helped her rise. Keeping a firm grip on her hand, he eased through the underbrush.

She should have been looking for bad men or watching the woods or...well, something. Instead, all she could think about was the feel of his palm against hers. How his presence provided a steady anchor in tumultuous waters. The way his fingers wrapped around her hand, offering more comfort than such a simple touch should.

She worked to put moisture back into her mouth. Weren't adventures supposed to be thrilling? Sending spikes of energy through her body? She felt none of that. Only radiating fear and the uncanny fixation on the wide shoulders in front of her. He'd remained calm, put her protection above his own, and taken charge of their situation. For once, she didn't feel like she needed to make all the decisions.

If they weren't running for their lives, she'd stop and kiss him.

They rounded the knobby pine and struck out toward her steamer, backs hunched as though that might stop a bullet. But no one followed. At least not that she could see.

Solomon waited at the rail, mouth tight. He thrust his chin toward the woods and gave the sign for a gun. Daniel kept his grip on her hand until they made it up the plank before releasing her.

"We are pulling out." Daniel spoke the order as though such a thing were natural, and her engineer never hesitated.

Solomon pivoted back to the engine room to stoke the coals. Buck appeared from the stairway leading to the upper deck, took one look at her face, and rushed to follow Solomon.

Camilla darted up the ladder to the pilothouse. They'd need to maneuver with only the bells. She wouldn't risk the whistle.

Lord, let the waters be quiet so we can turn downstream.

Daniel stuck close behind her, his footsteps mirroring her own. He slipped into the corner of the steering chamber, keeping close but out of the way.

As soon as the engine hum vibrated underneath her feet, she tilted the wheel, trusting Solomon to adjust their speed to make the turn across the river. Hopefully no one would be coming around the bend behind them.

They just needed to drift into the deeper waters and then—

A sharp whistle pierced the air.

Her heart jumped into her throat.

Daniel spun and braced his hands on the doorframe, gaze fixed behind them. "There's another boat!"

The whistle shrilled again.

Solomon increased the steam, pushing them out into the water. They could make it.

"What are you doing?" Daniel pointed out the window. "There's another boat coming."

"Too late." She bit the words and held fast to the wheel. If she slowed now, they would collide for sure. Her only hope was to beat the other boat deeper into the channel. And pray the others had time to maneuver their larger vessel out of the way.

"Camilla!" Daniel's shout snatched her eyes to the looming steamer.

Too close!

She spun the wheel hard, yanking the *Alma May* back toward the shore. She dared a glance behind.

The massive paddle wheeler plowed toward them. The whistle blasted again. The big boat lurched toward the center of the river to avoid the smaller packet hugging the inside of the meander. Puffs of smoke churned from the twin smokestacks. But they were coming much too fast.

She pulled twice on the rope to the bell below.

Full stop.

The engine rumbled, but they'd gathered too much steam. She adjusted the wheel. Could she squeeze between the other boat and the danger ahead?

"We aren't going to make it!" Daniel anchored himself to the doorframe, his body leaning out.

The other boat swayed close enough to hear the angry shouts. They had the right. She'd moved into the water without warning. In a blind bend.

She ground her teeth, her knuckles white on the spokes. Only two options, neither good. She could only pray the sands had shifted.

"Hold on!" She jerked the wheel.

"Are you going to ram us into—" Daniel stumbled as the packet snatched back toward the bank.

The paddle steamer let out another shrill whistle as they propelled past. The other boat slid by close enough to touch. A miracle they didn't collide.

"Wow. That was close." Daniel's voice hitched with a relieved laugh. "I could see their captain screaming at us from his pilothouse." He blew out a sharp breath. "That could have been disastrous."

"Brace yourself!" Camilla gripped the wheel hard, muscles tensing in preparation.

Despite Solomon cutting the engine, they'd gained too much momentum. No time to avoid what lay ahead and no way to make the turn without capsizing.

The bow crashed into the hidden sandbar with a sickening crack. Her chest slammed against the wheel, knocking the air from her lungs. Daniel shouted, and then a weight hit her back.

Alma May moaned as they tumbled to the floor in a heap. The planks beneath Camilla shuddered, then grew still.

Daniel scrambled off and knelt beside her. "Are you all right?"

She flopped to her back and gasped for air.

"You're hurt. Where?" His fingers probed along her scalp and nape. "Did you hit your head? I'm sorry I fell on you."

Her sore chest heaved, pulling in blessed air. She coughed and shook her head. "Just...lost...my breath."

He scooped her shoulders from the ground and settled her upper body against his chest. Concern radiated in his gaze. "Are you sure?"

She blinked up at him.

"Captain! I—oh." Finn scrambled to a halt at the pilothouse door, his gaze flicking between them. "Is she injured?"

Camilla pushed herself out of Daniel's embrace, even though part of her wanted to rest in the offered comfort longer. "I'm fine."

She brushed herself off and peered out the open front windows. The sandbar rose higher than she'd realized. So much for wishing it had washed away in the years since Papa mapped it.

"Tell Solomon we've run aground. Engines half steam, rudder right. Let's see if we can tip her back in the current."

"Yes, Captain." Finn cut another look at Daniel before scurrying away.

She spun the wheel all the way to the left, hoping to angle them off the bar and into the deeper waters.

"Will we be able to move?" Daniel stood behind her, focused on the swirling water below.

"Depends on if we can get her tipped or not."

The engines sputtered, and the paddle wheel at their rear began to chug.

If she could point the bow into the current and keep the paddles out of the sand, then they might tip the boat into the current. They'd float backward, but as long as another boat didn't come around the bend, they could push the engines and get turned around.

Alma May strained forward, sides quivering. A sickening screech lanced through Camilla's ears. She sounded the bell twice. Cut engines. The hull would rip apart if she forced the old gal too hard. Maybe if the water surged just enough...

Her grandfather's steamer rocked and shuddered, then settled into her prison with a groan.

Camilla closed her eyes. No good.

They were stuck.

Smuggie tucked the pistol back into his jacket as the lawyer and his dame scurried through the underbrush. That had been close. Too close.

He'd caught up to these fools almost on the doorstep of his crew's hideout before resorting to something drastic to scare them away. The big boss had said to trail them and find information at any cost, but he doubted that cost included one of their hidden smuggling ports. Now he'd have to deal with Dewy and Scat and explain why he'd been lurking in the woods instead of coming into camp the usual way.

He slapped a mosquito and cursed the creature's existence. Something that lived only to drain others didn't deserve to survive. Maybe the pest would be poisoned by the vices in his blood and meet its end.

The pair disappeared through thick underbrush, back toward the boat and away from his men.

No wonder the big boss had him following these two. Turned out they weren't after a treasure after all. They were looking to take down his operation. Good thing he got rid of them before one of the blokes saw them. Scat or Dewy would have put a bullet in both before even getting a good look at who had stumbled upon their hold.

They wouldn't care. They had their orders the same as he.

But Durkin wanted to see what these two knew, and as long as they were still living, Smuggie had to stay on their tail. At least until he had enough information and the big boss was ready to off them. If one of his men beat Durkin to the end of this game, he'd surely be the one to pay for it.

"Silent night!" He fired out the code word as soon as he heard footfalls. Whichever one of them hurried this way would shoot him as soon as he had a clean line of sight. Unplanned man in the woods was all the permission either needed to open fire, and Scat had an itchy trigger finger. More than most.

The pounding steps slowed. A figure emerged from underneath the brush a couple heartbeats later.

A breath leaked from Smuggie's chest. Dewy. If it'd been Scat, he'd already be dead. Code words or not.

Dewy lowered a pistol held at the ready. "Boss? Didn't know you was coming this way today."

"Do I need to clear all my plans with you?" Smuggie spat at the ground, his annoyance at the situation his quarry had put him into playing well enough into the ruse.

"No, sir. But I heard a shot." Dewy bested Smuggie by three inches and a good eighty pounds, but physical strength wasn't what put a bloke in charge around here. Brawn didn't get a man as far as brains, and neither Dewy nor Scat shared much smarts between them.

"Snake tried to bite me." Smuggie shoved his pistol into his waistband and then tried not to wince as the still-hot barrel collided with his skin.

Dewy scanned the area around Smuggie's feet, and his deep baritone dipped another octave. "Yes, sir."

Smuggie cast one last look at where the frightened couple had hit the woods, but the two intruders had hightailed it out. He needed to follow them, but he'd have to deal with matters here first. No use causing suspicion. Better Scat and Dewy think he dropped in for a surprise checkup. Always good if they wondered when he might show up and catch them doing things they shouldn't.

"What news on that shipment out of Georgia?"

Dewy slid his pistol back into his holster. "Came in right on schedule. Sixteen crates of white lightning from the hills. I swear them moonshiners are getting better. This here don't taste like sweat and acid."

"You tried it?"

Dewy shifted his feet. "Just the one bottle between us, like you said was our due."

Smuggie nodded. Easier to tell them it was their due for hard work than to let them know he used them to test every batch of homebrew to make sure it wasn't lethal. He'd heard more than one tale of the moonshine being poisonous. Better one of the low men keeled over than him. Or worse, one of Durkin's clients.

"Good man. Got a ship lined up for you. Coming in tonight."

"This one know we're loading?"

Smuggie fished a cigarette from his pack and rolled it between his fingers. "This is one of the outfitted kinds."

Smart idea, even if he did say so himself. Taking boats that came in for repairs and installing secret compartments with their owners none the wiser. His crew loaded their cargo onto the boats with the folks on board as innocent as babes. Law had no reason to search the vessels, but even if they did, they never had to worry someone might turn and rat them out.

"Yes, sir. We'll be ready." Dewy cast a glance behind him.

"Got something I need to check out?"

"No, sir." He cleared his throat. "Everything's fine. Well, except...except Scat and me don't agree on what you said was the orders, so if you don't mind telling the both of us together, that would be helpful."

Smuggie lit his cigarette and took a puff. "You saying I told each of you blokes something different?"

"No, sir." Dewy swung his head back and forth, sending greasy locks over his wide forehead. "I just know that, if he hears you say what you told me, then he'll realize he misunderstood you the first time."

Problem was, he had told Dewy and Scat two different things. Best way to smoke out a rat. Whatever information made its way back to him would lead him to the man with loose lips. But the tactic hadn't panned out. Maybe neither one of them had been the one to leak the rumor about that extra crate of Irish whiskey.

"Tell him I said I want the two of you working together on tonight's job. Follow the orders I already gave to you." Easy enough fix to pull Scat off a job that didn't exist nohow.

That seemed to mollify the bear, and Dewy grinned. "Sure thing, Boss."

"Now get back to work. I've got business to do."

"Yes, sir." He spun on his heel and trotted back the way he'd come.

Smuggie took another draw and then stalked in the other direction. With any luck, the steamer hadn't yet gotten too far downriver. Would they tuck tail and scurry back to Natchez, or did they have somewhere else to go searching? Someplace secret they didn't need to be?

How many of his waypoints had they discovered? The thought sent a chill down his back. The last thing he needed was for his operation to be outed by a couple of louts.

Briars tugged on his pants, and he cursed the snags they caused.

A shrill whistle, followed shortly by another rent the air. He paused. Maybe they were just now pulling into the water. But steamers didn't usually sound off that close together.

Another sharp screech.

Something must be wrong. He picked up his pace and peered around a tree at the water's edge. The ancient packet boat boiled black smoke and tilted toward the shore, hull dipping precariously toward the bank. A larger rear-wheel paddler blasted her whistle, coming around the river bend at impressive speed.

The collision was going to be catastrophic. He chuckled. Maybe he wouldn't have to worry about these two much longer anyway. And he couldn't possibly be blamed for their deaths if that lady captain rammed into another boat.

A sickening crunch followed by screeching metal bellowed above the roaring engines and churning paddles. He winced. Both boats would go down. Had to, with as bad as it sounded.

But the larger vessel shot past, hull still intact. It let out another angry whistle before hurtling upriver. The dame's boat screamed, well and good stuck on something beneath the water.

The boat puffed smoke, and the paddle wheel dipped into the water. But whatever held them remained fast. He pushed away from the tree and traversed the shadows for the length of the boat to get a look at the bow.

A gash cracked the hull, and brown water lapped at the wound.

He sucked his teeth and let a smile tickle over them. Looked like those two wouldn't be poking around anywhere sensitive now. He'd send the blokes to strip the boat down once the crew gave up and departed.

Then he'd finally be off babysitting duty.

N ot good. Daniel handed another bucket of water to Finn, who handed it off to Buck. The crack in the hull continued to seep, letting in water faster than they could dip it out. There'd need to be some repairs before they could hope to get the *Alma May* off the sandbar.

Camilla had taken Solomon, and the two of them used a skimmer to examine the outer hull while the others dipped the leaking water. Daniel lacked knowledge in boat repair, but even he could tell the old vessel would need more than a patch and some tar.

Cracks in the iron frame and fissures along the hull indicated it might need to dry dock for an extended time. What would that mean for Camilla and her crew? They were already struggling to stay afloat—so to speak—and repairs had to be costly. Not to mention she wouldn't be able to carry cargo any time soon.

If he didn't find the treasure, what would she do?

Another worry to add to those already pressing against the back of his skull and pounding into every waking thought. He had too many people counting on him, and he felt helpless to shoulder the need. Where was God when life crumbled around the edges? He'd always been a man of faith, and God had rewarded his efforts with a good job, a stable life, and peace. Had he sinned or misstepped in some way that brought all these trials upon him? Had he unwittingly earned God's wrath?

Finn paused with the next bucket. "We could do this all day, and it ain't going to help."

Buck winced. "You gonna be the one to tell Captain?"

"Ain't my place." Finn pinned Daniel with a meaningful look.

He rocked back on his heels. "What? You want me to tell her?"

Finn shared a look with Buck, who didn't offer an argument. They both stared at him.

"You're her crew. It should come from you. Besides, I doubt anyone will need to say anything." Why tell Camilla her boat had suffered a fatal blow? A tragedy she would clearly be able to see on her own. "Does this usually happen when a boat hits a sandbar?"

Finn rubbed his neck. "Don't think so. 'Least, not this bad. But *Alma May* here has seen better days. Might also have been a boulder or something else on that bar we couldn't see. Happens like that sometimes. You never know what's in the depths."

Which was why Camilla valued her father's notes on the river so highly. Knowing where hidden dangers lurked saved lives and property. Problem was, she'd known the bar was here but hadn't been able to avoid it. Not without crashing into the larger steamer barreling around the bend.

Finn handed his pail to Buck and waited for Daniel to fill the next. "We'll stay at this until she says otherwise. Keep busy and the like. Good surge might be able to get us off this bar, but with the damage, we won't be able to go far."

He dipped the water and passed the bucket to Finn as Buck returned with an empty one. "Maybe we should leave this so you can start packing up your belongings. We're going to need a towboat most likely. Better we get to dry land and wait on help."

Buck sucked his teeth. "You probably right. I'll see if I can find something to wedge in those cracks and slow the water. Finn, you start gathering our personal effects and put them on the deck. That way when the captain returns, we can help her with hers."

Daniel rose and wiped his wet hands on his trousers. "Has anyone gotten Lula from the captain's office? We can't leave her on board."

"I'm sure that feisty little terrier be just fine." Buck scratched the back of his neck. "But she's probably mighty unhappy."

"I think we still got some tar left in the engine room," Finn said to Buck before turning to Daniel. "You go get the dog."

"Should he gather the captain's belongings too?" Buck eyed the water pooling on the floor. "We might not have much time."

"That would be the best." Finn scratched his chin. "We need to be ready to go at a second's notice. What if another boat comes at us again?"

If another boat rounded the bend too fast, Daniel doubted they could do anything to stop the collision. The realization spiked through him like a barbed ten-penny nail.

"One of you get Camilla. Let her know she needs to gather whatever she can and prepare to leave the steamer for now." Daniel held up a staying hand before Finn could protest. "I'll not go into her private chamber without her permission."

But if she refused to pack her belongings and abandon her boat—the old nonsense of a captain always goes down with the ship or some such—then he'd haul her off this hunk of metal himself if he had to. Items could be replaced.

She could not.

His stomach knotted as the truth sunk claws through his center. Not the realization that life mattered more than property. What God created outweighing any of man's creations remained an undeniable fact. No, the twist tightening his entire inner being came with the sudden and irrefutable understanding that Camilla Lockhart could not be matched or substituted by any other in his life. Her swift intelligence, boundless kindness, and sweet spirit watered places within him he'd not even realized were parched. The very thought of losing her in any manner seared with enough heat to make him clench his teeth.

"You all right, Mr. Gray?"

Daniel cleared his throat and attempted to erase the life-altering realization from his features. "I'm fine."

The two men shared a look.

"Let's get moving." Daniel waved them toward the door. "We have a lot to accomplish in a short amount of time."

He could only pray Camilla would see reason. Assuming God heard his prayers anymore. He'd need to find a moment to go over his choices and discover at what point he'd lost the Creator's favor and beg mercy. He couldn't let his punishment affect Camilla and her crew.

Neither crewman appeared convinced, but they didn't have time to argue. Daniel hurried them from the cramped area beneath the deck to carry out their given assignments. He took the stairs to the upper deck two at a time and strode to the captain's quarters.

No sooner had the door swung on its hinges did tiny claws dig into his leg. Lula launched herself up at him, and he had to scramble to catch her before her momentum lost out to the lack of traction on the steep incline of his upright body. He snagged her against his waist and then adjusted her in his arms. She rewarded him with a lick to his cheek. He wiped it away.

The little dog quivered in his arms, clearly frightened by recent events. Poor creature. Had to be difficult, not understanding what happened. He patted her head and lowered her to the floor. He'd need to get her pillow. What else did Camilla keep in here for the dog?

He scanned the shelves. Would they be able to unload her books in time? They couldn't leave everything here or risk thieves. Abandoning even an empty vessel would result in scavengers taking pieces of it in the night.

Lula dug her feet against his knee.

"What?"

She twitched her ears and then began furiously digging again.

Did she want him to...? He bent his knees to pick her up. As soon as he dipped, she ran up his body again. Looked like he'd be gathering things one-handed.

Did Camilla have a leash? He tucked Lula against his side and scooted the pillow toward the door with his foot. He'd need to dump out the water in her bowl.

He rounded Camilla's desk, looking for more dog items.

Something shiny caught his eye. Two drawers on the desk had jarred open during the collision. He closed them and stooped before what rested on the floorboards underneath.

Sunlight glinted from the edges, beckoning him. He shifted the dog and scooped up the item before he let himself pretend he'd never seen it at all.

The metal felt cold against his palm. Lady Liberty's head encircled by stars seemed to thrum against his skin. Fire gathered in his chest and dried the moisture from his mouth.

Why did Camilla have an 1861 gold coin—just like the kind in the lost Hollis treasure—hidden in her office?

W hat was she going to do now? Camilla slogged her way back onto her grandfather's limping boat. Even with Daniel's fee and the money Mr. Copeland owed her, she'd never be able to afford the kind of repairs they were going to need. Not to mention what it would cost to haul the boat to shore. Assuming she didn't sink in the process.

Solomon gripped her shoulder when their boots hit the deck. His eyes said everything, but he splayed his fingers and touched his chin twice anyway.

Mama's.

Her heart pinched.

Keeping her gaze, he created a pitched roof with his fingers.

Mama's house.

He was offering for them to stay in Hattie's house. She hadn't been there since the day she'd found out Papa had died.

Hattie would have swaddled her in grandmotherly love and allowed the grief to flood the moors. Perhaps even giving that heartache a chance to settle rather than constantly beat against its bindings in her heart. But she'd been too consumed with surviving to slow down to grieve and too stubborn to admit having others help her would have been nice.

Camilla forced herself to swallow down the thickness in her throat and nodded. It would be a safe place to store their belongings and Papa's things and clear off *Alma May* until they could figure out what to do next.

And she was tired of letting her pride get in her way.

But where would they all sleep? Hattie's house was small, and neither of them could stay in such cramped quarters with three men. Even ones like family.

Finn scurried to her, hat clutched between reddened fingers. "Captain, the damage is..." His gaze darted to Solomon, who tipped his chin.

"I know, Finn. It's all right." No reason to make him say it.

"We're patching her up best we can. But we started gathering our things too." He scuffled his feet. "Just in case you wanted to head to shore."

Her stomach tripped. Of course, she needed to send her men to safety. Anything could happen while they were stuck on this sandbar. She scoured around in her depths until she located a modicum of courage and drew herself up.

"Load everything on the skimmer and get it to shore. Then bring me something to pack Papa's books in. We'll unload everything, and then you three will take it to Hattie's house for safekeeping."

Solomon crossed his arms, but she avoided his gaze. He would only say she had to come with them. Finn didn't move, words forming on his lips but not coming free.

She smacked her palms together. "Get moving, crewman! We don't have much time."

He ducked his head and hurried to do her bidding. She chided herself for being rude. But she was captain, and right now, she needed her men following her orders.

Not staring at her with pity.

She marched up the stairs to retrieve Lula from Papa's office. Then she'd need to find her valise and pack her few personal items. The most difficult project would be removing the books and contents of Papa's desk. But she couldn't risk keeping anything on board she'd need to protect from thieves.

The cabin door stood open, but Lula didn't bound out at the sound of Camilla's footsteps. Her breath snatched. Had she been injured in the collision?

She bolted inside to find Daniel behind Papa's desk with Lula draped over his arm. He stared down at something in his other hand, forehead etched with deep grooves.

Lula flicked her ears at Camilla's approach but didn't scramble to get down. She appeared unharmed.

"Is Lula hurt?"

Her words snatched Daniel's gaze from his palm to slam into hers with emerald fire. The intensity sent her back a step.

"What's wrong?"

"Where did you get this?" His voice held an edge she'd not heard from him before.

"Get what?"

He flipped his wrist and showed her a golden coin pinched between his fingers. She squinted and stepped closer.

"Is that a twenty-dollar coin?" Where had he gotten that? And why did he show it to her with such animosity?

His gaze narrowed. "It's a gold coin from 1861."

"War-era gold?" Despite their situation, excitement stirred. "Is it from your treasure? Where did you find it? Twenty dollars! Why didn't you tell me sooner?"

He clutched the coin in his palm. "I found it here."

The words hung between them before landing with a punch. "Where?"

"On the floor. The drawer must have come open when we hit the sandbar." A sliver of hardness left his voice.

"Wait. You thought I knew about that and was hiding it from you." She planted her hands on her hips. "You distrusted me so easily?"

His cheeks had the decency to redden.

"It seemed rather suspicious."

"And what possible reason would I have for keeping any clues from you? When you hired me for the job and when you promised twenty percent of the cut if I proved vital in finding it?"

He pressed his lips into a line.

She pointed a finger at him. "Have I given you any cause to immediately pin me with guilt?"

His chest expanded with a breath, and Lula squirmed. He placed the dog on the ground, and she hurried to Camilla. She bent and scooped the dog into her arms, and the comfort of soft fur and something to hold calmed a little of the fizzling in her nerves.

"My father is dead." The words seemed to scrape from his throat. "And your father has a piece of the gold they went to find."

Buzzing started in her chest and thrummed through her ears. "Are you implying he and Papa found the treasure, and then Papa took it all for himself?"

"It's possible that—"

"That what?" The words snapped from her lips. "They found a treasure, and Papa killed Mr. Dixon, then ran off with one gold piece, stashed it on the boat, and left again to get himself shot and killed and dumped at the riverbank?"

Daniel seamed his lips.

How dare he? What right did he have to go through Papa's things or fling accusations or not trust her or think Papa would ever do something so awful?

But why did Papa hide twenty dollars we could have used?

She shoved the thought aside and continued her deadlock of unwavering resolve against Mr. Gray.

"Captain! We got—" Buck darted into the room and shattered the stalemate. He paused in the doorway. His gaze jumped between her and Daniel before he cleared his throat. "Sorry to interrupt, but we got company. Might be trouble."

Of course. Why wouldn't it be?

Camilla stiffened her shoulders and spun on her heel. She'd deal with Daniel and his suspicions later. Right now, she had a boat to save, trouble to conquer, and a heart to shield.

Ice settled in Daniel's stomach and pulsed in numbing waves through his fingers. He closed his eyes to settle his senses. She was right. He'd cast immediate suspicion upon her. Or at least her father.

But hidden evidence didn't speak of innocence. Something bad had happened that night. And Captain Paul Lockhart harbored proof of the lost gold.

Perhaps.

What if he had come across this coin from somewhere else? Had used it to know what type of coin he was looking for? Or what if Father had found a small stash of the coins and it convinced him there must be more? What if he'd given this coin to Captain Paul Lockhart as payment toward his fee?

As more arguments he imagined an opposing counsel might ask volleyed through him, he pinched the bridge of his nose.

He should have thought of all these things and approached Camilla with questions, not accusations. Though he'd never actually accused her of anything. He'd simply asked where she'd gotten the gold. If in a somewhat cynical manner.

Shoving his hands in his pockets, he stalked from the room and down the stairs to see what trouble had found them now.

A willowy man with a low cap over his umber hair stood on the deck. He offered a hand to shake Solomon's. Daniel paused on the last stair. Did they know this man? Where had he come from? He didn't see another boat anchored nearby.

Dressed in a suit displaying moderate wealth, the newcomer offered Camilla a slight bow before assessing eyes skimmed over the deck. When his gaze landed on Daniel, a hint of recognition sparked. Then he returned his focus to the captain.

Did *he* know this man?

No, he hadn't met this fellow before. He would have remembered. He looked the type Camilla had called slick as an eel.

As though to punctuate his point, Lula let out a throaty growl.

The captain might be put out with him, but he strode forward to join the conversation anyway.

Solomon stepped to the side to give him room, though Camilla ignored him while she jostled the dog to shush her. Solomon made a gesture by placing one fist, thumb up, on his open palm and lifting both. It'd be nice to know what that meant. Daniel tilted his head to indicate his confusion, and Solomon cut a sidelong glance at the man while not moving his head.

Something to do with this man. He understood that much. But what? Did Solomon mean he distrusted the fellow? If so, Daniel felt the same.

Lula continued to growl, then let out a bark in defiance of Camilla's command to hush.

"As I was saying." A slight British accent underlined his voice. As though he'd been raised in England but had been away for some time. "Saw you blokes ran into some trouble. My men can get this vessel towed to our repair shop for you."

"And why would you do that?" Camilla's eyes flashed. She moved Lula away from the man and held her out toward Buck.

The older man scrambled forward and accepted the growling dog who succumbed to a fit of barking. Then he retreated with her to the deck behind the engine room.

Camilla must be even more distressed than he'd realized. He'd never seen her speak to anyone with such venom. Not even the unsavory Mr. Liles, the dockmaster who'd wanted her out of Natchez. At least he knew she wouldn't be hoodwinked into taking unscrupulous deals. She was far too clever.

"Business, of course." The man splayed long fingers.

Camilla's shoulders drooped, the poison of her earlier words draining away. "Thank you for the offer, but we'll need to make other arrangements."

"I'm willing to barter if finances are what's making you hesitate." He sucked his teeth, blue-eyed gaze dancing toward Daniel again.

This man was up to something.

"What did you say your name was?" He extracted his hands from his pockets and broadened his chest.

"Mr. Pike." His lips curved away from a yellowed smile. "And you are?"

Why did he get the feeling Mr. Pike already knew? "Daniel Gray."

"Pleasure to meet you, Mr. Gray. Now if you'll excuse me, I was making a deal with the captain of this vessel."

Camilla shot Daniel a look he couldn't decode. Did she want his help or want him to stay out of her business?

"What sort of barter?" Maybe if he asked, she'd see this man had nothing good in mind.

Mr. Pike's tarnished grin widened, and he shifted to speak only to Camilla. "We pay for the repairs, and in return, you make a few deliveries for us until the costs are covered."

Camilla narrowed her eyes.

"With a bit of interest for the trouble, of course," Mr. Pike hurried to add, clearly noticing her suspicion. "We do need to make a profit."

Her features eased. She wasn't considering the idea, was she? She couldn't be that desperate.

Daniel spoke up before she could open any doors she'd later regret. "That won't be necessary."

Solomon nodded before whatever Camilla was about to say broke free. She bit back her words and made a rapid series of gestures at the engineer.

Solomon followed her tirade with a finger pointed at Daniel, the same fist-on-palm lifted-hands signal he'd given before, and then a series of rapid finger movements.

Camilla glared at Daniel as though he'd been the one to sign whatever she didn't like.

He held her steely gaze. He'd seen this type of man before. The kind who took advantage of others' desperation and misfortune. They'd likely end up with shoddy repairs that cost more than twice what they should. Or a debt that never quite cleared until the next job.

"The captain respectfully declines." He refused to look away from Camilla even as he spoke to Mr. Pike.

Her eyes rounded at him speaking for her, but she pressed her lips into an unforgiving line. She swung her gaze back to Solomon for confirmation.

Solomon gestured between Daniel and Mr. Pike. Then he spread his hands and signaled to the shoreline. Daniel understood what that meant.

He directed Solomon's question at Mr. Pike.

"Where did you come from, anyway? Rather convenient for you to show up so soon after our running aground. Especially since there's no other boats anchored nearby."

Solomon gave a satisfied grunt.

Mr. Pike's nostrils flared, but the hardness in his face almost instantly turned to amused confusion. "I live nearby. Was coming down to fish when I saw what happened. Only wanted to help."

He tipped his hat when no one responded. "Well, then. I thought Captain Lockhart was the type of woman to make her own decisions. Didn't know she depended on her solicitor to do it for her. I'll be going, then."

Mr. Pike ambled toward the gangplank in a pair of nice leather shoes. The type a man didn't wear when he planned on fishing the Old Muddy's banks. He whistled as he hopped the rail and strolled down the plank that had been lowered onto the sandbar. Then he splashed through calf-deep water and onto the shore and disappeared into the woods.

"That was strange." Camilla blew a breath up her forehead.

"Yes," Daniel crossed his arms. "Especially since no one told him I was a lawyer."

Solomon mimed fishing.

"Right," Daniel agreed. "And no one goes fishing dressed like that. He must have come from that band of bootleggers we happened upon in the woods. He offered to fix your boat so you would be obligated to run illegal moonshine for him in return. We should alert the law."

But first they had to escape the sandbar, pray they weren't rammed by another boat in the process, and get the *Alma May* to safety. Before a group of criminals decided they'd sniffed too close.

23

Where was Papa's fortitude when she needed it? Camilla slid her hands along the side of her sturdy skirt before remembering she didn't have trouser pockets. Daniel opened the door to a blocky building and gestured her ahead of him. The warmth of his palm on her lower back helped with the upheaval in her stomach.

She'd never been inside a police station before. She waited near the door while Daniel spoke to a man in a blue double-breasted jacket with shiny copper buttons. She'd endured yesterday's trial of unloading her home, held herself together through a tearful reunion with Hattie last night that had caused cracks in the dam of her composure, and determinedly donned her best churchgoing outfit this morning.

Complete with uncomfortable T-straps she'd wobbled in twice. And gloves.

She picked at the lace near her wrist. The appreciation in Daniel's gaze when he'd arrived at Hattie's this morning almost made her wish she dressed like this more often.

"A detective will see us now." Daniel's voice so close to her ear made her jump. His hand settled against her back again. "Are you all right?"

Of course she was. She'd only lost her father and now her home and her head felt stuffed with so many confusing emotions it might burst at any moment. "Yes, sorry. Just thinking."

The concern in his eyes didn't dim, but he gave a nod and steered her toward a door in the rear past the waiting and receiving areas.

Her heels clicked against the stone floor as imposing walls loomed on either side. The officers bustling down the hall didn't seem to notice the humidity or the weight of despair, but they must be used to such things.

A fellow in a pressed uniform led them to the end of the tunnellike hallway and into a room that may as well have been a cell itself. Bare walls and a table with four durable chairs. Only a single window to let in clean sunshine while a gaslight in the corner battled the shadows with yellowed thrusts and parries.

The officer closed them inside without a word. Camilla stepped to the window, but the view consisted of the side of the neighboring brick wall and discarded rubbish.

"Are you sure you're all right?" Daniel regarded her from his position near the door. He ran a hand through his dark hair after tucking his hat under his arm. "You seem nervous."

Irrational annoyance volleyed up her throat. "And let me guess. You think I am nervous about being in a police station because I am secretly to blame for the loss of your treasure. Oh yes, and your father, though that seems secondary to you."

The horrible words shot through the air and landed hard enough to make him take a step back. Confusion and pain twisted together on his face as dense and intricate as a monkey's fist knot.

"Daniel, I'm sorry. I don't know why I said—"

The door opened, and an imposing figure filled the doorway. The man had to be a foot taller than she, with broad shoulders, a wide brow, and a generous mouth set in a determined line.

"Please take a seat, Miss Lockhart, Mr. Gray." The man's voice rumbled with authority, and she slid into the chair nearest the window.

Daniel hesitated, his intelligent eyes taking in the newcomer's tailored suit and short-cut hair. When Daniel sat next to her, his perfect posture, smooth features, and steady assurance made her blink.

But of course, Daniel would be used to rooms like this. Didn't lawyers sit in these meetings with criminals all the time? Her teeth clamped. And now he sat here with her.

She clenched the arms of her chair. What in the tarnation had gotten into her? Why the barrage of dark thoughts and unwarranted accusations? She closed her eyes and winged a short prayer heavenward for the Lord to help her to renew her mind, take every thought captive, and guard her tongue.

When she opened her eyes, she found the mountainous man regarding her thoughtfully. He seemed to take up half the table on his own. She cut a glance at Daniel, who also watched her. She lifted her chin a notch and waited for one of them to speak first.

"I'm Detective Mason McCready. Officer Sutton informed me you have information on suspected contraband and smugglers."

"Bootleggers." The word popped out of her mouth. "That's what y'all call them, right? We heard people in the woods. Then a well-dressed fella came out and said he'd fix my boat and we'd work out a deal. Seemed suspicious to us, seeing as how he came from nowhere. Oh, and there was shooting." She shifted to look at Daniel. "Right?"

Daniel's perfect poise never wavered. His hands relaxed on the table, his shoulders level, and his voice firm yet at ease.

"At approximately two o'clock yesterday afternoon, Captain Lockhart anchored the *Alma May* about eight miles north of

Natchez. She and I exited the vessel to explore a section of an oxbow in accordance with a family map I had in my possession. We heard voices and men talking about moving cargo and mentioning someone named Durkin."

The detective's eyes lit. The name had to be someone important.

"Suspecting these men were up to no good, Captain Lockhart and I abandoned our personal quest for family history and returned to the boat. In the process of pulling back out into the river, we were nearly overrun by a larger steamer. Due to Captain Lockhart's skill, we were able to avoid a collision. However, the boat ran aground on a hidden sandbar. Soon after, a man named Mr. Pike arrived and offered to tow the vessel and pay for repairs in exchange for Captain Lockhart making a few deliveries for him. The captain recognized a scheme was likely afoot, and so we came to report our findings first thing this morning."

Well, that certainly sounded better coming from him than it had from her. Gone was the man who stuffed his hands in his pockets and listened more than he spoke. This version of Daniel was confident and in charge. She liked that the same man could be both powerful and assured in this intimidating situation while also being known as a loving and playful uncle. And a man with a gentle touch and a passionate kiss.

Camilla blinked. Heavens. There went her thoughts again. Like chickens caught in a tornado.

Detective McCready plucked a small book from his breast pocket and jotted some notes. "Can you please describe Mr. Pike?"

Daniel looked at her, but she shook her head. He fared much better at this than she.

"White man, slightly taller than average, slim build. Medium-brown hair, clean-shaven, wide-set blue eyes. Slight British accent."

She would have merely described the fellow as rope-thin with a sharp nose and a slimy voice. Daniel had done much better.

"And the reason you were exploring the riverbank?"

"Personal family lore. We sought the location mentioned in an old document."

Why didn't he say anything about the treasure?

"For what purpose?"

The two men stared at one another. Should she say something? Before she could decide, Daniel spoke.

"There is a legend in my family about a lost sum of gold that's never been found. Odds are that no such heirloom exists, but I hired Captain Lockhart to take me up the Mississippi to assuage my curiosity nonetheless."

Detective McCready jotted more notes, then pushed away from the table. "Thank you for the information. My men will investigate this matter posthaste."

Camilla rose and marched to the door, careful not to let her stride length reveal her eagerness to get out of this room. As easily as men found cause for suspicion, she didn't want to give the detective any reason to wonder if she'd succumbed to any nefarious deeds.

When she reached the outdoors, she sucked a lungful of fresh air. Air tainted with the scents of horses, dust, and automobile smoke. She rubbed her gloved hands together as Daniel exited onto the street and secured a linen flat cap over his hair.

He cut a fine figure in his suit, blue tie, and shined shoes.

"That wasn't so terrible, though I must say I am glad it's over." She placed on a smile for his benefit.

Daniel regarded her with a level expression, his confident lawyer persona still in place. "Captain Lockhart, you and I are in need of a frank discussion. Would you kindly join me for coffee?"

Something in her stomach fluttered. She straightened her shoulders and dipped her chin with a single nod. She'd weathered worse than a man ending a contract and any hopes for romance with her. She'd withstand this as well. She couldn't pretend surprise. They'd suspected one another of secrecy and disingenuousness at nearly every turn. One could not build a friendship, let alone more, without trust. And no matter how hard they tried, neither of them could seem to go long without accusing the other. It would be best to part ways.

Besides, he'd hired her for her boat and knowledge of the river, and without the *Alma May* and now with the police raiding a bootlegging operation in the middle of their only clue, the job had turned belly-up.

They strolled along the sidewalk like a couple on a leisurely outing. She even let herself wonder what that would be like. To make a home on land, marry a good man, start a family. Do things like wear dresses and go out to breakfast rather than hauling cargo and eating fish stew before sunrise.

She'd been to Murphy's bakery to grab a few muffins as a nice surprise for the crew before, but she'd never sat at one of the pretty tables topped with white cloths and stem vases. Daniel pulled out a metal chair with a flower pattern welded into the back for her, and she sat while he went to order.

No one looked at her askance when she didn't come in wearing men's trousers, suspenders, and a newsboy cap. Why did a person's appearance matter so much to others? She was the same woman no matter what she wore. Perhaps life on land would be too constricting after all. How quickly would she get tired of heeled shoes and coiled hair heating the back of her neck?

Daniel arrived with two mugs emitting a delicious aroma and set them on the table. Then he returned with two frosted cinnamon rolls and placed one in front of her. He sat across from her and lifted his mug. Green eyes contained a current of emotion behind wisps of steam.

Perhaps she should save him the discomfort.

"I agree our contract should be terminated and our partnership henceforth severed."

One eyebrow twitched as he drew a slow sip. Then he lowered the yellow ceramic mug to the table.

She shifted her feet. "I understand that, without the use of my vessel and the complications arising from the criminals occupying the location of our only clue, such an agreement is no longer feasible under the original terms."

This time, he gave a thoughtful nod.

She cleared her throat, then took a sip of too-hot coffee to ease the scratchiness. "And given our rampant distrust of one another, I also understand your need to inform me any previously discussed inclinations toward romance at the conclusion of our contract are now over."

Daniel laced his fingers together on the table, gaze seeming to dig all the way to her heart.

"I'll sign a new agreement if you need me to." Not that she figured he would, but the unnerving silence dug around under her skin.

"Why do you distrust me, Camilla?" The soft words, so full of conviction, cut through any surface-level answer she might give.

"Because you could easily hurt me." Truth she'd not meant to speak landed between them. She swallowed against the sour taste it left behind.

Couples chattered around them, and sweet scents swirled in the air. But at their table, she sat on an island surrounded by uncertainty and a tempest of emotions she couldn't understand.

"Is that because you believe I sought you out thinking you had something to do with the disappearance of my father?" He spoke slowly as though each word pained him. "You believe I suspect your father of foul play and you had a hand in the entire scheme. Therefore, I am playing with your emotions and deceiving you into revealing incriminating evidence so I can get rid of you and take the treasure my father killed yours over."

"Of course not," she snapped.

His steady gaze wouldn't release hers. Something in her belly quivered. *Was* that what she'd believed? Somewhere in her heart, had she feared this stranger had come to finish whatever trouble her father had found himself in—that Daniel had deceived her along the way? Because in her hidden recesses, had she believed there must be no other explanation as to why a man such as he could care for a woman like her?

Perhaps. If so, she thought less of herself than she should, and she'd promised Papa she wouldn't let herself think that way. And...admitting Daniel had that much power over her inner workings meant he'd already anchored into her heart, even if that heart feared it was all a lie.

Did that make her weak? And woolly-headed?

She bristled. "*You* have suspected *me* at every turn. Just yesterday, you found a coin I'd never seen before and decided I had hidden it. Moreover, I had planned an elaborate scheme to trick you into coming to find me and hiring me so I could use you to get to the treasure your father found and then killed mine for."

Daniel set down his mug. "Whatever happened between our fathers, I don't believe you had anything to do with it."

She gripped her cup with fingers that wanted to tremble, and the fire left her veins. "Likewise." Her stiff shoulders deflated. "But that doesn't mean one didn't betray the other and regardless of what happened between them, it muddies the waters for us. We cannot trust one another because we blame our current pain on the other's family."

Daniel tapped a finger on the tablecloth. "Insightful. I believe you are correct."

Despite the logic insisting they were best off parting ways, his words still dropped like an anchor. "Very well. Then I suppose we are agreed."

"On which point? Thus far, you said several things I've not conceded to."

"Such as?" An annoying flare of hope lit deep within, and she did her best to quench it. It made no sense why she would continue to be drawn to a man she couldn't trust with her heart.

Except for the kindness and solid character he'd shown since they'd first met. The way he'd been tender to a tiny dog and a little boy. How he cared for those around him and sought to protect those he loved.

"While I do agree our arrangement must be altered due to the nature of our current circumstances," Daniel stated, "I'm not yet ready to give up the contract entirely."

She opened her mouth to protest but pursed her lips instead. She wanted to see what else he did or did not agree with.

"As to the more personal nature of our relationship, I have not strayed from my previous intentions. While I do acknowledge we have challenges to overcome, such is the nature of any partnership." His Adam's apple bobbed. "Or romance."

This time, she couldn't keep the words back. "You are still romantically interested in me? After all of this? Why?"

The edges of his mouth twitched. "That, for one." The humor left his tone, and his intense gaze remained locked onto hers. "I apologize for being a suspicious sort. I would blame it on my profession, but it is a personality trait I have always harbored. Perhaps it became a benefit to my work, but it can also be a hindrance. No matter what your father or mine did, it changes nothing about how I feel something intrinsic to the very nature of my soul when I am with you."

Her pulse tripped like it had also worn a new pair of heels and decided to go for a run. The man used a lot of fancy words, but the meaning had been clear. Something deep within her formed a connection with something within him despite everything else.

Was this what Papa had meant when he'd said that Mama had been his heart's match? That God had made their souls in harmony, and they resonated with one another in a way he'd been unable to explain?

Did her soul's harmony meld with Daniel's? Could that be why she continuously felt drawn to him even as she tried to deny his effect on her? Even as she tried to push him away?

"I..." She tried to regain moisture in her mouth. Without any luck, she took a sip of her coffee. Then another.

Daniel sat back in his chair, one side of his lips tilting. "Have I rendered the quick-witted captain speechless?"

Where had this confident, playful, and utterly charming man come from? "I like this version of you."

The smile slipped. "What?"

Had she offended him? "I mean, you always seem worried. Nervous, sometimes. But not today. Today you spoke to a beast of a man with perfect confidence. You're not only the smartest man I've ever known, but the kindest as well. Then today you added charming and in charge, and I think I finally know what women mean when they talk about swooning."

Daniel tilted his head back and laughed with a warm rumble radiating from his chest.

Her breath caught. Why had that been amusing? She'd revealed her affections for him, and he laughed?

He shook his head, and bright eyes met hers. "That, for second."

"What was for first?"

"First, you are direct and honest, which as I've said before I appreciate about you. For second, you see in me everything I want to be but fear I can never accomplish. Do you know what it does to a man to have a woman like you think such about him? It makes him feel as though he can take on the world."

"Oh." She turned over her lacy palm. "I only say what is true."

"And the fact that you believe it so—even while we still battle our suspicious and unbelieving natures—is what makes me want to do my best to live up to the assessment." He took her hand and held it between both of his. "I don't want to end our partnership and I don't want to halt our pursuit of a romantic relationship. Do you?"

"No." The word slipped out as more of a sigh, and she wanted to wallop herself for sounding like a lovestruck ninny.

Though perhaps she was.

And maybe...well, maybe that wasn't such a bad thing after all.

H e hated this creepy place. Smuggie cracked his knuckles and hugged himself close to the tree dripping in kudzu vines. A naggingly reoccurring thought needled his brain. He'd been reckless. Careless.

Why?

He'd thought about it for nearly two days now and couldn't come up with any feasible reason he'd given his name—his real name—to that lady captain. He hadn't used that name in years. Why had it slipped from his mouth? Sure, he'd known better than to use his nickname. That got thrown around too often to share with anyone outside of their line of work. But in the past, he'd always used a fake name.

How long before Durkin found out? He fingered one of the wide leaves of the invasive kudzu vine. Lot like Durkin, this vine. It hadn't come from here. Unsuspecting fools had brought it with them as something pretty. Figured it was harmless. Maybe it had been, way back in the early 1800s. Now it took over everything. It hung in vast sheets from the cliff face and covered trees whole. It spread its influence at a devastating rate. Pretty turning to deadly before anyone grew the wiser.

And once it got established, there was no getting rid of it.

The breeze ruffled through the leaves, a ghostly whisper in the still of night. He didn't like this part of the job. Usually got away with keeping himself out of it. But not this time.

A man's muffled scream mingled with the breeze and sent a tingle down his spine. When had he grown soft? Sounds of this side of the business didn't used to bother him.

Hard to be soft in a place called the Devil's Punchbowl. Crickets sang their lonely song, and in the quiet with nature's soothing sounds, he could almost forget evil lurked here. Evil that went far back before Durkin and his ilk.

He'd lived under the hill long enough to hear the tales. Stories generations old about river pirates and men like John Murrel and the Harpe brothers who used the hundred-foot gorge sheltered against the bluff as the perfect place to dispose of their victims.

Most of Durkin's men whispered about the ghost of the mistress. A few had even claimed to have seen her, though likely they saw only what the drink induced. Legend said a bloke named Joseph Hare discovered his mistress had been unfaithful, so he buried her here wearing nothing but the jewels he'd given her. Men with lesser minds claimed to see her walking about in the shadows, offering up her jewels to anyone who would relocate her body to the cemetery's hallowed ground a half mile away.

Worse than tales of unclad specters were the stories of the ten thousand who died here. He scanned the shadows clinging to the trees but couldn't tell where so many bodies might have been buried. Surely they couldn't have all been dumped into the gorge. Even a mystical pit said to have no true bottom until it reached hell would have filled to the brim with that many tortured souls. Story went that the Union army built a walled-off encampment for all the recently freed enslaved folks they found in Natchez. Might have been a good thing, except the army then left the poor people there to die of starvation, tainted water, and smallpox.

The wind tickled over his neck, and he shook his head. Bad night to be thinking of old stories. The modern ones were dreadful enough. As though to punctuate his thoughts, another muffled scream sounded from the hidden grove behind him. Shielded from the river by the crescent arms of the Punchbowl and sheltered by the two-hundred-foot sheer cliff behind, this place had become a lair for the evils of men. And all the old stories did well to keep the locals away.

Stories had a way of doing that. Got under a bloke's skin and the like. No one ate the abundance of wild peaches growing here for fear of what had fertilized the soil.

Boot steps crunched through the leaves, and he straightened. Didn't want Bones catching him slacking. He focused on the river, scanning for any intruders. Not that anyone who valued their head poked about out here.

Bones Jenkins kept the big boss's hands clean. Assuming, of course, one forgot God knew the inner workings of a man. The one who'd ordered evil stood just as guilty as the one who carried it out.

Now where had that thought come from? He hadn't thought of God since he'd been a boy at his mother's side in England and she'd filled his head with nonsense about a Creator who existed of light and love and who had so great a mercy as to sacrifice himself for the world.

He shoved aside a sudden rush of longing. If such a Creator existed, he'd surely turned his back on the world. Otherwise, men like Durkin wouldn't thrive, and boys like him wouldn't have grown into men who would have broken their mum's hearts.

"See anything?" Bones wiped a long blade on a cloth as he stepped into the moonlight at Smuggie's side.

"All's quiet. Not even a ghost this night."

Bones chuckled. "There'll be another soul to add to those tales soon enough. Help me toss him in."

Smuggie's stomach churned. "I have lookout duty. Get Erickson to help you."

An owl let out a screech, and Bones snickered when Smuggie jumped. "This place give you the willies, eh? How 'bout you smuggle me a crate of that Irish whiskey I heard you scored, and I won't tell nobody you got a yellow belly."

"Deal." The word shot out of him before he could catch it. He'd saved his fingers once. He wouldn't be able to do so again. But Bones didn't need to know that. If the big boss made good on his promise to deliver a free crate, then he could pass the bottles along to Bones. And if he didn't, well, that'd be a problem for another day.

Bones chuckled again and took two steps away. Tension leaked from Smuggie's spine, only to ratchet back into place when the man spoke.

"Oh, forgot to tell you. Boss wants you to bring them folks you been trailing to see me."

Ice trickled down his back. "He wants me to capture them?"

"How else you think folks get here?" Bones guffawed. "Ain't none of our guests here by choice."

"But I thought he wanted me to follow them and see if they found the treasure they were looking for." Why the sudden change in plans? When methodical murderers shifted tactics, something had to be afoot.

Bones shrugged. Pale moonlight glinted off the blade he held up to the light, inspecting it for lingering blood. "How should I know? I'm not paid to ask questions."

Implication perfectly clear, Smuggie grunted to cover up the thickness in his throat.

"Do it quick, yeah? I got the feeling this here thread needs to be snipped real soon before it starts causing trouble none of us want."

"Understood." Smuggie pivoted toward the bank and his escape out of this devil's den. "I'll take care of it."

Bones's laughter followed him like one of the Punchbowl's ghosts. Mouth dry, he avoided the shadows and clung to the faint reflection of light from above.

For the first time since he'd been a lad, he wished he remembered how his mother had taught him to pray. Probably wouldn't help none for a sad sod like him, but if there was any justice in the world, then maybe it would do some good for that kindhearted little bloke who was going to lose his uncle just like he'd lost his dad.

Smuggie jammed his hands into his coat pocket and searched around for a cigarette. He'd need a few tonight. And a full bottle of the good stuff. If he was lucky, he might even get to listen to the angel sing.

Maybe if he tried hard enough, he'd be able to smother the unnerving pressure begging him to find a way to escape his life as the puppet king under the hill.

"That boy don't deserve this fate. He's better than me." He tipped his head to the full moon. "Don't blame you for turning your back on me. But if you can do anything to help that kid..."

He bit off the words and shook his head. What a fool, talking to nothing and hoping it would help some boy he didn't even know. Just some little sucker who'd been naive enough to try to feed a hard-hearted criminal slinking in an alley. Not worth risking his neck for.

"Soft." He spat the word at the dusky ground. He'd grown too soft. Worse, he couldn't even nail down why his long-lost conscience had started prodding him.

The ghostly wind screeched through the trees, carrying with it the tortured cries of the innocent. It jammed cold fingers under his hat and sent it flying toward the pit he'd planned to avoid. The derby bounced over the dead leaves and leaped toward its demise.

He didn't try to catch it. Feet clamped to the ground by the eerie whistle slithering through the trees, he watched as his hat took a suicidal plunge. At the end of all of this, would he follow it down? Lose not only his fingers, but join the dozens he'd turned a blind eye to on their way to see the devil?

He'd earned no less. But that little boy with the big heart who wanted to make sure a stranger never went hungry deserved better.

Smuggie set his teeth and headed toward Natchez. Even if it sent him swimming in the Punchbowl sooner than he'd like, he'd make sure he got that boy out.

And maybe this time God would toss a crumb of mercy to someone more worthy than the rebellious lad from London who'd abandoned the one person who'd given him the only bit of light he'd ever had.

He was in no mood to argue. Daniel held out Mabel's gloves and nodded to the door. "Time to go."

She tapped the toe of her red shoe on the wood floor. Where had she gotten those? They'd barely had enough to feed everyone and keep the household running since selling the motorcar. "I already told you—I'm not going anywhere. You'll not haul us off to some ratty boardinghouse. He was my grandfather too, and I've just as much right to this house as you."

As though that had anything to do with it. From the dining room, Lucas's chatter filled the void. "Think of your son."

She arched a brow underneath the fine netting of a felt hat matching her shoes. "I am. Are you? While you are off playing childish games looking for treasure with your new mistress, I am the one here trying to hold our lives together."

Her words landed like a hammer. Mistress? Childish? Everything he'd done had been to find a way to get her out of the trouble on her heels. He clenched his jaw. But of course she didn't know that. He'd purposely made it so.

The breath heaved out of her chest, and her tone gentled. "That was unfair of me. I know you love Lucas and you are only doing what you think will help. But there must be an end to this foolishness. You'll only end up forfeiting what remains of our family's wealth trying to chase more. I can take care of Lucas and myself. You don't need to."

What did that mean? He narrowed his eyes at her tailored dress. Had he been too distracted to notice what had to be romantic gifts?

"Are you seeing a new man?"

She waved the question away with slender fingers. "If you really want to help us, then leave the house to me and Lucas and get the squatters out. Go back to your life. I promise I'll be fine on my own." Sweetness laced her words, and she stepped closer, heels clacking on the floor tread by generations of their family. "I know you want to help. This is what's best."

"You think what's *best* is for me to leave you and Lucas alone to fend for yourselves?" His nostrils flared. "What kind of coward do you take me to be?"

A crease formed between her eyebrows. "What are you talking about?"

He pinched the bridge of his nose. If telling her the truth was the only way to get her to see the danger, then he had no choice. "Your husband was involved in dishonest dealings. Men came to your house looking for money he owned. They've since made threats. I've been trying to find a way to pay the debt, but I am running out of time. Something is happening, Mabel. Let me take you and Lucas away until I know it's safe for you to return."

She blinked repeatedly, and then a shadow crossed her pale features. "What men came?"

"Not the gentlemanly sort."

"I see." She fingered pearls at her throat. "I've changed my mind. You may take me to town after all."

"I'm not taking you to town. You and Lucas are to pack your things, and we are leaving Natchez. I'll put you in a hotel in Stanton or—"

"No." Her haughty sniff raked his nerves. "You should have told me about this incident earlier. But like always, you think I'm some hapless woman with straw for brains who couldn't possibly be of any assistance. Not that you have any trouble seeking the aid of an uncouth captain who can't even dress properly for dinner and who eats with dogs."

She shouldered past him and flung open the door.

His blood pumped in hot waves up his neck to scorch his ears. How dare she speak about Camilla in such a manner? Especially when the captain had been nothing but kind to his vain sister. "Where are you going?"

"To fix the problem you've caused me." She tossed the words over her stiff shoulder.

He'd caused? Had she lost her mind? He started after her, leaving the door gaping behind him. "You don't understand what these men are like. You can't just sweet-talk them with honeyed words and think all your problems will go away."

She spun on her heel, eyes flashing. "What would you know about it? My honeyed words have gotten me more than you can imagine."

That didn't sound good at all. "What have you done?"

"Only what I need to for me and my son." She tipped her chin. "No different from what I have always done. While you were busy with your schooling and your career, I learned a different skill. How to use the only privileges granted to me in my favor."

"What does that mean?" A sour stone settled in his gut. How much had she hidden from him?

"You always were blind, little brother. You never could see past the way you wanted things to be to the way they are."

He crossed the distance between them and took her elbow, her gloves still clenched in his other fist. At least she didn't snatch away this time. "For whatever I have done or haven't done that has caused you this hurt and anger, I'm sorry. I'm sorry I didn't tell you about those men. I was only trying to protect you."

She sighed and patted his cheek like he'd aged no more than Lucas. "I know you were. But you need to stay out of this and let me handle it. There are things a woman can accomplish that a man cannot." Her voice edged with steel as he began to shake his head. "Unless you plan on also manhandling me and tossing me into a locked room, there's nothing you can do about it."

Heat scorched through his chest. "Did Lucas Sr. do that to you?"

Sadness dimmed her irises for an instant. "You never did see what happened in the rooms beyond the books you had your nose in."

But he hadn't lived with her since before he went to university. His mouth dried even as bile inched up his throat. She couldn't mean what she implied. "Are you saying...?"

The sadness in her eyes hardened. "Finally you understand." She stepped away from him and stalked through the gate and down the narrow road along the cliff's edge.

Mind reeling, he stared as she marched off. Half-formed memories he'd subconsciously tried to bury did their best to resurface. Their father keeping her tucked away in her room for days on end. Her inability to go on social calls without Father present or receive any gentlemen callers he hadn't first put through rigorous testing. Daniel had dismissed the behavior as a father's concern for the safety and reputation of his only daughter. But had it been worse?

How had he not seen the truth? Why didn't he shield her? The sour feeling in his gut churned.

What do I do now, Lord?

Focusing on the peaceful river beyond, he tried to offer up a better prayer but scattered little more than incoherent thoughts heavenward.

"What bee buzzed under your bonnet?"

The familiar teasing snatched him from a petition for his sister's safety and for wisdom to move through this situation. He opened his eyes to Camilla tapping a finger on her crossed arms. How long had he been standing here with his eyes closed, gripping his sister's gloves like they were his only anchor to sanity?

"Want to talk about it?" Camilla smiled at him from underneath the brim of a flat cap, her long hair tied up in its customary braid.

The muscle in his jaw twitched. How could he explain he'd been a complete fool and made things worse for everyone?

"Guess not." Camilla rocked back on her heels. "All right, then. I'll talk instead. I'm going to be staying with Hattie until we figure out what to do about *Alma May*. Mr. Copeland still owes me a goodly sum. After restocking, paying my crew, and doing the necessary patch jobs, we still have a little left over from the first portion of your payment. Enough, I believe, to cover the extensive repairs and dry dock fees."

"Good." He returned his gaze to the river. One worry to lift from her shoulders.

"House is a mite cramped, what with Hattie, her son and Finn and Buck there."

He glanced her way, but the statement didn't need a response, so he watched a lazy paddle wheel dip into the water. Did the people on the boat down below know how lucky they were to spend the day drifting along a peaceful current?

She shifted to catch his gaze. "I'll come right out and ask, then. Can Finn and Buck take a room here? They are good at repairs and can work to earn their keep. I couldn't help but notice the house could use some fresh paint and sanding and the yard hadn't seen a gardening tool in some time. My men can help with other chores as well to earn their supper. It won't be for more than a few days, I hope. At least until I can figure out something else."

Wait. What? His attention snapped to her. She wanted the crew of the *Alma May* to stay here?

"You know them to be good Christian men." She spread her hands. "Just in case anyone might be worried about boarding men in a house with so many women."

"What?" He shook his head. "Of course I know they are good men. That's not it."

She touched his arm. "What's wrong?"

"You might have been right about my sister." Hurt and anger seared each syllable, but he couldn't keep the emotion from his tone. Not from her. Not when she looked at him with such boundless compassion. "And likely my father."

"Oh." Her lips puckered.

His fingers clenched into fists. "How could I have been so blind? I should have seen how possessive he could be. How he went to any lengths to be obeyed."

From the house, the soft sounds of Stella's rich voice wafted through in a beautifully haunting tune. At least Lucas didn't know anything about the turmoil.

Camilla stepped closer. "Who wanted to be obeyed?"

"My father. Maybe Mabel married a man just like him. Possessive. I never saw that side of Lucas Sr. Had no reason to suspect. But you never truly know what a man might be behind closed doors. His involvement with operations outside the law is proof enough I didn't know him. Still, I don't think he hurt her. But he might've tried to control her. Make her do things she otherwise wouldn't. I should have seen it. At least with my father if not with Lucas Sr." He shook the gloves. He wasn't making much sense. But his thoughts and memories jumbled and took logical sentences out of his grasp.

She rubbed a soothing stroke along his sleeve. "Did you and Mabel have an argument?"

He pulled away from her and ran a hand over his face. "She knew about those men who made threats. I told her today about them looking for a debt to be repaid, and she didn't seem surprised. Whatever was going on, she knew about it. She's gone to do something to handle it."

Camilla pressed her lips into a line, her gaze following the trail. Wherever Mabel had gone, she must not have crossed paths with Camilla. He should've followed her, but he'd been too twisted up.

How like him to center his focus on his turmoil and ignore others' needs.

Help me to be better, Lord.

"I must stop refusing to see what is in front of me." He steeled his spine. "I should've been thinking like a lawyer on a case all along."

"You already do. You've always had an objective way of seeing things. Mostly." Her wobbly smile faltered when he didn't respond. "Do you think what's going on with your sister is connected to your father and his hunt for the treasure?"

"One line from my grandfather's writings keeps haunting me." He couldn't get it out of his head. All last night, he'd tossed as the words pressed upon his brain. "'He's close. Too close. Can't let him see what died with the gold.' That's what Grandfather wrote. The more I think about it, the more I am sure he couldn't have been talking about lost gold a half-century old. So, what died with the gold?"

Camilla tucked her hands behind her and faced the river. The paddle wheeler had made its way past, leaving nothing but ripples. "I'm not given to believing in coincidence, so the fact that a band of outlaws is currently occupying the location on the treasure map doesn't bode well. I was too preoccupied with the untimely death of my boat to sift through those implications at the time, but I've had plenty of time since." Her tone took on a cautious edge. "Should we go talk to the detective again?"

He clamped the gloves tighter. They should. But knowing what he should do didn't make it any easier.

"Sorry." Her cheeks colored. "I don't mean I want to go to him and fling around accusations about your family. But if Mabel might be connected to those men we found when we followed your grandfather's map, then she could be in danger."

Daniel faced his grandfather's house—and faced a different, more ominous picture. "I don't think our fathers were ever looking for the Hollis treasure. They were after something else. Likely, they ran into the criminals we discovered, and it got them killed."

"Which means my father died for a lie." Camilla's pain knifed through him. "Mr. Gray—under the false name of Mr. Dixon—tricked him into thinking they were looking for a treasure. He wouldn't have helped otherwise. What do you think they were after?"

"Still gold, if my grandfather's words are to be believed. And since I'm not given to trusting the concept of coincidence either, it must be connected to the men we happened upon. Those are probably the same men who have been following us."

Camilla shivered despite the heat. "Was your father after whatever those men were smuggling? What about the gold coin you found in Papa's cabin?"

"I don't know. But it all must be connected somehow, and my sister is a part of it." He pinched the bridge of his nose. "Bring your crew and your belongings. Until this is over, we stay together."

"I told Hattie I would stay with her."

"And bring danger to her door?"

Her features tightened. Would she refuse? Like Mabel?

But he couldn't force her to listen either. No matter what she decided, he would find a way to protect her. And those she cared about.

Somehow.

Camilla studied his face, then gave a nod. "Very well. I respect your judgment. Tomorrow we'll pack up and relocate here."

He hated the slump of her shoulders. "If it hadn't been for that man who came offering to make repairs..."

She rested her hand on his arm again. "I know. We are both tangled in whatever this is. We stick together."

He cleared his throat. "I'm sorry I brought you into this mess."

"All part of the adventurous life of a riverboat captain." She winked.

Her poor attempt at humor didn't fool him, and he pulled her into an embrace. She melted against him as though she'd been made to fit into that very spot near his heart.

He spoke against the top of her head, determination welling from his core. "I'll fix it, I promise. Just...stay with me. Please."

She wrapped her arms around him and stroked his back. "I'm here."

Daniel eased back a few heartbeats later and cupped her chin. "You're a good woman, my dear captain. Better than a man like me deserves."

Words to express what had been gathering within him tried to make their way up his throat but were rerouted when her lips brushed his.

Achingly soft, the kiss held a promise deeper than their growing friendship. A million words were spoken in that simple touch and the brush of her thumb along his jaw. Lord knew he didn't deserve her trust or her heart, but he would do everything in his power to shield and honor both. The weight of the darkness shrouding him lifted as she lowered back onto the flat of her feet and offered him a warrior's encouraging smile.

No matter what challenges still lay ahead, they could face them.

Together.

H e hated crouching in the shadows like a wolf waiting to devour a lamb. Smuggie tucked his hat under his arm and lingered behind the kitchen of the well-to-do mansion the little boy lived inside. He hadn't been able to forget the way the lad had called to him in the alley, wanting to make sure a stranger didn't need help. Or go hungry.

Good lads like that didn't deserve what Durkin had planned. He'd done a little poking around. The lawyer happened to be the brother of Mabel, wife of Lucas "Sticky" Shoemaker.

So there was more to this situation than Durkin let on. But he couldn't stand by and see that kid left with no family and no options except the fake kindness of the big boss. Too well did he know how that situation would unfold.

Mum would say such coincidences were really the hand of Providence, and before now, he wouldn't have believed her. Not that he'd believed anything she'd tried to teach him in his youth.

A light flickered through the kitchen. He tensed. Shouldn't be long now. On the nights he'd been waiting for Mr. Gray and Miss Lockhart to leave the house, he'd made note of the family's routine.

His stomach churned. How long had it been since he'd taken a risk for someone else's benefit? Not since he'd stopped George Hammond from clobbering a boy half his age when they'd both been twelve. That had only been about a month after Mum first got sick. Broken heart had been what caused it. Made her body too weak to fight it off.

If only he hadn't taken Nate with him that day. At six, his little brother had been too small to run with the older lads. Hadn't been able to keep up when they'd dashed across the street to avoid the merchant calling for the police when Hank had pickpocketed him.

Smuggie had heard the thunder of hooves too late. Hadn't been able to get to Nate in time. He sometimes still felt that limp and broken body in his arms. Mum never said she blamed him, but she must have.

Why wouldn't she? He should have made Nate stay home.

Then Mum got sick from her broken heart and couldn't do her work as a seamstress anymore. He wasn't as good a pickpocket as Hank. So, after nearly a week without a crumb in his stomach and Mum getting weaker the thinner her broth became, he struck out on his own to find work to feed her. When he'd come home a few days later with news he'd found factory work, she was dead.

He'd left the house with her in it and ran to the docks. Hadn't even waited around to see if she'd had a proper burial. Took the first boat heading away from England that would allow lads to work for scraps to eat and their passage in its belly.

Surely the God Mum had loved wouldn't turn her out of heaven because her worthless son hadn't put her in hallowed ground. Would he?

Smuggie shook off the memories. He couldn't make up for what he'd already done. But he might save another unsuspecting lad from working for Durkin. He had to play this situation just right if he didn't want to end up in the Devil's Punchbowl himself.

A second later, the rear door opened. The shuffle of little feet accompanied the bobbing light heading to the woodpile. Then a round face with innocent eyes appeared within the halo. The lad looked like Nate with that ready smile and big heart. He hadn't been able to save his brother. But maybe he could do something for this boy.

"Psst, lad."

The boy hesitated and held up his lamp. "Who's there?"

"The man you offered a wooden penny to. You remember that?"

The little bloke glanced back toward the house. If he called for help now, Smuggie would have to run, and then there'd be no escape for the lad and his mum.

Smuggie stepped closer, palms open to show he didn't carry a weapon. "You made sure I got a nice meal. That was kind of you. I wanted to say thank you."

"Oh. God tells us we should all share." The boy's light circled Smuggie in its embrace. "I remember you. Come on in and have supper with us. Stella won't mind."

Good-hearted lad. "I'm afraid I can't tonight. Thank you, though. I came to—"

"We got plenty, mister. I promise we do. Mama says we don't, but that's just because she liked how it was before. When my father was around, she went to a lot of parties, and we never ate frog legs. But I don't mind frog legs so much. Especially when I get to help catch the frogs. Bo says I have to help clean them next time, though."

Someone else bustled around the kitchen. Likely the lad's nursemaid. "That's great, lad. But I need you to listen."

"My name's Lucas."

After his father. Something unfamiliar twisted in Smuggie's stomach he didn't care for, bringing a sense of urgency. "Lucas. Please listen. You need to tell your mum to take you out of town."

"Why?" He thrust the lamp higher, illuminating Smuggie's face. "I overheard Uncle Danny saying the same thing to Mama this morning. She said no. Is something wrong?"

How much truth did he tell? If he shared too much and terrified the child, Durkin would find out someone had tinkered with the plan. It wouldn't take much to identify who. "No, not really. It's just important that she takes you somewhere fun."

"I like fun. Father was going to take me to a baseball game, but I never got to go. I don't think Mama is going to take me. Besides, season is over, and Uncle Danny doesn't really like baseball." His shoulders slumped. "Not like Father did."

"You tell her it's important."

Lucas's little brows gathered above his nose. "Mister, I don't know what it was like with your mama. But I ask for stuff all the time, and she says no. She already said no to Uncle Danny when he wanted to go somewhere, so she'll just get mad at me and tell me to do extra arithmetic. I don't like arithmetic, even though Stella tries real hard to teach me. I don't want to have to do more on account of pestering."

This wasn't going to work. He'd have to go a different route. "Tell your mum some bad men are causing trouble around here. Tell her she needs to take you away to keep you both safe."

It would be good if the lad's mum and uncle both left so he didn't lose any more family. But if the others got to Mr. Gray before Smuggie could figure out a subtle warning, then at least the boy still had his mother. A boy needed his mother.

Lucas took a step back. "What bad men? Why would they come here?"

A lie that he didn't know worked its way up his throat, but Smuggie swallowed it down. "Your mum will understand. Those bad men knew your father. Since he's gone, they will want to talk to your mum and uncle. But if your family isn't here for a few days, then the trouble will go away, and you can come home safe."

He hoped. If Durkin got rid of the lawyer and the captain for whatever he had against them, then the whole thing would be done. Unless for some reason Durkin had beef against Sticky's wife. Sticky's sticky fingers had skimmed too much from the books, and Durkin found out. It didn't have anything to do with the treasure the others were after, though, so Durkin wouldn't have cause to go after the boy and his mum. Even if she'd known anything, she was just a dame.

It would blow over. Hopefully.

"Just listen, lad. You were kind to me. I'm trying to do the same for you."

"Lucas?" A female voice cut through the buzzing cicadas. "What's taking you so long with that wood?"

The boy turned, and Smuggie melted back into the shadows.

"That man we gave a wood penny is here. I told him he could come to supper."

"What?" Alarm sparked in the woman's voice. "You get back here right now."

Smuggie slipped past a scraggly young oak and edged toward the road hugging the rear of the property, then picked up his pace.

"But, Stella, he's—hey! Where'd he go?"

He'd done his best. Now he'd have to wait and see if his efforts had done any good. He shot a glance at the stars above. He'd talked to God and tried to do something noble. If anyone up there actually looked down, now would be a good time to prove it.

"**D** aniel!"

Stella's alarmed cry brought him out of the hidden room in his grandfather's study where he'd been racking his brain to figure out any additional clues.

He kicked the camouflaged door closed behind him just as she darted inside. "What's wrong?"

Stella waved behind her. "A strange man's out there! Lucas was getting the wood and—"

His pulse railroaded through his veins and sent a shock up his spine. He bolted past her and into the hallway before a single panicked word breached his tight throat. "Lucas?"

If he'd been taken...

Why hadn't he insisted Mabel and Lucas stay somewhere else until he unraveled this mess of trouble?

"He's fine." Stella caught his elbow as he snatched the doorknob. "I have him up in my room." She wagged her head. "Lucas said he saw the same man we talked to in an alley a few days back."

The heat thrumming through him turned cold. "What man? Why wasn't I informed about this?"

She wrung her hands. "Didn't think much about it at the time. Lucas saw a hobo and worried about the man not having anything to eat. I made him come along but told the hobo he could get something to fill his belly at Mama's. Then we went on our way. Didn't even see him good in that dark alley. Don't know how he'd know where we live."

Could he be the same man who had snooped around the house? How else could he have known where Lucas lived? Had men been following the boy too?

Daniel pivoted and started up the stairs to check on Lucas and Mabel. With his nephew safely inside, he didn't need to rush out into the darkness without a weapon or a plan to search for a kidnapper.

He met Buck and Finn on the landing. They shared a room at the end of the hall since Violet and Daisy hadn't minded moving in with Stella for a short time. Camilla had insisted she needed a night alone with Hattie for women's talk, so she planned to come tomorrow.

Daniel gestured to the crewmen. "You two head back to Hattie's and get Camilla."

At least he wouldn't need to decide between going after her and staying here to keep watch over Lucas and the other women.

Finn scratched his head. "What for?"

So Daniel could keep her close. Make certain she stayed safe. Solomon could surely protect her. But he needed the peace of mind of seeing that for himself. "Something suspicious is going on, and we need to all be together. Safety in numbers and all. Tell Solomon and his mother to come along as well. We need to plan."

Buck's eyes widened, and he gripped Finn's shoulder, stifling any protest the other man might make. Not that he seemed inclined to objection. Both men bounded past him down the stairs without further questions. Their loyalty to their captain extended past the riverbanks.

"Wait!" Daniel jogged down after them and then into the study. He couldn't send them off without a means of defending themselves, should trouble meet them on the way.

He found what he needed in the second drawer of Grandfather's desk. He only had two pistols in the house, so he couldn't give a weapon to each man, but hopefully, they wouldn't need one at all.

He hefted the revolver and checked the cylinder. Full. He snapped it closed and joined the men in the entry hall.

He thrust the gun toward the older of the two. "Take this."

Buck shook his head. "I promised never to hold a weapon again."

Too much emotion clogged those words for Daniel to explore, so he lifted the pistol toward Finn.

The redhead had no such hesitation and tucked the weapon inside his jacket. Solemn eyes caught fire in their blue depths. "We'll fetch the others and be back as quick as we can."

Daniel grasped Finn's shoulder. "Be careful."

They hurried out the front door, and after engaging the lock behind them, Daniel took the stairs two at a time. He found Stella, Daisy, Violet, Mabel, and Lucas crammed into Stella's room. Mabel stared out the window, fiddling with a long strand of golden beads around her neck. Daisy, Violet, and Stella huddled near the wardrobe, speaking in hushed tones.

Lucas jumped up and down on the mattress, making a mess of the bedclothes and leaving dirt and leaves on the blanket.

All eyes turned to Daniel. Stella whispered to the two younger girls, and they scurried out, each with a wide-eyed stare.

He caught Daisy as she passed. "You girls stay upstairs. Don't go outside."

Daisy blinked large dark eyes. "All right, Mr. Gray. We'll stay put."

He nodded his thanks and closed the door behind them.

"Lucas." Daniel kept his tone light. "Let's have a little talk."

The boy flopped down to sit cross-legged in the center of the bed. "Are you going to ask me about that homeless fella too?"

"I am. And I need you to tell me every single thing you remember."

"All right." He scrunched his nose. "I was playing with my yo-yo, trying to get it to come back up and not just drop down each time. It's not much fun when you only get to watch it go down, and then you have to wind it back up."

Daniel patted the boy's shoulder. "How about we start with when you went outside to get the firewood."

"Yes, sir." Lucas found a dried leaf and crumbled it between his fingers. "Stella told me to put up the toy and get on with my chores, so I did like she said. I lit the lamp we keep by the back door and made sure both of my shoes were tied."

Daniel clenched his teeth and forced himself not to interrupt. He had told the boy to tell him everything. A child his age had no way of knowing how to separate important facts from the mundane.

"I went outside, and I checked to see that the door closed behind me. Stella don't like it if I forget that part because she says I invite all the outside bugs to come on in and make themselves comfortable in our kitchen where they don't belong."

Lucas glanced at Stella, who encouraged him to continue.

"I got down the steps and about halfway to the woodpile when someone said 'Psst, lad.' I stopped because I couldn't see him real good. I thought about running back to the kitchen, but then I figured a bad man wouldn't have called out to me. Bad guys in stories are always sneaky, and they grab children without announcing their presence."

Daniel crossed his arms. Lucas had a point. But why come talk to a child if he didn't have nefarious intentions?

He'd tried not to worry the others, since so far, the only thing to rouse suspicion had been a faint cigarette smell and a barking dog. He should have warned Stella not to let Lucas out of her sight.

"Then the man said he'd talked to me before. I was kind to him and Miss Stella gave him a free meal, so he came to thank me. I thought it was a little strange he knew where I lived, but he seemed nice so I stayed." He puffed his chest. "I'm real smart, though, Uncle Danny. Just like my father taught me, I kept out of reach in case he thought about trying to grab me. But he didn't do nothing. Just stood there sticking his hands in his pockets like you always do when you're thinking about something super hard."

Stella cocked an eyebrow.

"That's a good observation. Thank you." Daniel jabbed his fingers through his already mussed hair. "Then what happened?"

Lucas plucked at the blanket. "I told him he could come in to eat. That's probably why he came, him being hungry again and all, and I knew y'all grown-ups would want to know about a man in our yard."

"You should have run away as soon as you saw him." Mabel's tight words made Lucas hunch forward, but she never took her focus off the window to notice.

Daniel cut her a glance she didn't see. "Go on, Lucas. What did the man do next?"

"He told me I should tell Mama to take me somewhere fun." He cocked his head. "But he said it funny like. He said 'mum' instead of mom or mama."

A tingle snaked along Daniel's spine. British. Like the man who'd come onto the *Alma May* after it ran aground. The man they'd described to the detective. Could that also be the cigarette man? "Do you remember what he looked like? Or what clothing he wore?"

Lucas tilted his head, mouth puckered. "He had brown hair and...blue eyes. Maybe green? But not brown. And he had on a jacket with a...white shirt under. No tie. No hat."

Could be the same man. "Did he smell like he smokes tobacco?"

"Don't remember."

"That's all right. You're doing well." He patted the boy's shoulder. "And the man said you should tell your mother to leave?"

Mabel remained silent, her focus stubbornly set on the window. Why would the men who'd been following them give a warning to the boy and not one of the adults? Or had Mabel received one and ignored it?

Lucas swung his feet and knocked them along the side of the bed frame. "I told him you had already asked Mama to go away and she told you no. If I asked, I'd just get in trouble. He got upset and said bad men were coming, so it was important I told her. He didn't tell me why. Then Stella called me, and he disappeared."

Stella rubbed her hands along her arms. "I'm sorry. I shouldn't have sent him out there by himself."

"This is my fault, not yours. I should have told you about my suspicions of being followed. I didn't want to worry anyone—and look what could have happened." Daniel stood from where he'd crouched by the bed. "Mabel? Do you know anything about this?"

She snatched her head around. "Why would I know anything about strange men in our yard?"

He glared his silent question, and she clamped her jaw. Fine. They would discuss it in private. He focused on his nephew.

"I'm thankful you're safe. But let's not talk to strangers who show up in the dark from now on. People who don't announce themselves in the light don't have honorable motives. Understand?"

Lucas nodded, big eyes sad. "I'm sorry. I just didn't want anyone to go hungry. That's awful. Your stomach growling and gnawing so hard you want to cry but you know you shouldn't." He wagged his head. "No one should have to feel like that."

What? How would the boy know anything about that kind of hunger?

"Enough, Lucas." Mabel stalked past Stella and held out her hand. "Come with me to our room."

He scooted off the bed with downcast eyes and took his mother's hand. Daniel followed them out of the room and down the hall.

Someone had opened the gaslights on high, banishing every possible shadow. The incident must have rattled Stella enough to push past her normal frugal ways.

Mabel opened the door to the room their grandmother once used, ushered Lucas inside, then closed it, and faced Daniel with a stiff spine.

Words leapt out of him. "What does Lucas know about being so hungry his stomach gnawed?"

His sister notched her chin. "I'm surprised he remembers so far back. And anyway, he's exaggerating."

"You never said you and Lucas Sr. were having financial troubles."

She toyed with her necklace. "Men do have their pride, you know. He had a bad year, but he made it right. Promised he'd take care of me, and I'd never go without again. He made good on that." She stabbed him with a glare. "I won't go back to that situation ever again. Wondering if we will be able to eat."

That explained why she'd been so determined to stay in Grandfather's house. He'd missed a lot when he'd buried himself in his practice. He shifted the topic back to the matter at hand. "Where did you go today?"

"To see a friend." She swallowed, but her eyes remained defiant.

"What sort of friend?"

"Why does that matter to you?" After reading his features, she drew a long breath and let it out slowly. "Look, I know you mean well. But I told you, I can handle things."

His fingers curled against his palm. "So 'handling things' is strange men talking to your son and telling him bad men are coming? What if Lucas had been taken, Mabel? What then?"

"What about you?" she snapped. "You knew about men coming to my house and about someone lurking around here and you never said anything! You knew something could have happened to Lucas going around at night by himself, and you couldn't even be honest with me then! All you do is give me orders and expect me to obey them without telling me what's going on."

The accusations landed with knifing blows. She was right. He should have told her. Why did he always think he could handle everything on his own?

Guilt wrenched through him. He called himself a man of faith, but he'd charged forward without praying for wisdom or seeking God's will in any of the decisions he'd made in the past year. Perhaps that, and not God's punishment, had caused some of the trouble crouching at their doorstep.

"I'm sorry, Mabel." He sought and held her gaze. "I should have told you about the men who came to your house that day and the reason I kept hunting for treasure despite the abysmal odds of finding lost gold. And I should have told you I suspected someone had been sneaking around our home. Lucas being in danger tonight is my fault. Please forgive me."

At length, her shoulders fell. Then the hard lines around her mouth softened. Her chin quivered. "No one is going to hurt Lucas."

"How do you know?"

"He promised." She twisted her hands together.

"He?" Daniel unlocked his clenched teeth. "I need you to tell me the entire truth."

Mabel's eyes flashed like she wanted to throw his concealment of pertinent information in his face, and she pressed her lips together.

"I should have told you sooner, and again, I'm sorry for not being more forthright." He touched her elbow. "But this keeps getting worse. First the brutes saying we had to pay off a debt.

Then someone following me. Now this with Lucas. Have you known about this trouble all along?"

"Some of it." Tears glistened, but her posture remained stiff. "I found out about my husband's business associates after he died. He only did what he had to for us. His family. They shouldn't have killed him for it. I learned who he worked for. He has a house here in Natchez."

"Who does?" Daniel's stomach churned, but he did his best to keep his emotions from showing.

He must have failed, because Mabel planted her hands on her hips. "Mr. Durkin has taken a liking to me. He knows I didn't know anything about what happened. He feels sorry some of his men acted too rashly. He's going to make it up to me. He has the authority to make all of this go away. Just trust me, will you?"

"And in exchange?" Daniel gripped her arm. "What does he want from you to make it all go away?"

"That's none of your concern."

"The devil, it isn't!" He released her and stepped back, heat boiling in his chest. Rash words never helped. He hadn't lost control of his tongue like that in years.

She shied back and scuffed her shoe against the carpet running the length of the hall.

Blast his temper. He jabbed his fingers through his hair. He wouldn't be like their father, regardless of how angry he became. He gentled his tone. "Forgive me. I shouldn't have spoken so crassly."

Her throat worked as she swallowed. After a few tense heartbeats, she wiped out the mark she'd scraped into the carpet.

"Men like that are dangerous, Mabel." He let all his fear for her hang on his words. "They take and they don't give. One wrong move, and you end up with bruises or worse. I've seen it a dozen times in my profession. Promise me you won't go back to see him again."

"Without the money, there isn't..." She rubbed her eyes when her voice cracked. The defiance leaked out of her, and her resignation knifed into Daniel's heart. "This is the only way I can pay the debt and protect my son."

"That's a lie." Daniel tipped her chin so she could read the truth in his gaze. "He wants you to think you don't have a choice, but you do. I'm here. We'll find a way out of this."

But without the treasure, how would they pay anything back? They'd need help.

Lord, please.

His heart cry came out paltry at best. But perhaps God would have mercy on him.

He took a step back and let a little of his inner desperation seep into his words. "Tomorrow morning, we are going to talk to Detective McCready. Let the law bring justice."

Her eyes flared at the edges, a gasp slipping loose. "No. You can't—"

"Think of Lucas." His soft words halted her protest. "His mother living as a criminal's mistress, always on edge, wondering if any perceived slight might get her harmed? At least until her lover grows tired of her and tosses her aside for the next woman without a penny to her name? Then what will happen to your son?"

Mabel's lips quivered.

He pushed on. She had to see. Needed to understand. "Can you risk your son growing into a young man with criminals around to influence him? What happens when he's old enough to get brought into the operation? When that's the only way to make sure his mother stays safe?"

She squeezed her eyes shut. Tears leaked down her cheeks. "All right."

"Good. We'll go over everything once we are all here. Gather our information so in the morning we can—"

Something banged downstairs and they both jumped. He ushered Mabel into the room. "Stay here. Stay quiet. I won't let anyone upstairs."

As soon as he heard the lock engage, he bolted to the stairs. Someone banged a fist on the door. Did he have time to get to the other pistol? Why hadn't he already put it in his pocket? He needed to be more logical. Make sure he—

"Mr. Gray! Open up!"

Finn?

"Solomon's hurt!"

Daniel dashed down the remainder of the stairs, tripped on the last one, and landed hard on his knees. Ignoring the pain, he gained his feet.

Finn pounded on the door again.

Daniel flung it open to find Buck and Finn sweating and heaving, Solomon propped up between him. Blood seeped between the big man's fingers, clutched to his side.

"My baby!" A tiny woman scooted around them, her face pinched in terror. This must be Hattie, Solomon's mother. "The doctor. We need a doctor!"

Daniel ushered them inside, the sharp scent of blood clogging his senses. "To the parlor. Put him on the couch in there." He glanced out the door, and his chest tightened. Oh no. "Where is Camilla?"

The elderly woman wrung her hands, tears rolling down her face. "They done took her! Shot my boy and took her."

Daniel's stomach hit his toes. His chest constricted as though his heart had been ripped away and his body fought to hold on. *Please, God. No.*

If anything had happened to her, he'd never forgive himself.

P ain radiated from Camilla's skull and through her teeth. Awareness seeped back into her with foggy sensations. Her entire body tingled, like little prickles invading her skin. Hard ground bit into her back. Her fingers twitched against a dirty floor.

Voices sounded nearby. Echoing as though in a cavernous room.

Where...?

Her muscles tensed, body preparing to flee. Escape. She'd been taken and—

No. She must be still.

Think. She held her breath and forced her eyes to remain closed. She'd be helpless without her wits. She'd been at Hattie's. They'd been having a heart-to-heart. She'd gone out to get water for tea.

There'd been a shout. Pain.

The voices came closer. Her body strained, itching to move. To escape.

Be still!

If they didn't know she could hear them, she might learn something. Gain insight on how to escape. Maybe they would leave if they thought her still unconscious.

"But it doesn't make any sense," a man said. His words dipped low, but something about them seemed familiar.

But what?

She clenched her teeth.

Think!

She concentrated on the hard ground beneath her. Anything to force her slogging mind to function at full steam. She had to ignore the throbbing in her skull and reorient her focus. A pebble digging into her shoulder blade. Hands bound in front of her with coarse rope. Earthy scents and the faint sound of whistling wind. Cold leaching through her simple blouse and trousers. Light flickered, causing a red glow through her eyelids.

As her foggy mind began to clear the haze, energy zipped through her system. She barely caught her eyes from popping wide to assess her situation.

Be calm.

Slow breaths in and out.

Lord, I need help.

Her mouth felt filled with sand, but she didn't dare swallow in case someone watched. Unconscious people didn't swallow.

"I know what we were told." The man's voice moved closer. "I'm just saying it doesn't make a lick of sense."

Where had she heard...? Recognition slammed into her gut. On the boat after they ran aground. The man in the suit. What was his name? Right. Pike.

A slippery fish in a nice suit with a hint of British in his words.

"Makes perfect sense to me," another deeper voice responded. "I handle snoops all the time. Nothing new about it."

Metal scraped against a hard surface, and her stomach clenched.

"But why now? I thought he wanted them to lead him to some kind of treasure," Mr. Pike replied. A boot scuffed the ground.

Dare she take a peek? As slowly as she could and careful to remain as still as possible, she opened her eyes into the narrowest of slits. Blurry shapes took form not far off, the closest with his back turned to her.

Yellowed light pirouetted along the rough gray walls. No, not walls. The sides of a cave. Where had they taken her? Somewhere past her feet, water dripped.

"Look, we ain't paid to ask questions, Smuggie. You know that. We are paid to do a job. And keep our lips locked about it. What's gotten into you?"

The loaded question hung between them for a few heartbeats before Mr. Pike—who the other man had referred to as Smuggie—grunted. "I prefer my women on stage or in my arms. Not tied and tossed in the corner."

She closed her eyes again lest the mention of her draw their gazes.

A dark chuckle rose from the first man. "Fun is what you want, yeah? Well, how about you and I make a deal, and I'll take longer than normal to prepare my tools."

Ice slithered through her core and wrapped fingers around her heart.

Lord, no!

Despite her best effort, her breath quickened. How would she be able to escape two men? Especially with her hands bound. Had Hattie or Solomon seen the men take her? Would they have sent for help? She barely remembered going to the well when pain had fractured through her skull and everything went black.

They'd taken her because of the treasure? Why? She hadn't found anything.

Bile churned in her belly. Why hadn't she abandoned the foolish quest? She'd known better, yet she'd still followed the same path that had gotten Papa killed.

I'm sorry.

Maybe she apologized to a father who couldn't hear her. Or to herself. Or maybe as a heart-cry repentance. Perhaps all of that rolled together. A tear leaked from her eye and slid down to her ear.

Would she be tortured, abused, and murdered, never to be found again? Boots scraped closer and she tensed. She'd fight. Take him unaware. Slam her head into his nose if he got close enough or...or...

"I know you're awake." The whisper barely slipped into her ears as a figure loomed over her. "But he doesn't. Stay still, and I'll do what I can to help you."

Camilla's eyes flew wide. The narrow face of a man not much older than she stared down at her. His lips drew into a grim line. He didn't have lust swimming in his gaze. Only fear. Her breath came in and out of her lungs so quickly her heart might burst.

"I'm sorry about this." He grunted and then reached for the buttons on her blouse.

She screamed as he ripped open the first two. She writhed against him as he pinned one shoulder down.

"I'll try to get him to let me take you outside." Alcohol wafted on the breath that hovered over her face. "Then you can run. But if you fight here, there won't be anything I can do."

His words came short and fast as he kept his back to the other man and pretended to be doing something other than talking.

She couldn't trust him, of course. But this might give her a chance. Even with the panic undulating under her skin, she didn't dare fight yet. If she could gain her feet outside, then she might be able to run away. Even though he likely only toyed with her, she would make him underestimate her.

When she didn't get up, he gave an almost imperceptible nod and lifted from his haunches to face the other man.

"Can't do nothing with you hanging about, you know." His voice dropped to a thick and rough cadence. "I'm taking her out to the woods, and then I'll toss her back in here to you when I'm done."

Metal scraped again. Her heart quivered as the source of the noise registered. A sharpening knife.

"Got to come to an agreement first." The amusement lacing the other man's words made the bile roiling in Camilla's stomach climb into her throat.

Seconds passed. Mr. Pike rubbed his chin. "Pretty one. And fresh too if I don't miss my guess. All right. I'd say that's worth a case."

The first man grunted. "If that's true, then a lamb is worth more."

Pike scratched the back of his head.

Would he decide the price the man wanted wasn't worth the effort? If she could at least get into the open, there might be hope.

"Fine. Two cases."

"Make it four, and you have a deal."

Mr. Pike snorted. "There's plenty of skirts under the hill willing to show some leg. Durkin will notice four cases, and no dame is worth my fingers."

Durkin? She filed the name away for the police. She shifted to get a better look at the beast crouched in the shadows.

Please, Lord. Let me make it out of here and to the police.

"Yeah, all right." Metal rasped again as the hulking man drew a six-inch blade along a whetstone.

His cold eyes met hers, and her heart tried to fold in on itself. "She's awake, which'll be more fun for ya, but best you take the gag, just in case, yeah?" He tossed a bloodstained rag at the slender man, and an evil grin curled the edges of his lips. "You'll owe me, you know."

Pike let out a low sound like one of Lula's growls. "Our deal covers debts. Take it or leave it."

Oh, Lula. Was she still safely inside Hattie's house?

Tears coursed down Camilla's face and gathered in her ears. Whatever else the men said became jumbled through the thrumming blood. A moment later, Mr. Pike appeared over her again.

"Sorry about this too." He grabbed the hair on the top of her head and snatched her head from the hard floor. She let out a sharp cry as her scalp lit fire.

He shoved a vile cloth between her teeth and secured it in a tight knot behind her head. Then he thrust his arms underneath her shoulders and knees and lifted her off the ground.

She swung her bound fists and connected to his ear. He grunted and faltered.

"Hang on now." The larger man stepped closer, his looming form casting a wide shadow. "This one here's got spunk. Might be more trouble than she's worth."

The grip around her tightened, pinning her against Mr. Pike's hard body. "More fun that way. Got to be a little sport in it."

The other man's eyebrows dipped toward his nose. "Never heard of you being that type."

Her captor shrugged. "I'm a smuggler. I'm whoever you want to see."

The icy words flooded through her. She'd been tricked. He never planned to let her go. She thrashed against him, but his grip remained firm. The pain in her head reared, galloping through her temples with abandon.

Please, God. Save me.

How long before the doctor arrived? Frustration boiled in Daniel's chest. He needed to search for Camilla. The longer they delayed the more they risked irreparable harm befalling her. He checked the mantel clock in his parlor once again and tried to focus. Solomon needed his attention, yet his mind kept running through all he'd learned about Camilla's disappearance.

She'd gone to get water from the well.

Lula had started barking.

Solomon had run outside and been shot.

A few scuffed leaves and boot prints led to the road where tire marks indicated an automobile. She'd clearly been abducted.

But by who? And why? The men who'd been following them hoping to usurp the treasure if they ever found it? Daniel and Camilla hadn't found anything new, so that couldn't be the reason. It had to be something to do with the criminals they'd stumbled upon in the woods.

His blood congealed in his veins. Where would they have gone? There must be thousands of places scoundrels could hide her. And what would they do to a woman alone? The thought curdled his stomach. If they hurt her...

A knock pounded on the door, and he nearly bolted out of his shoes. He hurried past Hattie and into the receiving hall, blowing the tangy scent of blood out of his nostrils.

Dr. Wellburn doffed a hat from a receding gray hairline as Daniel jerked the door on its hinges. The man who'd given his grandfather personal care tucked his fedora under his arm and adjusted his medical bag. "The patient?"

Finn scrambled in behind the doctor as Daniel gestured toward the parlor. "He's been shot. We've compressed the wound to staunch as much of the bleeding as we could."

The stately physician strode into the room, his polished shoes falling in measured steps across the carpeting. He nodded politely to Hattie. "Step aside, please, ma'am, so I may assess the patient."

Solomon grunted and hefted his frame into a sitting position, causing his nostrils to flare and his mouth to compress.

"Easy there." Dr. Wellburn adjusted spectacles on the bridge of his nose and leaned closer. "Tell me what happened."

"He was shot. That's what!" Hattie leaned over the doctor's shoulder, peering at the wad of kitchen towels Stella had provided to stem the bleeding.

Despite the pain he must be in, Solomon gave his mother a flat look. He lifted his right arm to sign something, but winced, and abandoned the effort.

"Solomon speaks in hand gestures." Daniel met the doctor's gaze. "According to the others, he heard a commotion outside his mother's house and ran to see what happened. A man with a gun fired wildly behind him as he was running away. His two friends brought him here, and we sent for you immediately."

"I see." The doctor adjusted his spectacles below his gathered brows.

He didn't ask why they'd brought the man across town to Daniel's house instead of taking him to the charity hospital.

He hadn't asked them, though funding seemed the simplest explanation.

The doctor plucked a pair of scissors from a leather bag he'd placed next to Solomon's shoes. The silver shears made quick work of Solomon's denim shirt, exposing a seeping wound in hard muscles.

Daniel turned away when the doctor started poking around the wound and Solomon's face contorted.

The doctor's words brought a rush of relief. "You are very blessed. The bullet missed most of your vitals. It entered beneath the lungs. Appears to be a small caliber lodged against your costal cartilage. The bone is nicked, but once I remove the projectile, you will heal nicely."

Not wanting to witness the doctor do his work, Daniel stepped out of the parlor and slid the door closed behind him. Since Solomon had care, he could start the search. First, he'd need to go to the law. No sense wandering aimlessly on his own. That wouldn't do anyone any good.

Finn and Buck waited in the receiving hall, eyes questioning.

"Doctor says he will make a full recovery."

Buck's lips moved in what looked like a prayer of thanks, and Finn's shoulders sagged.

"When Dr. Wellburn finishes his work, please tell him to leave his bill, and I will take care of it in the morning." Daniel plucked his hat from the rack near the door.

"Are you going to the police to find the captain?" Buck's mouth tightened around the words, causing lines that aged him past his years.

"Stay here and protect the others, will you?"

With a nod, Buck positioned himself at the base of the stairs while Finn stood guard at the parlor door. Daniel tugged on his hat and stepped out into the hot night.

I'm sorry, Lord. Whatever I have done or not done to bring this trouble upon us, please forgive me. Keep Camilla safe, and

227

don't let her pay for my mistakes. Please give me wisdom and show me what to do next.

His insides churned as he hurried down the path into town. Every shadow grasped for him with clawing fingers, each rustle of the wind a Klaxon call of danger. With his senses on edge and nightmarish images dancing through his head, he couldn't dispel the oppressive feeling. The distance stretched before him, never seeming to grow shorter even as he continued to increase his pace.

He finally reached the police station and burst inside. Behind the counter, a young officer in blue leapt to his feet and put a hand to the holster on his hip.

Daniel thrust his empty hands high. "There's been an abduction, and my friend has been shot. We need immediate help!"

The officer shouted to the men behind him. Two officers entered through a doorway to Daniel's left. The wider of the two, a man whose face indicated his years of experience, spoke with a deep baritone.

"Your name, sir?"

"Daniel Gray. The man shot is currently at my residence and under the care of a physician. We need to send a search party for Camilla Lockhart immediately."

The other officer, a man in his midforties with a thick mustache, jotted notes while the first man asked Daniel a series of unnecessary questions about how he knew the victims and his whereabouts during the crime.

"And you were not present for any of these events?" The officer's forehead folded into tight wrinkles. "Why didn't one of the witnesses come to make a report?"

Daniel unlocked teeth that tried to clench and forced his tone to remain even. "Solomon needed the other two men to carry him. Then they went for the doctor. His mother is understandably staying with him while the doctor tends his wounds. You need to start looking for Camilla."

The other officer scribbled notes, his pencil scratching languidly across the page.

"And why send you instead of one of these others who had been present for the shooting?"

Daniel's fingers curled into his palms. "What does that matter? You can question all of us as much as you want. After we find Camilla!"

A large form stepped up to him seemingly out of thin air, and Daniel startled as he glanced at the imposing form of Detective McCready. He blew a breath out of his nose. "Detective. They have taken Captain Lockhart. I suspect it's the same men we told you about earlier."

The Detective shared a look with the other officers. "I'll handle this."

The older man hesitated, but the younger closed his note-book and spun on his heel and disappeared behind the partition. The older officer pinched his lips but then followed, leaving Daniel with the detective.

Detective McCready's piercing gaze settled on him again. "You believe the smugglers abducted Miss Lockhart? And what's this about a shooting?"

"Camilla went out to get water. Solomon, her engineer, heard a commotion and went outside. He saw a man fleeing who then turned and shot at him. Camilla was gone."

"And why do you believe the smugglers are involved?"

Tension radiated through his neck and shoulders. "Who else would it be?"

The detective lifted a brow as though to ask the same question of Daniel, but as he had no other explanation, he kept the man's steady gaze.

After a brief stalemate, the detective volleyed orders over the partition. "Smith, Pollard, and Helsen, gather a team and start questioning Durkin's men. He's behind this, and we might have the opportunity to catch him."

The name slammed into Daniel's chest and leaked out between his lips. "Durkin?"

McCready's heavy gaze raked over him. "Kingpin of the operation I believe is responsible."

Daniel forced words past his dry throat. "My sister... she's been seeing a man named Durkin." His stomach dropped. "And that's the name we heard those men use in the woods."

Why hadn't he realized it sooner? He tightened his stomach against the bile churning inside.

McCready's face clouded, and he called for another officer.

The pieces fell into place. There'd been no coincidences. The members of his family had been entwined with a smuggling ring, and it had gotten his father and brother-in-law killed. Then Captain Paul Lockhart. Now it might cost Camilla her life as well.

"Mr. Gray?" The officer's clipped tone pulled Daniel from his swirling thoughts. "I need you to come with me."

He pivoted toward the door. "I'm going to help find Camilla."

Detective McCready's meaty hand settled on his shoulder, eyes warm with a compassion that didn't match the hard lines of his face. "I need you to give the officers every detail you can. That will go the farthest in helping us locate her."

"But—"

"And then you need to lead them to your sister. For her protection. Under no circumstances is she to contact Mr. Durkin again. Do you understand?"

Heat scorched through his limbs. They were wasting time. "She's at home. They can question her there. You need me to show you where we found those bootleggers. Maybe that's where they took Camilla."

"I know the place." He squeezed Daniel's shoulder. "Let us do our job."

The bile rose to his throat. Every muscle within him strained to run out into the night and tear the town apart until he found her. But what could a disgraced lawyer with no combat or detective skills do? Perhaps there was one thing. Before he could let his usual skeptical tendencies outweigh boldness in faith, he closed his eyes.

"God, please lead these men to Camilla and save her from any harm that might come her way. Give them supernatural insight and, if you are willing, please bring swift justice to those behind these crimes."

When Daniel reopened his eyes, Detective McCready's gaze held steel. Then he jerked his chin in a single nod. "Amen."

Armed with the best protection Daniel could hope for, the bear of a man stalked out the door. Activity erupted behind him, and soon the officers on duty were mounting up a party.

Daniel bowed his head. He'd done all he knew to do. The rest of this mess, like everything else in his life, he'd have to yield to God.

The night settled over Camilla like a heavy shroud, transforming the landscape into a haunting, ethereal realm. She'd been right about being held in a cave, and wherever they were, she had to be near the river. The air swirled with the musky scent of decaying leaves, an unmistakable perfume of forgotten sorrows tangled with the familiar undertones of the silty Mississippi.

Mist slithered across the nearby murky waters, weaving its ghostly fingers around the gnarled roots of a cypress tree as if caressing secrets hidden within the ancient heartwood.

Mr. Pike's grip remained firm yet not painful as his boots thumped an even rhythm across the moist ground. Humidity clung to every exposed inch of her skin like a clammy embrace. She squeezed her eyes shut and sent up another prayer for divine intervention as he carried her farther away from the cave and into the woods beyond.

Beneath the oppressive gloom, a symphony of insects echoed in harmony with the drumming of her heart. The chorus of throaty bullfrogs mingled with the haunting cries of water-bound creatures, their calls a discordant melody.

The moon, a pale luminescent orb, cast faint beams of light through the knotted canopy above, unruly tendrils reaching down to graze the indigo waters. If she could make it to the riverbank, she could swim to safety. Get her bearings or maybe even flag down a friendly vessel.

The Mighty Mississippi had been her home for decades. Now it had to be her salvation.

No. God alone would be her salvation. But perhaps he'd use her skills in the water to facilitate a miracle.

Mr. Pike's hot breath swept across her face as he glanced back toward the cave and edged farther into the dense over-growth. They were moving away from the water.

Bile burned up her throat, but she had to remain calm. Lure him into a sense of security by underestimating her. As soon as he put her feet on the ground, she'd make a run for it.

The moonlight's spectral glow revealed the twisted gnarls of ancient roots creeping out from the mire, like skeletal fingers clawing toward the surface, seeking release from their watery prison. She could only pray she wouldn't find herself buried with them.

Mr. Pike stopped, his chest rising and falling against her with the effort of carrying her so far. Had he taken her where no one would hear her scream? She bit down on the filthy rag in her mouth.

"I need you to promise not to scream, or you'll get us both killed." Mr. Pike's eyes filled with worry in the moonlight.

Was it possible he did mean to set her free? Why?

She blinked at him, unable to do anything else with the way her insides quivered.

Give me strength, please, Lord.

Pike's gaze shifted over the shadowed landscape. "I didn't plan on any of this. I was just a lad who needed to survive. Then I was a greedy youth with high ambitions and bendable morals. I don't even know what I am now." He set her feet on the ground.

"But for all the things I've done, I would never force myself on a woman."

Camilla gained her footing and prepared to bolt, but the pleading in his gaze arrested her.

"There ain't no treasure, miss. Nothing but a tangle of secrets you don't want no part of. Get your fella and his family and get out of here."

Her heart fluttered as he held her arm in one hand and fiddled with something at his side. Could she snatch away from him and slip into the shadows? Surely he would catch her in a matter of steps.

A glint of metal caught in the moonlight. Was that...?

A scream tore its way from her chest and up her throat and lodged against the filthy rag.

"Easy. I don't want to cut you." With a quick raspy sound, her hands came free.

Camilla stumbled back a step and came up against a tree. The man pointed behind her.

"Just through the trees, there is the road. Go left, and you'll reach the city cemetery." He sheathed the knife underneath his jacket. "I'll stall him as long as I can. It's not enough, but it's the best I can do."

She needed to run. Flee before he changed his mind. Yet her feet wouldn't move. Perhaps the panic had rendered her numb, or God had granted her a little of that peace no one could understand, because she removed the gag from her mouth and words she wouldn't have expected came free.

"God has mercy on those who call on his name."

The man's jaw went slack.

Panic slammed back into her chest, and she whirled around. Her feet caught on roots and shadows as she plunged into the darkness.

Her heart drummed, matching the rhythm of her labored breaths. She pushed herself forward, stumbling through the thick underbrush. Fear coursed through her veins like venom, paralyzing every rational thought that attempted to surface.

Any moment his fingers would grab her. He'd laugh as he lived out the cruel game of cat and mouse. She couldn't risk slowing or taking a straight path.

He couldn't let her go. And even if he did, no doubt the devilish man in the cave would come for her. She'd seen their secret camp hidden deep within the woods, concealed among the ancient trees and twisted roots. They'd want to silence her forever.

Branches whipped at her face, leaving angry welts in their scathing wake, but she didn't dare slow down. Her mind conjured haunting whispers and ghostly figures lurking just beyond the reach of her vision.

Please, God. Guide my feet.

The forest closed in around her, suffocating. Shadows danced menacingly, mocking her desperate attempt to outrun the inevitable.

Up ahead, the tangle of overgrown kudzu thinned. She veered left where a steep incline had her nearly crawling, using her hands to assist her scramble. If she'd been below a ravine near the riverbank, then higher ground would surely take her closer to Natchez and safety.

Tears blurred the edges of her vision, mingling with the sweat and dirt on her cheeks. But despair could not extinguish the flicker of hope burning deep within her. No shouts came. No footsteps pounded closer.

Summoning her last vestiges of strength, Camilla surged forward and burst through the tangle of vines. Moonlight cascaded across a slithering line of dirt.

The road. Just as he'd said.

She turned left and jogged, rocks crunching beneath her boots. Only a lonely owl answered her winded cries for help. Her chest burned, and sweat streaked down her face. She'd escaped.

But what if they'd taken her somewhere miles from town? How long had she been unconscious? Surely they couldn't have a murderous cave so close to Natchez without anyone knowing.

Up ahead, bony fingers reached toward the sky. She squinted in the milky light. What were those...?

Headstones. The cemetery.

A cry of relief poured through her dry lips. People didn't bury loved ones far from civilization. And if the iron fence gave any indication, she hadn't left Natchez at all.

Souls did not haunt their body's resting place, but she still didn't want to traipse near on a night like tonight. Keeping to the other side of the road, she willed her heaving lungs to gather more dusty air and increased her pace.

Up ahead, flickers of light glowed promises of salvation. She could make it. Her feet pounded on as she ignored the burn in her lungs.

A growling rose up behind her, shattering the slumber of the dead and startling a flock of crows. Two glowing eyes rounded the bend.

Not eyes. Headlights.

The roar of a motorcar's engine churned a cloud of dust as the vehicle barreled her way. Friendly folks who would whisk her from this nightmare? Or her captors already on her trail?

God help her. She couldn't run much more.

Sucking air, Camilla dove for the shadows at the edge of the gravel and crouched in the ditch. Better she make it to town on her own where crowds offered safety than risk seeking help from strangers on a deserted road in the middle of the night. She pressed her body to the ground, scents of dirt and grass clogging her nostrils as her lungs fought to fill and release.

The lights approached, carrying the sound of crunching tires.

Just as she thought they would safely pass, the motorcar slowed.

And a bright beam of light swept over her.

S muggie added one final thought and then scrawled his name at the bottom of the page. He dropped the pen in the holder on his writing desk in his apartment, though it wouldn't matter now if he left the entire place in disarray. One letter for Bella, the singer with the angel's voice and kind eyes who had rebuffed him but never judged him. The other would be for the little boy's uncle and the police. A decision like this, once made, couldn't be reversed. He could only pray that, if there really were a God looking down on him, Mum and the lady captain had been right.

Maybe this one act of courage would bring him the mercy he sought.

The haze of cigarette smoke lingered in the air. Past his apartment walls, the club below would be bustling with an electrifying energy. Illegal liquor flowed through the veins of his world, and the temptation of a drink to dull the sting of what he was doing called like a siren.

His fingers shook as he folded Bella's letter and reached for a second page.

He should hurry. It wouldn't be long before Bones came for him. Then Durkin. He had to make his break before they caught up to him. He probably wouldn't be safe anywhere. Maybe if he caught a boat home. Started life over again in London.

He had no usable skills aside from the illegal, but he could learn. Find something that would have made his mother and brother proud. He glanced toward the pressed tin tiles on the ceiling. Did God look down and approve? Obvious signs of an all-knowing being would be more helpful than relying on these strange gut feelings overpowering his senses.

The clock on his wall chimed two, and he let his gaze roam the room that had, only days ago, felt like his kingdom. Over-stuffed furniture with gaudy gold edging. Expensive-looking vases from countries he'd never visited. A built-in bar brazenly boasting glasses and hooch as though he never feared the law could crack Durkin's shield. A shiny haven of self-indulgence.

Why did it now feel so empty? Like a golden cup encrusted in jewels on the outside yet filled with filth and decay inside.

He jotted another note on his letter to Mr. Gray, giving the location of the Devil's Punchbowl and the names of the men who ranked in the operation. None of the lower fellas would matter, since Durkin saw them as expendable. But if he lost several of his trusted men at once, it might be enough to make something stick.

Rumors circulated that the law had sniffed around Durkin before but couldn't find substantial evidence to bring him down. Certain officers looked the other way or shipments disappeared, and Durkin slipped through their nets each time.

One man had gotten closer than the others. What had his name been? McCullen? McCray? He couldn't remember. Some detective. He jotted another thought on the paper. Maybe Gray would find a decent copper who didn't have a hand in Durkin's pockets. One more notation of a more personal matter, and it was done. He folded the paper and stuffed it in his pocket. Then he snagged a carpetbag from the bed and jammed his hat atop his hair.

He wrestled the back window open enough to fit the bag through and tossed it in the abandoned alley. Wouldn't do him any favors if people noticed him leaving with luggage. That would raise too many questions. After struggling to get the protesting window closed again, he dusted his hands and strode through his home of the past four years. He closed the door on his old life, the soft click a gong of finality.

No going back now.

The first floor of the building masqueraded as a general wares' shop, while the real business carried on below street level. He locked the door to the stairs at the rear of the warehouse and descended to the basement. He'd need to make an appearance. Let the watchdogs see him going about business as usual to waylay any suspicions about his loyalty once he went missing. Might buy him extra time.

Smooth saxophone melted into a soulful voice, and he paused at the bottom of the stairs by the bar. Through the blur of cigar smoke, flecks of light caught on the fringe of Bella's blue gown, cascading motes of diamonds at her feet.

Flappers with their gaudy lip rouge wove around men in suits and fedoras, exchanging loaded glances and seductive whispers. He'd always seen this place as a haven of freedom from the oppression of the dull world beyond. But tonight...

The men's eyes looked tired. The women's faces pulled tight with lines of unease. Dancers lost themselves on the lacquered floor, their movements jerky and desperate.

"Good crowd tonight, eh?" A male voice much too close to him sent a scamper up his spine.

Smuggie barely caught himself from showing his surprise at having been snuck up on. He cast Tom an annoyed glance. "Well enough. Make sure you keep an eye on that one there." He thumbed toward the far corner where a man held a glass he clearly hadn't touched. The ice had melted. "He doesn't seem to be enjoying himself."

The bartender followed Smuggie's line of sight. "Got it, boss. We'll make sure he's no canary."

Smuggie hooked casual thumbs through his suspenders. "Got business tonight with a few ripples. Make sure things stay smooth here."

"You got it." Tom flung his towel over his shoulder and sauntered to the other end of the bar.

Nights like this happened occasionally, where someone had to take a trip to the Punchbowl. Smuggie's job generally involved keeping tongues liquored and eyes turned. Tom wouldn't think anything of the instructions. Ripples meant taking out someone who got a little loose in the tongue and was causing trouble. Another way they spoke in code. He'd thought it clever, once. Now it seemed like malicious children playing evil games.

Staying close to the truth would cover his hide for a while. They were dealing with ripples, and he had taken the woman out to the woods. All legitimate in the eyes of the operation. Maybe by morning when they started to put the pieces of his betrayal together, he'd be far enough downriver to make a clean break.

The throbbing brass resonated over the room, and he cast one last look at Bella's smooth cognac features. An angel too beautiful to taint with his presence any longer.

God, if you are there, get her out of this place. Give her a better life somewhere else.

Maybe the prayer would work. Maybe not. Either way, he had to make his move without risking a goodbye. Not that he would want to sully her with his company anyway.

His heart raced, matching the sudden upswing in the tempo as Bella took a break and the musicians belted something jaunty. Every nerve in his body screamed to get moving, but he schooled his features into a bored look of composure. Scanning the patrons as he would on any regular night, he waited. He watched the dancers and drinkers with their masks of deceit and shallow laughter.

Then he wove through the crowd, slow enough not to draw attention but fast enough not to be stopped for conversation. On the far side, the door leading to the tunnel that would take him to street level yawned open. He slipped past the sagging door and into the dim hallway.

The enforcer at the other end barely cast him a glance before opening the door onto the street. It closed behind him. He sucked in a lungful of air laden with cat urine and discarded stomach contents and strode to the rear of the building to retrieve his bag. He'd drop the letter at Gray's house and hoof it through the woods downriver. Once he got far enough from Natchez, he'd catch a vessel headed south.

Each step weighed an eternity, as if the grimy bricks beneath him conspired to slow his escape. The pungent stench of betrayal hung heavy in the air, threatening to saturate his lungs and choke him with its intoxicating bitterness.

He could turn back. Make an excuse about losing the girl. He could pull it off. He'd spent most of his life crafting lies.

But for some unfathomable reason, the idea soured his stomach. Maybe Mum made enough petitions up there in heaven to knife through his armor of selfishness at last. He'd do this one good deed. For her.

He shouldered the bag and slipped through the shadows. The walk to the Gray house didn't take long. Lights glowed throughout the lower levels, and a one-horse cart parked out front. Visitors? At this hour? He hesitated in the shadows, the sharp drop of the ravine to his back.

A silvery moon peered shyly through a veil of clouds, casting ethereal light upon the winding river now flowing with a hushed murmur. He held still, his senses attuned to every sound, every subtle shift in the surrounding symphony of nature.

The distant croaking of frogs echoed through the night, harmonizing with the gentle swaying of the pine branches, which whispered their secrets to the breeze. The river, alive with sparkling ripples, murmured tales of forgotten souls.

A figure moved inside past the window. Smuggie squinted at the form. One of the crewmen from the *Alma May*? Why were they staying at the Gray house?

The front door creaked open, and two figures stepped outside. Smuggie crouched in the bushes and strained to hear the words.

"Keep the bandages clean and try to dissuade your son from too much movement." An older man settled a hat over gray hair and nodded to a short, dark-skinned woman.

"Thank you, Doctor. Mr. Gray said for you to leave your fee amount with us, and he'd take care of it come morning." The short woman twisted her hands together.

"Thank you."

She opened her mouth as though to say more, but the doctor strode down the steps and onto the walk before she had the chance. He paused and untied his horse's reins, gaze lingering on the shadowy place Smuggie hid.

He held his breath.

Then the doctor swung up into the seat and backed the cart out of the yard. The wheels crunched dirt as the vehicle rolled away. When Smuggie returned his focus to the house, the front door had closed again.

He plucked the two letters from his coat and ran a finger over them. He'd rather have left Bella's at the club, but that would have been too risky. The post office downriver would have to do.

But no. What had he been thinking? That would give Durkin a clue about which way he'd gone. He'd find the letter for certain. Would see where it had made post. Might even bring harm to Bella, thinking she knew something about Smuggie's betrayal.

He ran his finger over his confession of feelings he hadn't thought himself capable of and then ripped the page in half. Then tore it again and again until confetti slipped through his fingers and tangled in the wind.

Better he not burden her anyway. She needed to be as far from his stain as possible.

He tapped the other letter against his palm, the one meant for the detective.

Could he trust the lawyer? In most things, probably not. But he'd seen the way the man looked at Miss Lockhart. He would take any information about her whereabouts right to the coppers. This was the best he could do. He didn't have much time.

He crept toward the front of the house. The miniature watchdog better not be on duty to alert the household of his presence. With a resolute breath, he mounted the mansion steps, leaving only the echoes of his footsteps behind on the riverbank.

Then he dropped the letter on the threshold, banged on the door, and bolted back to the shadows.

T he air inside the police station clung to every pore of Daniel's skin, heavy with the scent of stale coffee. The murmur of conversation and the occasional cry from a far-off holding cell muffled the sharp click of typewriter keys drifting in through the open door to the receiving area.

A faded city map hung on peeling paint, and despite the heat this time of year, the chill in the room caused the fine hairs on the back of his neck to stand on end. Or perhaps that came from the thoughts churning through him.

Please, God. Keep Camilla safe.

If any harm came to her, he'd—Well, he didn't know what he'd do. They'd only just gotten to know one another. But she invaded his thoughts, disrupting his once orderly existence. Camilla had stormed her way into his heart, and now he couldn't imagine life without her. Admiration of her spunk and spirit had turned into fascination, which morphed into something much deeper.

He loved her.

But would she even have him, knowing whatever illegal mess his family had tangled in must have caused her father's death?

Could she forgive him? And how could he expect her to want to become part of the family responsible for such heartache?

Muted footsteps echoed down the corridor, growing louder with each passing second. The heavy wooden door creaked and swung open, revealing a surly detective showcasing a furrowed brow and lines etched deep into his weathered face. An air of suspicion cut through the tension-filled air.

"Daniel Gray?"

He met the man's icy gaze. "Yes."

"You have information on the Durkin gang and the where-abouts of the missing bank robbery?"

"Bank robbery?" He shifted on the stark metal chair. "I don't know anything about that."

"Hmm." The man's voice rolled like gravel from his throat. "Says here young detective McCready believes you know about a stash of missing loot from a bank robbery in St. Louis a few months back."

"Captain Lockhart and I were looking for a treasure men-tioned in my family's lore. I don't know anything about a bur-glary."

The officer settled his hardened frame into the chair across from Daniel, narrowed eyes deepening the wrinkles around their edges. "What can you tell me about Mr. Durkin?"

"My sister has been seeing him, and it appears he's been giving her expensive gifts. She promised me she wouldn't see him again."

"How did the relationship begin?"

Daniel tamped down the urge to withhold information for the sake of saving his family's reputation. "From what I've gathered, her late-husband, Lucas, hit a rough financial patch and started working for some unscrupulous men. Somewhere along the way, it went sour, and next thing we know, Lucas has an untime-ly fatal accident. Two men came to Mabel's house soon after Lucas's death. I was handling her affairs. They've made threats. I took Mabel and my nephew to live with me in the house I inherited from my grandfather. Some old writings I found of my grandfather's hinted he knew the whereabouts of a lost family treasure. I thought, if I found it, I could pay off any of Lucas's debts and make sure my sister and nephew could start a new life."

The aged detective jotted down notes as Daniel spoke, then read back over them. "And you then told the officers you'd discovered a smuggling operation?"

"Camilla and I followed a map into the swamplands outside the city. We may have stumbled upon a bootlegging operation. We then reported that information to the authorities. Tonight, my nephew was approached by a man who told him to tell his mother to take him out of the city, Captain Lockhart was abducted, and her engineer shot. Her crew is at my house."

"How did you come to discover Durkin was involved in any of this?"

"I overheard the bootleggers in the woods mention the name. Then Mabel told me she'd been seeing him and her husband's boss promised to take care of her and release her from Lucas's debts. I begged her not to see the man again. Then Solomon showed up wounded and told us Camilla had been taken, so I came here." He rubbed the tense muscles throbbing in his neck. "I know you are just doing your job going back over all of this. But the woman I love is missing, and we need to focus on finding her."

The officer sat back in his chair. "That is precisely what I'm doing, young man. We believe the Durkin gang, your treasure hunt, and the robbery stash are connected. Any information you have can help us find the missing lady."

He'd give anything to make sure they saved Camilla. He dredged up every detail he could recall about their hunt for the treasure, even revealing his grandfather's hidden room. Through it all, the aged policeman jotted notes, nodding now and then.

When every ounce of insight and scrap of memory had been reamed from him, the officer stood. "Thank you. I'd like to question your sister as well, find out what else she knows."

"And Camilla?" He clenched his fists. "We must hurry before..."

The officer opened the door and gestured Daniel through. "A search is already underway."

That didn't help ease the tightness in his chest. Nothing would until she was found.

The man's eyes softened. "Take heart, mister. Good men here will do everything they can to find your lady."

Daniel locked his teeth together, not trusting himself to words. When they exited the station, a rumbling paddy wagon waited. White lettering emblazoned on the side of the black motorcar. Police Patrol. The round headlights punctured the night scape, offering hope.

He climbed through the open doorframe behind the flat front window panels. Maybe they didn't have closing doors on these things to make getting in and out faster. A redheaded officer behind the wheel thumbed for Daniel to circle around to the rear. A partition sectioned the front two seats from the containment area in the back.

He ground his teeth and hopped down, then rounded the vehicle and popped the latch on one of the two rear doors. After hefting himself inside, he settled on one of the benches and twisted to face out the line of windows.

The older officer who'd questioned him—he never did ask the man's name—strode out of the station. His gaze landed on Daniel in the back like a criminal. Then he hopped into the motorcar with surprising spryness. The engine roared, and they trundled down the street.

They reached his house quickly, thanks to the increase of speed the paddy wagon provided over walking. What would the neighbors think if they looked out the window and saw him arriving in a police vehicle meant to cart wrongdoers off to jail?

They stopped at the end of the river road, and the engine noise died. Daniel tried the vehicle's rear door, only to find it locked. He clamped his tongue between his teeth as he waited for one of the officers to release him.

Finally free, he leapt from the vehicle and waved the officers to follow as he jogged to the house. Every second mattered. With each pump of his heart, unwelcome visions of harm befalling Camilla jolted through him.

He shouted his presence and pounded the door, not caring if he disturbed the neighbors. Someone opened it before he could fish the key from his pocket.

Inside the receiving hall, Hattie returned to where Buck and Finn stared at an unfolded sheet of paper. Her hand flew to her throat. "Got something here you're goin' to want to see, Mr. Gray. Looks like a letter. Oh, and you done brought the police with you."

Buck slipped into the nearby parlor where Solomon recovered. Finn eyed the two officers, then settled himself outside the parlor doorway. What did the two have to fear from the police? Maybe they had a distrust due to Buck's past. Not something Daniel had time to contemplate.

He took the letter and scanned the contents.

Mr. Gray,

They took the captain to the Devil's Punchbowl. Bones there is in charge of dispelling ~~ripples~~ problems. I cut her free and told her where to run if she'll listen. Told you already to get the boy and his mum out of here. These are the high men who work for the big boss. That's Durkin. Watch out because some of the coppers are on his payroll. There's one detective I think is clean. Name is McSomething.

Here's the blokes that will cripple him if you can take them down. Others are more easy to replace.

Marcus Day—Goes by Bones

Samuel Elroy—Sammie

Jonathan Cray—Toothpick

Peter Mackleroy—Butch

Durkin is also after a fella they call Scissors. Name's Jacob Something. He double-crossed Durkin and another big boss named Mickey over a bank load out of St. Louis. Word is Mickey got put in the slammer over it. Durkin thinks the treasure you and Lockhart are after is the missing stash. Don't know how that goes together but thought it might help.

Get the kid out of there. Don't let Durkin take him and turn him into a wretch.

Best of luck to you.

The Punchbowl is south of the cemetery under the ravine. Got a cave there tucked under the kudzu. Take men. You'll need them.

Daniel passed the paper to the elder of the two officers accompanying him and focused on Hattie. "Where'd you get this?"

"There was a pounding on the door. Found it on the porch with no one in sight. Not more than a couple of minutes before you showed up."

His fists tightened, and he looked at Finn. "Didn't I tell you not to open the door?"

The redheaded man shrugged. "Looked out the window. Didn't see no one there." He thumbed at the letter. "I don't read good. Does that letter have anything to do with the captain?"

"It gives us an idea of where they took her. This cave and the... Punchbowl. Whatever that is." Frustration boiled. "We must leave at once."

The officer met his gaze. "Heard of the Punchbowl. Says here he cut her free. We'll pull some men from the station."

"Hope this isn't a trap." Daniel jabbed his trembling fingers through his hair. "But this letter names men and tells where they took Camilla. Maybe even why. They think she knows something about a missing bank robbery."

Finn's face scrunched, but he didn't reply.

The aged policeman rambled off instructions to the younger officer, who hurried out the door to gather the other policemen to go after Camilla. Daniel started toward the door when the old-timer caught his arm. "Leave the work to the lawmen, lad."

"She'll be frightened." Daniel bit off the words. "I should be there."

The officer's grip remained firm. "You'll only be in the way. Trust us to do our job."

His being strained toward the door closing on his opportunity to bolt, but he forced himself to remain. How did he know who to trust anymore?

Was he making the right decision? Only God knew.

Please, God, be willing to save her.

Insides rendering to shreds, he freed a tight breath. "My sister, Mabel, is upstairs."

The officer gave a sympathy-laden nod and released Daniel's arm. They traversed the stairs, and Daniel paused at the top. Would Mabel cooperate? He cleared his throat and lowered his voice to almost a whisper. "My sister can be...flighty. You'll need to treat her with a soft touch." He took another step and then paused. "What is your name so I can introduce you?"

"Patrick O'Leary."

Daniel led Officer O'Leary down the hushed hall and rapped gently on Mabel's door. Lucas flung it open an instant later, his little eyes going round.

"Oh, the police are here? Y'all sure are worried about that hobo. Did he do something wrong? Was him talking to me wrong? Father said I shouldn't talk to men I don't know, but I sometimes forget things like that. I'm really sorry, Uncle Danny."

The tirade of words came to a close, and Daniel ruffled the boy's hair. He should be sleeping at this hour, but he could hardly blame the child for having too much energy to try. "Don't worry. This nice officer is just here to talk. Why don't you go down to Stella's room and visit with her?"

He doubted the women would be sleeping either.

Lucas poked his head to see around Daniel. He narrowed his eyes at Officer O'Leary. "What's he want to talk to Mama for? She never saw that hobo. That was me."

Astute little man. "Lucas. There'll be time to answer your questions later. Right now, I need you to do as I say."

He cast one look at his mother, who stood at the far end of the room fiddling with her pearls. Mabel didn't seem to notice, her owlish gaze fixed on the policeman.

Lucas sighed. "All right." He marched past Daniel and stared up at Officer O'Leary. "My father said coppers was like a church potluck. Some of them ain't half bad, but the rest were as crooked as a squash neck. What kind are you?"

"Lucas!" Daniel nearly choked. The boy had clearly mixed up whatever metaphor his father had been trying to use, but the meaning was painfully clear. "That is impolite."

A spark of humor lit Officer O'Leary's eyes, but his voice remained grave. "I'm the God-fearing kind who takes his vows to protect the innocent and bring the lawless to justice seriously."

Lucas studied him. "That's good then."

Hefting a brave set to his shoulders, he continued down the hall and rapped on Stella's door. She granted him entrance, frowning at the officer in their house. Then she ushered the boy inside and closed the door.

Daniel addressed Mabel, who hadn't moved from the rear of the room. "This is Officer O'Leary. He has questions for you about Mr. Durkin."

Mabel backed up a step.

The officer stepped into the room. "Perhaps you'd be more comfortable speaking down below? In a less personal space?"

She scanned the room, which stood in disarray. The bed-clothes had been flung back, and dresses and hats were strewn about. Had she been packing to leave?

A quick headshake sent her pearls swaying. "I have nothing to say."

The officer arched a brow at Daniel.

"Mabel. He's here to help. The only way to resolve all of this is for the police to be involved. You know that."

Her eyes flashed. "If you stayed out of it, everything would've been fine."

That made her sound guilty.

Mabel crossed her arms. "I have nothing to say. My husband is dead, and whatever trouble he had died with him. I'm a grieving widow, and I would thank you to let me alone to try to make a new life for me and my son."

"Does this new life involve a man named Arnold 'Dimples' Durkin, who has murdered over a dozen people, including two of his mistresses? One of whom he left tied naked to a pole in the center of town?"

Mabel's face paled and her mouth worked. No words came out.

Officer O'Leary's already gravelly voice hardened further. "Think long and hard, ma'am, about protecting a man who has been nothing but an evil scourge on this city. If not for the good of others or your family or even yourself, then for that boy you got there and what might happen if you let a man like Durkin go free."

Mabel's lips parted and her chin trembled. After a desperate glance at Daniel, she nodded. "All right. I don't know how much it will help, but I'll tell you what I know. Little as it is."

Relief uncoiled in Daniel's chest. With the letter and Mabel's account, they'd be that much closer to bringing down the men who had taken Camilla.

He could only pray they made it in time.

The moon hung low in the inky sky, casting long, ghostly shadows across the ground Camilla pressed her body into. Had they found her already? Damp soil mingled with the distant fragrance of wildflowers loved ones had placed on headstones. She tried to force her breathing to slow. Her heart pounded so loudly they might hear it over the motorcar's engine.

Would they keep going? What would she do if they stopped?

Her trousers bore the marks of her dash through the woods, hanging ragged below the knee. Every muscle in her body ached.

She huddled in the darkness, pressing her belly to the ground and peering through the tall grass, her eyes affixed on the impending headlights. Her chest constricted, strangling her breath. Likely decent people approached, curious about a form they could see in the grass. They'd probably help. Take her to the police station in town. Fuss over the state of her clothing and matted hair.

Probably.

But she couldn't afford to take any chances and end up back in that cave.

The automobile glided closer, its engine emitting a low, steady hum that blended with the night symphony of crickets. Shadows danced against the vehicle's sleek, dark exterior, their fleeting movements mirroring her racing thoughts.

She couldn't chance it.

Keeping her form as hunched as possible, she slunk from her hiding spot and then darted into the neighboring woods, her feet slapping against the damp earth. Her heart pounded in her ears, drowning out even the sound of her frantic breath. Every rustle of foliage could mean pursuit.

She slipped behind the line of trees. There. She'd made it out of the path of the oncoming lights and—

A shout.

Her heart tripped. Decent folks out for a midnight drive wouldn't be hollering at her. She lurched deeper into the shadows, roots catching her boots and sending her crashing to the ground. Whatever the voices yelled out behind her drowned beneath the thrum in her ears. Then the crash of their pounding steps breached the tree line, breaking sticks and making no effort at stealth.

She pushed her body into the fastest run she could manage in the dark. To her left, shafts of moonlight poked through the branches. If she kept the road in sight, she could follow it closer to town. Getting lost in the woods wouldn't do her any favors.

Camilla risked a glance over her shoulder. Two looming shapes fought against the shadows and tangling undergrowth. Their silhouettes merged with a flickering beam of light. A flashlight?

How could she escape them now? She pushed harder, ignoring the briars catching on her arms and leaving stinging trails.

Elongated shadows swung like pendulums. Her pursuers illuminated the ground behind her, casting her shadow into her path. Her legs screamed with exertion, but the menacing figures closed the distance with alarming speed.

She wouldn't make it.

Her burning legs betrayed her, and her ankle twisted on the uneven ground. She stumbled, her body collapsing to the earth and sliding in the dirt and dew.

A masculine voice shouted something, but the words wouldn't register. The light swept over her, and the nearest body appeared at her feet.

She let out a piercing shriek, the best her heaving lungs could afford. She sucked in another lungful, preparing to fight, scratch, or whatever else she—

"Police!" one of the men bellowed.

The next scream died in her throat.

The shadowy form bobbed behind the blinding light, but no hands reached to grab her. A brisk voice unimpeded from their sprint washed over her. "Are you harmed?"

Harmed? Yes. She gathered her knees beneath her and struggled to rise.

Were they truly the law?

Please, God. Let it be so.

Relief wrestled with terror, and her shoulders began to shake. Another shadow man reached out from her side, and she jumped back, nearly falling again. Warm fingers encased her elbow, gentle rather than possessive.

"I'm Officer Abner, and this is my partner, Officer Smith. Are you Camilla Lockhart?"

The beam of light from the first man swept over to the one at her side and settled on the man's relaxed brows and warm brown eyes. A gentle smile tugged at the corners of his lips, mirroring the care and sincerity in a gaze meant to put her at ease. Her focus dropped from his face to the shiny buttons on his policeman's uniform, and the pent-up breath left her in a rush.

Law officers.

Good men.

Safety.

Her knees threatened to give way beneath her, but the officer kept her from slipping to the ground in a melted heap.

"Camilla Lockhart?"

She nodded, chest still heaving.

Officer Abner guided her steps back onto the road, the abandoned motorcar rumbling not far away.

Thank you, Lord.

If the police hadn't happened upon her and it had been those horrible men instead...

She pushed the thought aside. Her body quivered as they opened the rear door. Then she collapsed against the Ford's interior.

The next minutes passed in a blur as they drove to the police station and then led her inside to a dimly lit room. Her head pounded, and the slick sweat on her skin cooled, leaving her trembling.

They drowned her in questions, one after another. She worked to calm her quivering body and attempted to relay every detail and relive every horror, no matter how grueling. Anything she could tell them to catch the men responsible. They asked if she needed a doctor to tend her cuts and bruises, but she assured them she'd be fine.

What she needed most was to get out of here and back to those she cared about. Hattie, Solomon, Buck, and Finn, and...Daniel. Her chest tightened at the thought of him. Had the criminals come after him too? He hadn't been at the cave with her, but that didn't mean he hadn't ended up like Papa, face down in the river and...

Her breathing came in sharp painful bursts, and she had to close her eyes.

Please, God. Let him be safe.

What would she do if she lost him too? Somehow in the short time they'd known one another, he had brushed away the shadows in the recesses of her heart and settled his steady presence in their place. His gentle strength, quick wit, and generous soul had blanketed her in a way she'd never anticipated. She wanted more time with him to see what this tangle of emotions meant.

"Miss Lockhart?" The concerned use of her name brought her eyes open, and she forced herself to focus.

"Forgive me. It's been a trying evening."

"Of course, miss." A sheepish crinkle formed at the corners of his eyes. "We're nearly finished."

She swallowed the bile burning at the back of her throat. "Would you repeat the last question?"

After she'd described her captors and the place where they'd held her, the torrent of questioning came to an end.

Officer Abner finished scribbling in his notebook. He closed the cover and rose. "That will do for now."

"Do you know what happened to my friends?" The question she'd been too afraid to voice squeaked from her lips.

One bushy brow lifted. "The people in the residence from which you were taken?"

She swallowed the lump in her throat and met his eyes, praying she wouldn't find septic sympathy there. His blue eyes remained clear of the kind of pity that meant her loved ones had faced a worse fate, and her heart tripped over itself.

"According to the report, one witness unharmed. One suffered a pistol shot but has been seen to by a doctor."

The hope rising in her chest plummeted to her toes. "Who? What...?"

The stoic lines of the man's face softened. "I'll have to look for the exact names, but the man who was shot is reported to be recovering."

"Solomon." His name came out in a groan. Her hands trembled. She had to get out of here and find out what happened. Help somehow. "May I go now?"

The officer dipped his chin. "One of our officers will escort you to your residence."

She didn't have a residence, but she wouldn't explain. She rose and took a second to steady herself. "Wait. You said a doctor saw my friend. Is he at the hospital?"

The man gestured her from the room and down a long dim hallway without answering. When they reached the front of the station, he conferred with an elderly officer in low tones. Camilla fidgeted with the ragged hem of her blouse, which had long come free of her waistband.

On any other occasion, she'd be mortified by the dirt caking her clothing and the long strip of flesh exposed on her thigh. But right now, ripped pants and mud hardly mattered.

The older officer motioned for her to follow him, and they stepped out into the night.

"Wait here while I fire the engine."

Camilla wrapped her arms around herself while he turned the crank on the front of the motorcar she'd recently exited. After a crabby grinding of gears, the engine sputtered to life and then roared with vigor.

Twin lamps over the fenders shot beams of light over the cobbled street. The officer opened the passenger door for her. "Let's get you home, miss."

Home.

What home did she have without Papa and the *Alma May*? She settled in the seat and wrapped her arms around her as loneliness surged like ice water.

But no. She wasn't alone. Even in the absence of her beloved crew and the grandmotherly affection of Hattie, she didn't face her trials on her own. The Creator of the universe held her close. She hadn't been alone in that cave. God had worked to create a way to escape. He'd inexplicably softened the heart of one of the criminals and led the authorities to her.

No, she was never truly alone.

Warmth pooled through her and loosened some of the tension in her chest.

Beyond the bobbing headlamps on the motorcar, they passed the edge of town and started down the river road.

She stiffened. "This isn't the way to Hattie's house. The place where I was abducted." She twisted in the seat to point in the other direction. "She lives on the outskirts of town, not here by the river."

The driver nodded. "Yes, miss. I'm taking you to your friends. Isn't that what you asked?"

Large houses took shape near the ravine ahead where the drivable road dwindled into a walking path. They'd gone to Daniel's? Why?

She thought the officer might stop and leave her to walk the rest of the way, but he opened her door and left the vehicle lights on to illuminate their path. He escorted her up the front porch and rapped on the door.

When it swung open, her insides liquefied.

Daniel's eyes widened in his stricken face. His hair stood on edge in disarray.

She'd never seen anyone more appealing.

Without a word, he leapt through the doorway and scooped her into his arms, his strength pressing her tight as though he thought he would never see her again. His fingers slid up her back past her matted hair and settled at the base of her neck, and she melted into him.

The tears came then. Sobs poured out, raw and unfettered and leached from the depths of her soul. At some point, the officer mumbled instructions that Daniel responded to, but she hadn't the strength to pay much heed to the exchange. He held her until the night waned and the torrent subsided. When nothing remained and her breathing, at last, came in a slow rhythm, she extracted herself from the comfort of his embrace. She smeared a tattered sleeve over her eyes. What a mess she must appear.

He kissed her forehead, his eyes twin pools of worry and...something more. "Let's get you inside so you can rest."

He didn't pepper her with questions. Bless him for that. She sniffled and managed a nod.

After helping her stand, he tucked her close against his side and led her into the house. No sooner did she breach the threshold than a familiar voice reached out to envelop her.

"My girl!" At Hattie's shrill cry, Daniel released her into Hattie's waiting embrace.

They held one another, and then Hattie eased her back to peer into her face. "Oh, sweet child. I prayed and prayed. A few scratches, but nothing more, right?"

A smile tried to twitch at one corner of Camilla's mouth as she nodded. Thank God, nothing more.

Her relief waned at the pointed absence of the others. "What happened? Where's Solomon?"

Hattie patted her cheek. "Doctor already got the bullet out of my boy, and you know him. He's tough as they come. Doctor says as long as Solomon isn't too stubborn, he'll heal up right nice."

Fresh tears leaked down Camilla's cheeks. "I'm so sorry. All of this is my fault."

"Hush, child." Hattie's eyes crinkled at the edges. "Ain't a lick of this your fault."

Camilla pressed her lips into a line, too tired to argue the truth. But if she hadn't gone after that cursed treasure, none of this would have happened.

"Camilla." Hattie's stern use of her name snapped Camilla's gaze from the floor and back to the wise eyes fixed on her face. "If you think you have enough control to order the lives and choices of others and to manipulate the series of events in this world, then you think a bit too highly of yourself than you ought."

Her lips parted. Thought too highly of herself?

"Child, you aren't to blame for the actions of evil men. What happened to your papa was a tragedy, and what happened tonight is the same. There's a lot of tragedy in this life. But it doesn't mean we carry the blame for every bad thing that happens. Sometimes it's just the way of this fallen world."

A strange choking noise came out of Daniel, which he tried to cover by clearing his throat.

He probably blamed himself too. With a tearful smile, Camilla held her hand out to him. He gripped her fingers, and she pulled him to her.

She wrapped an arm around Hattie and the other around Daniel and breathed in the strength their presence provided. Then she steeled her spine and stepped out of their protective circle. "I'd like to see Solomon."

The welcoming scent of coffee warmed Daniel's insides, and the hot brew pushed the fog from his sleepless brain. Dew clung to the grass, and even from his place on the porch, he could hear Solomon's steady snore emanating through the cracked parlor window. They'd offered him the bed in the room the other two men shared, but he'd insisted the couch suited fine. Likely, the daunting task of climbing stairs prompted the decision.

The door creaked, and Daniel pivoted, hoping to find Camilla also seeking the beauty of the first touch of dawn. Instead, his sister clutched a shawl around her shoulders, and her red-rimmed eyes sought his. He motioned for her to join him at the rail.

They stood in silence, admiring the light glittering off the expanse of the Mississippi.

"Do you think it's over now?" Mabel's leaden words plunked between them, rippling through the peace.

"I hope so. The law is in pursuit of Mr. Durkin, and with the information from our Good Samaritan, they should be able to make arrests."

Her nod came slowly. "Men like that aren't easily ensnared." She gripped the porch rail. "I'm sorry. I thought hinting to Durkin we might find our family treasure would help. Give him confidence I could clear the debt on my own. I didn't know it would put you and Captain Lockhart in danger."

Tears leaked from her eyes, and she brushed them away.

"I promise I don't know anything about some bank robbery in St. Louis. I don't think my Lucas had anything to do with that." Her headshake sent a frayed curl over her shoulder.

That explained why Durkin had been following their every move. Maybe he suspected Lucas Sr. had taken the money from the robbery along with whatever else he'd skimmed.

"It's all right." Daniel tucked her into a brief side hug. "I'm sure the law will bring swift justice, especially with all the information we've given them."

Mabel dipped her chin, eyes brimming. "I've decided Lucas and I should stay with Great-Aunt Flora for a time."

He hadn't thought about their elderly relative in Maryland for a long time, but she'd always taken a shine to Mabel. Perhaps the two had stayed in touch.

"That shouldn't be necessary. I doubt Mr. Durkin will try to come here."

Mabel pulled at her shawl. "I need time, brother. Time to grieve and heal and separate myself from vices that have crept into my bones."

He wouldn't argue. Not with the way her chin trembled and lines squinched around her eyes. "I'm sure you're right. Probably for the best as keeping Lucas under constraint here might be difficult. At least until all these men are safely serving their due time."

But he'd sure miss Lucas. The boy brought joy and adventure into their lives.

"For the best," Mabel repeated, her words ringing with an echo of finality.

He cupped her elbow, guiding her to meet his gaze. "When it's well and over, I want you and Lucas to come back. I'd like all of us to stay here on the river together. If that's what you want."

She tucked a lock of hair behind her ear. "Time out in the country under Aunt Flo's careful eye and away from...certain temptations will do me good. And hopefully by next summer, I'll be ready to be the mother I should be for Lucas." She drew a long breath. "I'll wire Aunt Flo today, but I don't think she will refuse me. And with her seven daughters around, Lucas will have cousins to play with and responsible mothers to help look after him."

He offered an encouraging smile. "That's brave of you, Mabel. You'll make him proud."

Tears glimmered in her eyes. "I hope so. He's such a good boy."

"That he is. I will miss him."

She smirked. "He'll complain heartily about leaving. But our visit will give you time to establish your practice here and pursue *other* personal matters."

Personal matters. Like Camilla. The thought of her tweaked his chest, and he glanced toward the house.

"Don't be timid, brother, if that's what you're thinking." Mabel's fresh smile lit the shadows under her eyes. "A lady like the captain will appreciate a man who is decisive with his feelings for her and who doesn't care if the entire world knows it." She bobbed her chin, her eyes clearer than he'd seen them in weeks. "Don't lose your opportunity by waffling or waiting for some time in the future when things are better. One thing I know about life is that you can never anticipate what a day will hold. If you wait for everything to be perfect, you'll wait forever."

He bumped her shoulder with his. "Thank you for the wise advice."

They stared at the water. Then he mustered his courage to broach a topic they'd always avoided. But if there was to be healing, then they must first expose the wounds.

"I'm sorry I turned a blind eye to how our father treated you, and I'm disgusted with myself for not realizing the type of man you married. You are too sweet to be misused as you have. You deserve a man who will honor you and treat you like the treasure you are. As your brother, I should have done a better job protecting you."

She wrapped an arm around his waist and pulled him against her side, resting her head on his shoulder. "I'm learning that part of life is the circumstances we've been given, but the other part is the decisions we made and how we chose to handle our trials. I'm not without blame for how my life has gone. Perhaps if I hadn't been so rebellious, Father wouldn't have thought he needed to keep me confined. Lucas wasn't a bad man. Misguided, maybe. He looked for the easy way out of any trouble, and I fear I share his inclinations. Pray I will get better about being patient and wise with my decisions as I try to put in the hard work of reordering my life."

Daniel gave her a gentle squeeze. "I shall pray for you daily."

Gleaming rays of light peeked over the treetops and dusted the sky in sparkling gold and rose. A breeze toyed with the steam rising from his mug, and he took a long sip, enjoying the simple pleasure. Mabel was right. Building a life and a law practice here would be arduous work. Overcoming the damage caused by his bruised reputation and starting from scratch would be a challenge.

But it'd be worth it.

"Too bad there wasn't a real treasure." Mabel sighed. "That would have been something."

He leaned against the rail. "Too much to hope that whoever had their hands on that gold didn't spend it a long time ago."

"True." A half-hearted laugh bubbled free. "I'm sure I would have."

"But what I don't understand is the hidden room. It had to be there for something, right?"

Mabel focused on him, her eyes warm. "That's one of the things I love most about you. Sometimes you don't see the corruption right in front of you."

He opened his mouth to protest—after all, such ignorance was not at all a good thing—but her next words stopped him.

"Hidden rooms are where men keep their records and their stashes when they need to hold something during transit. I'm rather certain Lucas did not stumble upon the men he came to work with. Grandfather must have been an important man in the operation." She caught his eye. "Little hints Mr. Durkin let slip during our time together. I think our father found out about it. Maybe he did think he was after a lost family treasure, but he ended up unearthing family secrets instead."

Same as he and Camilla had.

Mabel pushed away from the rail. "Father and Grandfather are both gone, and those troubles died with them. You have a new start here. Let whatever is hidden remain that way."

She pressed a light kiss to his cheek. "I'm going to town to wire Aunt Flo." She held up a hand. "And before you protest, both of Captain Lockhart's able crewmen have offered to escort me while Stella keeps Lucas occupied with his studies."

He watched her glide away, proud of her determination. He lifted a prayer, asking God to grant her wisdom and protection along the way.

He drained the last of his coffee, and a short time later when the door opened again, Camilla stepped through. His heartbeat spluttered. She'd had a bath, and someone had tended to her scratches. She'd tamed her long hair into her customary braid but wore one of Mabel's dresses rather than her usual slacks and blouse.

"You look lovely." The words were out before he could stop them.

Camilla's lips quirked in a suppressed smile. She smoothed a palm over the yellow fabric. "Prefer your ladies in dresses and pumps, do you?"

He smirked. "I prefer you, no matter if you want to wear trousers or ball gowns."

Her face sobered and she studied him. "You really mean that, don't you?"

"Of course I do." A nervous chuckle rattled around behind his ribs. "Your inner loveliness radiates into everything you do. The clothes you wear don't change that."

Mabel's words still fresh on his mind, he set his mug on the rail and then closed the distance between them, coming to stand only a stride away. "Captain Camilla Lockhart, I find you to be the most intriguing woman God ever created. You challenge me and inspire me to be a better man. You are smart, kind, and perfect in a way I never thought a person could be. You've stolen my heart, and for as long as I live and breathe, it will be yours and yours alone."

Her lips parted, and she blinked at him.

His disorderly pulse heaved in his ears. He'd laid out everything at her feet. He knew his shortcomings and his family's failings. The messy history and painful past. But none of that changed how he longed for her to be at his side. He'd spend a lifetime attempting to right wrongs and soothe aches for as long as she'd let him.

"Daniel, I..."

She hesitated, thoughts churning in the velvety depths of her eyes he couldn't decipher. She had every right to reject him. To leave and never have anything more to do with him or his family and their—

Camilla pressed her warmth into him and slid her hands over his shoulders and her fingers into his hair. With a gentle nudge, she offered for him to lower his mouth to hers.

She smelled of sunshine and tasted of light and wholeness, and he wrapped his arms around her, not ever wanting to let her go. He deepened the kiss, every promise of his heart that words couldn't say finding a different form of expression.

Whatever the future might hold and whatever trials may come, he could face any of them with such a precious blessing by his side.

Three days had passed since the harrowing night she'd been taken, and Camilla finally awoke feeling as though she'd slept soundlessly without nightmares stealing her rest. She stretched underneath the thin summer blanket and cracked her eyelids to an empty room. The ball of fur near her knees unrolled, and Lula's snout wriggled out from underneath.

Camilla stroked the dog's ears. Mabel had been awfully kind to let them all stay here. She hadn't even complained about Lula sleeping in the bed. Well, to be fair, she might not know about that.

Buck and Finn had fetched Camilla's poor pup from Hattie's house as soon as daylight had broken the darkness of the night she'd been abducted. Lula had howled like a banshee once she saw Camilla and refused to be parted from her side since. She was thankful for the comfort her little friend offered.

Canine company aside, there hadn't been much privacy anyway, what with so many people staying in one house. Daniel occupied his grandfather's room while Mabel and Lucas shared the adjoining room Daniel's grandmother once used. That left the three guest rooms for a host of visitors as well as the parlor couch for Solomon's temporary hospital bed.

Not that she'd minded sharing the corner room with Hattie while Stella, Daisy, and Violet took the other. Finn and Buck occupied the smallest room—once a nursery—farthest down the hall and across from Daniel. Having people around comforted the frayed edges of her nerves.

Sunshine poured through the large windows and gleamed on the river beyond one while the other overlooked the edge of the untamed garden, which wrapped the rear and both sides of the house. She lowered her feet to the rug and wiggled her toes. Then she stretched the aches from her sore muscles.

The door swung open, and Hattie bustled in. "'Bout time you got up."

Her wink and laughed words left no doubt she'd been the one to make sure Camilla slept late. She offered the older woman a smile of thanks.

"Get dressed. We got things to discuss." Hattie fished around in her skirt pocket. She handed Camilla a creased envelope. "And this came for you. Buck picked it up from the post."

Her name covered a majority of the manila paper in firm, blocky script. She slipped her finger through the seal and pulled out a single sheet of paper. Huh. She skimmed the contents.

"Well, I'll be."

"What?" Hattie peered over her shoulder, even though she'd never learned to read. "Something wrong?"

"On the contrary." Camilla shook the paper. "Seems I actually received my payment for our last shipment. Truthfully, I thought I'd never see the day. I even started to think Mr. Copeland was tangled up with all these other criminals in Natchez. But this letter claims he's transferred the entire amount to the bank."

"That's good, right?" Hattie busied herself making up the bed, fluffing pillows.

Lula rumbled her protest, but Hattie ignored her, scooping up the pup and placing her on the floor. Lula stretched with her front paws splayed in front of her, then plopped down on the rug.

"Of course." So why did the words feel heavy in her mouth?

She frowned at the page. Perhaps because now that she had enough money to make the repairs to Papa's boat, she had decisions to make. Ones she hadn't yet wanted to consider.

"Um-hmm." Hattie shook out the coverlet and laid it back on the bed, then turned to face Camilla. "It's time Solomon and I be getting on home."

Camilla paused. "I understand. Thank you for staying with me while things settled."

Everyone had the right to get back to their usual lives. Unfortunately, she had no idea what that meant in her own life. Where would she go now?

Mabel had offered to let Camilla stay in her and Lucas's room once she and her son left for a trip up North. But she didn't know how she felt about that yet. She'd never resided in one place long, and the room could swallow three of her cabins on the *Alma May*.

But neither could she impose on Hattie's small cabin, and since she'd gotten her money from Mr. Copeland, she could afford to pay a boarding fee. At least for a short time.

"Lots of thoughts churning behind those pretty eyes." Hattie propped a hand on her hip.

"Just thinking about the future." Camilla snagged a green dress and ducked behind the privacy screen to change. "There's a lot to consider."

"Including one handsome young lawyer, I imagine."

At Hattie's wistful tone, Camilla couldn't help but smile. "Yes, that's part of it." She hauled her sleeping gown off, hung it over the partition, then shimmied into her underclothes. "I haven't known him long."

"But?"

Camilla tugged the cotton frock over her head and tied the bow behind her back. "But...snakes and saltwater. That fella's making me have to do a lot of thinking, that's what."

She huffed and exited the changing area to where Hattie had started dusting. Where had she gotten the rag? Likely, she thought the chore would help repay their lodging, food, and Solomon's doctor bill. Camilla moved to stop Hattie since Daniel would never require repayment, but she stopped herself.

Sometimes people needed to extend their love and thanks in their own way. Stopping Hattie would only rob her of providing a blessing.

"Love's only partly about thinking, my girl." Hattie smoothed the rag around the edge of the writing desk. "Rest of it is about feeling and praying."

The feeling part had come in a flood. The praying part...well, she'd done a little of that. But perhaps not enough. She rubbed the back of her neck. "How do you know if you love someone?"

"You know." Hattie's deep-brown eyes twinkled, and the corner of her mouth tilted.

That didn't help in the least. "How?"

Hattie lifted her brows, then wriggled them in the same way she'd done to Camilla as a girl. The look that meant "you know you just don't want to say it."

Camilla stifled a groan. Fine. Hattie knew her too well. "He makes me feel safe, like I can accomplish anything, knowing he's there to support me. He's gentle and kind, smart and strong. I've never met anyone like him. My insides feel like turbulent waters whenever he looks at me with those soul-deep green eyes. And then when he kisses me..." The words dissolved into a helpless shrug. "I don't know...I get all warm and jittery at the same time."

"Sounds like love to me." Hattie waved the rag at her. "You told him yet?"

Camilla shook her head.

"He tell you yet?"

"Not exactly. He never said he loved me. Just that I had his heart and always would."

Now Hattie rolled her eyes. "If he's showing you love and respect and he's telling you you hold his heart, then you know everything you need to. Question is, do you feel the same?"

She did. But that didn't stop the pounding worry or the fear of the unknown. "But what about my boat and my crew? I worked hard for my license."

Hattie's rag stilled on the desk. "What does that have to do with Mr. Gray?"

"Love means marriage, right? And married women cook and keep house and live on land."

Hattie studied Camilla, then tilted her head back, and laughed.

Really. What was funny about that?

"Girl, smart as you are, you can be thickheaded about some things." Hattie plucked the rag again, this time going to attack nonexistent dust on the windowsill. "Just because other folks choose to live their own lives that way don't mean you have to. Mr. Gray knows you're a steamboat captain. If he was looking for a kitchen mouse, he wouldn't have picked you."

Perhaps she had a point. "I'll think on it." She caught Hattie's eye. "And pray."

"Good girl." Hattie patted her arm. "Now come on downstairs so we can have a talk with the fellas. They got something they want to say to you."

Camilla didn't much like the sound of that. Nerves in check and a pleasant expression plastered in place, she finished readying herself for the day and then strolled down the stairs, Lula trotting at her heels. After Camilla let the dog out and waited for Lula to finish her personal business in the front yard, she followed the familiar masculine voices to the parlor.

Solomon sat on the couch, a smile on his broad lips and hands gesturing quickly. Buck and Finn guffawed over something he'd said while Hattie moved her dustrag attack to the shelves near the hearth. When Solomon noticed Camilla lingering in the doorway, he beckoned her inside.

The other two men grew sober as she settled herself on the couch.

Solomon gestured to his mother, then to his side. Next, he signed "home" and "new start" with slow and deliberate movements. Buck and Finn both kept their gazes locked on the woven carpet.

Hattie finished her dusting and settled in the chair next to them. Solomon motioned for her to take over, but she waved the suggestion aside. "This here is your row to hoe, my son. Not mine."

Solomon drew a long breath and signed.

I've thought and prayed, and I am ready for a new chapter in life. I want to stay around here, be close to Mama. Help her around the house and maybe...

He spread his palms with a sheepish look.

Maybe find a woman who looks at me like you look at Mr. Gray and start a family of my own someday.

Her stomach sunk to her toes. "You won't be our engineer anymore?"

"We ain't abandoning you, Captain." Buck twisted his cap between his fingers.

"We?" She included Finn in a sweeping gesture. "You two are looking to start families too?"

Buck snorted. "Too late for that for me." The lines around his eyes crinkled. "But it ain't too late to find my brothers. Maybe help them with our pa's farm. Might be good to be around family again now that I'm a changed man. If they'll have me."

Her throat thickened. "They would be fools not to."

"Thanks, Captain. It's been an honor working for you."

Swallowing down tears, she focused on Finn. "And you?"

"Thinking about trying out for a captain license of my own." He scratched the back of his head. "Been learning a lot, and you've been great to teach me. Don't want you to see it as a betrayal, me learning from you and then leaving you shorthanded."

Camilla grinned and then stood to tug him into a quick hug. "That's wonderful! I'm proud of you, Finn. I know you can do it."

"You do?" He shifted his feet. "You aren't angry?"

"Of course not." She slapped at his arm. "What teacher wouldn't be proud to see her student succeed? You'll be a fine captain."

"Thank you." Moisture glimmered in his eyes, and he ducked his chin.

But what would she do without a crew? Sure, she could hire another, but it wouldn't be the same. So many changes. She drew a fortifying breath, then sat back down next to Solomon. After a loaded moment, he continued.

Been praying a lot here on this couch, Solomon signed. *And I have an idea.*

As he laid out the details of an interesting plan, the idea anchored into Camilla's heart. Could it work? What would Daniel think?

They talked late into the morning until Stella rang the bell for the midday meal. Camilla rose, feeling lighter than she anticipated after such a shift in currents. She wrapped an arm around Solomon's back and squeezed, careful of his wound.

"You've been a great friend to me, Solomon. I hope we can always remain that way even if we don't live on the same boat."

He gave her a look like she'd gone mad if she thought anything else. Then he grinned and motioned her out the door.

I'm starving.

Lula yipped in agreement, as though she understood the hand gestures. Likely she'd caught a whiff of whatever Stella had fried. Camilla chuckled as she followed the others to the dining room filled with laughter and conversation.

She glanced toward the ceiling as everyone else filed inside. "I figure you've got a plan in all this, God," she whispered. "Sure would be helpful if you'd help me know what it is. A little wisdom and guidance, if you please."

No voice came down from heaven, and no insights struck her like lightning. But peace settled on her heart, and a sense of rightness swelled in her soul.

And for now, that was enough.

What was he missing? Daniel stood in the hidden room concealed behind the shelf in his grandfather's office, sunlight illuminating dust motes in beams of light. Despite all that had happened and what they'd discovered about the criminal dealings his family had become entangled with, he couldn't shake feeling there had to be more to this hidden room. It must have existed long before his grandfather got involved with Durkin.

While he searched the space again, Camilla combed through Grandfather's office. They'd been at it most of the morning without any luck. Still, his intuition insisted a piece of this puzzle had yet to be uncovered.

He tapped his toe on the floor. He simply had to be missing something...

Wait.

Why did the floor sound...hollow? His pulse quickened. "Camilla!"

She popped her head through the door, Grandfather's journal splayed open in her palms. "Find something?"

He tapped his foot harder on the place in the center of the room. Then did the same at the edge before repeating the stomp at the middle. "Does that sound different to you?"

Her arched brows dove toward her nose. Her cheeks still bore thin scratches from her ordeal, but her spirits had brightened in the days since.

She flashed a grin. "Hidden trapdoor inside a secret room?"

"Grab me something to pry up the carpet."

Camilla fished around in her pocket and then flipped open a six-inch blade.

What in the heavens? His lips parted, but no words escaped. Where had she gotten that?

"What?" She wiggled the silver metal. "A gift from Finn. He said a gal should always be prepared for nefarious bootleggers and the like."

Despite the humor in her tone, he hated that such thoughts haunted her. He'd do everything in his power to ensure she felt safe from now on. He took the blade without comment and crouched on the floor. He inserted the tip beneath the carpet edge and twisted. The weave lifted without much trouble, and after scooting and repositioning, he rolled up the square of old carpeting and passed it to Camilla. She tossed it behind her with an unceremonious thud.

They stared down at the door set into the floorboards, nearly unnoticeable except for a tarnished loop of metal flush with the wood grain.

Camilla bounced on her toes. "Open it!"

His fingers looped around the cold iron, and he tugged. With a groan, the boards parted, revealing a depression about the size of a hatbox.

His heart sank. So much for opening a chest full of gold.

"What's in there?" Camilla dropped to her knees and peered inside. "Is that a book?"

Daniel reached inside and pulled out a leather-bound volume coated in dust. He handed it over to Camilla so she could take it into the better lighting of the study while he felt around for anything else in the compartment.

His fingers brushed a small box wedged near the corner, and his nerves skittered. A jewelry box? He set it by his knees and explored every inch of the interior but discovered nothing else. He secured the box under his arm and pushed to his feet.

Camilla stood near the window, tilting the opened book to the light. Eyes glimmering, she glanced at him as he emerged from the secret closet. "It's a diary. I think it might be Dorothy's."

"Might be." He held up the jewelry box. "This was in there too."

She plunked the book on Grandfather's desk. "Well, what are you waiting for? Open it!"

He scooted past her and set the box on the writing surface so they could both see. Roughly four inches by six, the finely crafted container showcased inlaid dark wood set against a lighter oak. Centered on the lid, a detailed magnolia made of mother-of-pearl caught the light. Daniel released a delicate latch and creaked the lid against protesting hinges.

"Ohhh." Camilla leaned closer.

Inside, a collection of tarnished jewelry sparkled in the light. He let out a low whistle. "She must have hidden all her valuables to keep them from being commandeered by soldiers."

Camilla plucked a large emerald ring from the velvet lining. "Then why leave them hidden after the war ended?"

"Remember when she told her husband the rebel soldiers had stolen everything? Maybe she meant to take her jewels with her when she eloped with her lover but then that never happened."

Camilla slipped the ring on her finger and wiggled it to catch the facets on fire in the sunlight. "But she never did, and her husband eventually died. I'd have taken these back out and worn them."

Whatever the reason, quite a few valuable pieces were in here. A pearl necklace, several brooches crusted in various jewels, and at least a half dozen rings. One, in particular, caught his eye, and he swiped the golden band from the box and slipped it into his pocket while Camilla examined a brooch shaped like a bee with black and yellow gems.

He fingered the little band wrapped in watery blue aquamarine and diamonds. Would it fit her? He could take it to a jeweler and have it sized before proposing.

Doubt snaked through the rising hope. Would she even want a hidden family heirloom instead of something new? The story and the glimmering watery look of the ring in his pocket seemed to suit her better than anything he could purchase.

Camilla placed the brooch back into the box and grinned at him. "It might not be a shipping crate full of gold, but I bet you can get a hefty sum for those items. And since the police are on Durkin's trail, you won't have to worry about paying off any debts. You can sell all of this and start a new practice here in Natchez."

As hope lit her eyes, his chest constricted. He'd rather see her dreams realized first. "Might even be enough to cover the repairs on the *Alma May* as well."

Her lips twisted. "About that..." She rubbed her arms. "Mr. Copeland's payment came through with the bank transfer like he promised. I'll admit, with everything else we've encountered, I thought he had to be tangled up with bootleggers and criminals too. I didn't think we'd ever get paid. But the money is there, sitting in my account."

"That's good, right?" He scratched the back of his head. Why didn't she look pleased?

"Certainly." She dropped her gaze, and the next words came out in nearly a whisper. "Would it be dishonoring my father if I sold the *Alma May* for scrap instead of investing in the repairs?"

He squeezed her shoulder. "Of course not. Your father would want you to do what you thought best for your business. I'm sure he wouldn't mind you buying another boat."

She nodded thoughtfully. Then her countenance brightened. "I'm thinking of a ferry. You know, something carrying nice smiling people downriver instead of herds of cattle."

When her nose wrinkled, he couldn't help but chuckle. "Sounds like a fine idea."

Her tone gathered excitement. "We could charge a fare and deliver people up and down a stretch of the Mississippi, then dock at home each night." Her tone shifted to something akin to shyness. "Maybe I wouldn't even have to live on board."

The tingling in his stomach increased. "You'd like to work during the day on the water but live in town?"

Intense brown eyes slammed into him. "Thinking about it."

Did that mean she wanted to stay closer to Natchez? To him? He couldn't help the grin that bunched his cheeks like a schoolboy. "That's a grand idea!"

Her shoulders relaxed, and she cast him a coy grin. "Maybe we'll find treasure after all, and I can get the percent you promised. I'm sure I've more than covered the clause about participation. Wouldn't you say?"

He couldn't resist pulling her close and brushing a gentle kiss against her lips. "That you have."

Desire to return to kissing stirred, but he didn't find her lips again. Instead, he watched emotions play behind her eyes. He'd been giving her time, but she still hadn't responded to his declaration of love. If sorrow or sympathy reigned in those glowing depths, he'd bow out. But no woman had ever gazed upon him with such devotion. So, he would wait. He'd endure every second she needed.

His pulse thrummed, pounding through his core. But before it could fire up too much heat, she spun away.

Camilla sucked in a breath and dropped the lid on the jewelry box. "Maybe the diary has some clues?"

Hadn't he just vowed patience? He doused the longing. Soon they would need to discuss what bloomed between them, but for now, he allowed the subject change. Camilla plucked the book from the desk and peeled back the cracked leather cover.

Daniel peered over her shoulder and examined the pages, his fingertips tracing the delicate script. Camilla's shoulder pressed into his side, warm against his ribs.

He forced himself to focus on anything other than her nearness and skimmed the entry.

My memory has so failed with the horrors of these times, so I have concluded I shall be obliged to keep a diary. Simple things such as the common daily occurrences and dates necessary in all our domestic and business affairs. As I propose to write every evening, no doubt it will abound with minute details, which might appear unnecessary, but I often find the little things to be of great importance.

"Ha!" Camilla pointed to the entry. "If that's not a cover-up for keeping secret records for spying, then I don't know what is."

She might be right. Especially with all the family rumors they'd heard about Dorothy over the years. He motioned to the couch near the cold hearth, and Camilla bounded over to it.

She settled and patted the cushion close to her. "Why don't you read it aloud, since your eyes are better than mine."

"Still opposed to spectacles? You'd look quite fetching with them."

She gave him a sour face, and he held up a palm in surrender. He settled on the seat and flipped to the next entry, dated July of 1864.

"'Two rebels came dashing up the road. I did not have to wait long till I saw them come back with three workhorses from the stables. Charlie talked with them, and I overheard the conclusion none of these horses would answer their purpose at all. The handsome man was Captain Belton from Lorman. He said he had run away from the farm to join the army. Keeping true to my husband's loyalties, I told him "What a pity you did not run to the right side." He gave me the brightest smile and said he had done so.'"

Camilla tapped a finger on her chin. "Do you think this Captain Belton is the Confederate man who became her lover and later betrayed her?"

"Good possibility." He flipped to another page.

He continued reading a series of entries with nothing more than common occurrences, references to the comings and goings of the two armies, and allusions to Lincoln and his policies. Some entries seemed to be about clandestine meetings, but they were too vague to garner much more than suspicion about Dorothy's work as a spy.

After roughly an hour of deciphering faded ink and fragile pages, they uncovered something useful.

Daniel squinted at the faint script starting to tax his eyesight. "Look at this. It seems like a bunch of clues."

Camilla leaned closer. "'Follow the path to where the roses bloom.'" Her breath caught. "Do you think this will lead to the treasure?"

He kept his voice even, despite the anticipation rising in him to match her enthusiasm. "Possibly, but there's more here."

She snagged the book from his hands. "Come on. We'll go out to the rose garden and see if we can follow a trail of clues."

This would likely lead to nothing more than disappointment, but he'd take any excuse to spend the day adventuring with her. She stuck the book under her arm and bounded out of the room, her customary thick braid bouncing against her white blouse.

He followed her through the rear door and out to the rose garden in need of drastic tending. They scanned the cluster of thorny bushes.

"Do you see anything matching this next line?" Camilla pointed. "'When the times circle and shadow us, the zenith will point the way.'"

What shadow? "Times and zenith. Sounds like a—" His gaze snagged on something hidden in a tangle of thorny foliage. "There!"

They edged closer, and the form of a rusted sundial took shape.

"Of course!" He hurried to it. "Times and shadows has to be referring to the sundial."

Camilla frowned. "How are we going to follow where it points when that thing is tilted and nearly choked under all those vines?"

He winked. "With the art of deduction." He quirked a finger in the air when she rolled her eyes. "When the sun is at its zenith, it's directly overhead. And when it's noon on a sundial, the shadow points due north." He situated himself with his back to the dial. "That way."

"Quite clever, Mr. Gray." She followed his line of sight to an ancient live oak. "That must be it!"

They hurried to the tree's dipping branches, and Daniel read the next clue. "'From shade's embrace take twenty paces east to where the earth drinks deeply and secrets lie still.'"

Camilla faced the right direction. The Mississippi River flowed to the west, and north led to the edge of the property adjoining the neighbors.

She fit hands to hips. "Was this property always the same size? What if the treasure is buried on land sold to one of your neighbors?"

"A possibility." He could only shrug. After all of this, either they would find something, or they wouldn't. "We'll just have to see. What's the next clue?"

Camilla traced her finger along the page. "'Within the depths, all is revealed.'" She puckered her lips. "What depths?"

"'Where the earth drinks deeply'..." He tapped a finger on his thigh. "Let's mark out the twenty paces east and see if we notice anything."

They made their way through the wooded area bordering the neighbor's land and came to a low, circular stone wall. His pulse quickened. "It's a cistern!"

"That's 'where the earth drinks'? And 'secrets lie still'?" She toed the crumbling wall.

Daniel winked. "A great place to hide a strongbox."

"It still makes no sense." Camilla wrinkled her nose. "Why not just say 'Go look in the cistern'?"

Daniel squinted down into the murky darkness. "I'd guess Dorothy had a propensity for histrionics."

A grunt escaped her chest. "And maybe she was right about her mental acuity. Do you think she somehow *forgot* about her jewelry and the treasure?"

"Maybe." After reading all the ramblings in her diary, it was hard to say if Dorothy had suffered some type of mental break or not. "The stories say she told her daughter everything on her death bed. But either Mary dismissed the claims as madness or she never found anything."

Camilla braced her hands on the stone wall and lifted her leg. "Well, down we go, I suppose."

He caught her shoulder. "A little preparation first? If a treasure has been down there for over fifty years, I doubt it's going to disappear in the time it takes to gather a rope and lantern."

She laughed. "That is one of the many things I love about you, Daniel Gray. You are the logical match to my impulsiveness."

He froze.

Camilla fiddled with the end of her braid. Then she huffed and dropped it, her intense gaze crashing into his. "I do love you, you know. With all my heart. I just don't know what to do about it. I've been praying a lot, like Hattie said. But God hasn't laid out a series of instructions yet."

Humor bubbled in his chest, but he tamped it down. "Are you saying you're waiting for the Almighty to tell you your entire future before you can let me know we feel the same for one another?"

She puckered her lips. "When you put it like that, it sounds ridiculous."

He held out his hand, and she slipped her fingers into his. He guided her back toward the house. "I've been doing a lot of praying myself, and I believe you are the one for me, Captain Lockhart. I don't know what the future holds, but I do know I want you in it."

"I want that too." Her words came out breathy.

"Then you keep praying to make sure God agrees." He squeezed her fingers. "Just promise me you won't hold out for the Creator to wire you a detailed list of the events of your life first. I don't think it works that way."

"I promise." Smirking, she bumped his shoulder. "I'm learning to leave room for trust."

Daniel fingered the ring in his pocket and then sent a little prayer heavenward of his own. He also still had a lot to learn about trust himself.

Squelch. Camilla's boots hit the bottom of the cistern, and she had to grab the slime-coated wall to keep her balance. She sloshed around in knee-deep water that smelled of sour leaves and rot, giving room for Daniel to descend the rope behind her. There had to be maggots and mosquito larva swimming around in here.

Daniel plopped down next to her, and she pressed her fingers under her nose at the stench arising from disturbed the layers of rotting vegetation.

She studied the muck. "Do you really think there's treasure here?"

Would they have to sift through decades of sludge to liberate dirty coins one at a time? Hopefully Dorothy had put them in a container and not scattered them down here like forgotten wishes.

Daniel lifted his lantern, casting shadows over brick walls coated in moss and slime. Couldn't be a large box. She could stretch out both arms and nearly touch the walls. They tapered to a rounded opening about four feet above her head.

"Probably nothing here. Surely someone getting water would have noticed." Daniel toed his boot around in the sloppy mixture of silty ground and decomposing foliage.

"Who knows? Maybe Dorothy quit using it on purpose." Camilla edged her foot through the wet leaves, dislodging another wave of stink. "Then after she died, her daughter moved away, didn't she? Other family members lived in the house? What if they didn't know about it back here?"

Daniel shrugged, bobbing the light. "Possible. Though I'd have more hope if it'd been filled in or hidden."

He had a point. She glanced up at the sunlight trying to poke through. "How deep are these usually?"

Daniel followed her gaze and then lowered it again to the ground. "Hmm. About twelve feet, if I remember correctly. Which would make this one roughly three feet too shallow." He flashed her a grin. "Hang on while I go get us a shovel."

Before she could respond, the man handed her the lantern and shimmied up the rope and out with as much skill as any rigging monkey. She nearly shouted how impressed she was with his physical ability before the realization she stood in a cavern alone stole her breath.

She shook the sudden sensation away. No. This wasn't the Devil's Punchbowl or the cave where they'd taken her that night. She could climb the rope at any moment and escape.

The logical thought eased the tightness in her chest.

Still, she closed her eyes and thought about open boat decks and fresh air until Daniel's voice came again.

"Got it!" His handsome face appeared in the circle of light. "I'll hand it down to you."

She lifted her free hand to receive the lowered handle. Once her fingers wrapped around the wood, Daniel swung his leg over and slid down the rope. He landed in the leaves with a sickening squishy noise. Her momentary unease dissipated as soon as he stood by her side. The tingling in her nerves flowed into excitement.

What if after all the dead ends and disappointments, they discovered the treasure right here? On property Daniel owned, where it couldn't be disputed?

She handed him the shovel, and he poked the tip around. Making a slow search pattern, he started in the center and worked his way in a circle toward the edges. Her heart sank more with each stab.

What if they never found anything? There weren't any more clues if they didn't find Dorothy's gold here.

The sense of peace swelling within her lately surged anew.

Whether or not they found anything of value didn't matter. They didn't need the treasure. They'd been blessed with so much already. Her gaze settled on Daniel.

This man.

He possessed a kindness running to his core. He was honest and dashing. Protective yet not restrictive. God had given her a wonderful opportunity to share her life with someone amazing. How could she not seize her chance?

She grabbed his arm. "Daniel. I—"

Thud!

Her breath caught. Daniel's eyes widened, and he poked the same place again. Another thump.

"There's something here!" His excitement quickened her pulse.

He collected a shovelful of dirt and leaves and tossed it to the side. The viscous ground replaced what had been removed, flowing back into the indent before Daniel could lower the tool again. He tried three more times anyway before giving up.

"Hold up the light." He propped the shovel against the wall.

She did as instructed. Then she held her breath as he plunged his bare hand beneath the festering surface.

"Yes." He felt around. "There's something here and..." He snatched against a weight. "I have the handle!"

Camilla couldn't help bouncing on her toes. "Pull it out."

He stopped tugging and shifted his weight. "I need you to grab the other side so we can lift it."

She nearly dropped the light in her haste to tromp around to the opposite side. She thrust her hand into the slimy ground.

There! Her fingers met something hard. She swiped dirt and grime out of the way until she could hold the slender metal. "I have it."

"Ready? On my count, we lift."

"Now!" She snatched upward, too excited to waste another second.

Daniel nearly lost his balance but recovered and put his muscles into the effort. They heaved, jolted, and wiggled, finally dislodging his corner of a metal strongbox.

"It's heavy!" She panted. "That's a good sign, right?"

He grunted. "Get the end of the rope."

Right. Good idea. She let her end go and snagged the dangling rope. Thankfully, he'd given enough slack for her to free the end from the slurry and pull it to the strongbox. She looped the end through the handle and tied a perfect bowline knot like Papa had taught her.

Daniel straightened, hands on his back. "This is going to be a pain to pull out of here. We're going to need help."

Solomon would have been the best for the project, but his gunshot wound hadn't yet healed. Stella and the two girls wouldn't offer much by way of muscle.

"What should we do?" She blew a stray piece of hair off her nose. "I'm not sure adding three more women to the task will help."

After a reluctant nod, he flashed a smile. "I have an idea." He gestured to the rope. "It should still be safe for us to climb out with the end tied."

Warm hands encircled her waist, and her boots made a sucking sound as Daniel lifted her out of the mire. She grabbed the rope above her head, and with his help lifting her knees, she pulled herself out and over the rim. He followed.

Daniel brushed his hands against his trousers. "We'll hurry down to the livery and hire out one of the draft horses for an hour. That should do the trick."

He started marching away when Camilla caught his arm. "Wait."

A little line formed between his brows, and he cast an impatient glance at the cistern.

She parroted his earlier sentiment. "A few more moments won't hurt, right?"

The corners of his mouth twitched. "I find patience harder to come by since we've discovered the treasure. I'm dying to open that box."

She took both of his grimy hands in hers. "Before we do, I have something to say, and I don't want whatever is in there or not in there to change anything."

Intense green eyes flecked with gold shone down at her.

"If there is a treasure in there, I don't ever want you to think I said what I'm about to because of it." She dipped her chin and angled her most serious glare at him. "Do you understand?"

Those tempting lips quivered again, but he pressed them into a serious line. "Yes, ma'am."

"Captain."

A crack of laughter burst from his throat. "Captain. My apologies."

She allowed a coy smile. "Now, Mr. Gray, as I was saying. I want you to hear this with the utmost sincerity." She swallowed the thickness in her throat. "I love you, and I'd like you to ask me to marry you."

Camilla straightened her shoulders. There. She'd laid out her heart before him to do with as he would, treasure or no, uncertainties and all.

His eyebrows shot toward his hairline, mussed with their adventure. "You would?"

This time, all she could manage was a nod, what with all the emotions trying to clog her throat.

He released her hands and fished something out of his pocket, then frowned down at it. "Rats. Now I've gotten it dirty."

The light caught a delicate band of alternating blue and clear gems. He'd been carrying a ring around in his pocket? Waiting for a chance to propose?

He lowered himself to one knee and held the ring up, and her heart buzzed. "I'd be honored if you would be my wife and allow me to spend my days attempting to become the kind of husband you deserve."

She threw herself into his arms, not even caring they were both smeared in mud.

This was it. Daniel patted the Belgian horse's beige neck and tied him to the wizened oak with the leather lead rope. The two-foot-by-two-foot strongbox hadn't proven taxing for the heavy-hoofed animal, and after a bit of wrestling and wriggling, he and Camilla had plunked the heavy chest to the ground.

By the time they'd rented the horse and freed their prize, the day had grown late. Even with the sun dipping beneath the trees, the Mississippi heat remained relentless.

Camilla wiped an arm across her sweating brow and then knelt in the secluded corner of the property by the iron-wrapped box, peering at the latch. "I expected a hefty lock."

"There isn't one?" He knelt beside her and smeared the mud from the latch. "There's a keyhole here."

Her shoulders slumped. "Of course there would be." She groaned. "And I bet the key is hidden somewhere else, with a bunch of silly clues to follow."

Perhaps. But then again...

He ran his fingers over the box. Only about a foot deep, it had been exceptionally heavy for its size. That could only mean one thing.

Daniel pushed the latch, if for no other reason than to be sure. The button protested the grit but gave way. The latch sprung free.

They stared at one another. Had it really been so easy?

Knees pressed into the damp earth, he grasped the top corners of the banded box and lifted. The hinges resisted his effort but soon screeched open.

Camilla gasped.

Inside, golden coins caught the day's fading light.

She clenched his arm. "Are you seeing this?"

He wrapped an arm around her shoulders, emotion congealing in his throat. They'd found it. The lost family treasure. Right here in their own yard all along. On top of the coins, a yellowed envelope displayed the name "Mary" in flowing penmanship.

Camilla plucked the letter from the pile, wiped her hands down her trousers, and then released the seal on the back. "It's a letter to her daughter." She squinted and then held it out to him. "Read it, please?"

Daniel angled the paper to the light and read aloud.

"'My dearest Mary, here I leave to you my legacy. May this letter find you prosperous and well. Likely I am no longer with you and have given you the location of your inheritance in secret either in my private diary after my passing—if such were unexpected—or in my instructions prior to my death. I used what I needed to, mind. I don't know how much of what remained you found in my storeroom, but I aimed to be careful to use only a portion. That which belonged to me, gifted as my dowry by my father.'"

"So that was what was in those little boxes in the hidden room." Camilla puffed her cheeks. "Dorothy kept her gold in them and must have used it throughout her life."

"But only what she believed belonged to her from her dowry." Daniel swatted a mosquito. "Did Mary never find that either? Maybe my grandfather discovered the room and the gold."

"Which explains where Papa got one of those coins."

He scratched his chin. "And what likely convinced my father the treasure was real."

Daniel returned to reading the letter.

"'Hopefully, you have come of age, and this blood money will be cleaned in your hands. I'm sure you must have a lot of questions. I am not perfect, and we all have our sins to atone for. As recompense for my own, I never touched the greed that consumed me, choosing instead to live out my days without it in penance.

"'I deserve the broken heart doled out as punishment for my infidelity. And Captain Belton deserved the crate of river stones he shipped to New Orleans the night he thought to abandon me and carry off my gold.

"'I still don't know if he deserved to die by fire and find no rest at the bottom of the Mississippi. Perhaps there simply is no mercy for some sins.'"

Camilla sucked in a quick breath. "So that's what it meant in the story you told me. About how she swindled him in return."

Daniel nodded. "Everyone thought the gold went down on the *Carolina*, but she'd sent him off with a crate of rocks instead."

"Goodness." Camilla stared at the glittering coins matching the one he'd found on her boat. Then she shook away whatever thought plagued her. "Keep reading."

He focused on the yellowed page. "But my penance isn't yours to share. There are five hundred gold coins here. Not useless paper money."

He let out a low whistle. "No wonder this thing weighs so much."

Camilla plucked one of the coins from the box and rolled it around in her fingers.

There had to be a fortune in there. He refocused on the letter.

"'I pray you can start a new life for yourself, living independent of anyone else. You are the mistress of your destiny. May what burdened me be freedom for you. With all the love of my heart, Mother.'"

Daniel folded the letter and tucked it back inside the envelope. "I suppose that solves the mystery. Dorothy kept most of the treasure to hand down to her daughter after her death so she didn't have to face the consequences of explaining where it came from and the sins of her affair to her child. But Mary hadn't believed her and attributed the claims to her mother's high fever. So, no one ever found the treasure."

Camilla flipped the coin back into the box. "How much do you suppose this is worth?"

He pulled her to her feet and wrapped an arm around her waist. "Oh, I'd say it'll buy a wedding dress. And a cake. And perhaps a few decorations for the house."

She snuggled into him. "And pay to open a new law practice."

"And purchase a shiny new ferry boat. Top of the line."

She looked up at him, eyes shining. "A whole new life for all of us. Mabel won't have to worry."

Always thinking of others. He pecked her cheek, then ran his thumb over the ring on her left hand. "A new life for all of us."

The cicadas picked up their evening song, and they held each other. All along, God hadn't been punishing him. He'd seen his troubling circumstances as consequences for his lackluster faith. When in truth, those very trials had urged him to remember the peace found in relying on the Creator through his struggles.

He nuzzled Camilla's hair. "I'm thankful for you, my soon-to-be bride."

She squeezed him in return. "As I am for you. God is good."

"That he is." Weight settled in his stomach. He'd start off their life together by confiding his inner battles with his partner. "I've realized I've been angry with God because I saw all the troubles with my law practice and my family as some kind of punishment. And since I hadn't done anything wrong to result in the loss of my business, I assumed God had decided to shun me for my lukewarm faith."

Camilla twisted to look up at him, compassion in her eyes. But she gave him a moment to collect the rest of his thoughts.

He pressed on. "Terrible things have happened. Our fathers' deaths. My family's involvement in criminal activities—the extent of which is still to be determined."

A warm breeze skittered over her hair, sending a lock to tickle his nose. Camilla brushed it away. "That's probably what the line in your grandfather's journal meant. He didn't want your father discovering what died with the gold because it was likely people." A shiver ran through her. "God only knows how many people were tossed down the dreadful sinkhole."

He gathered her close. The back of his eyes burned for the horrors Father must have suffered. Only the comfort of knowing his father had a robust faith and would now reside in heaven kept the worst of the grief at bay.

"Through all those awful things," he said against the warmth of her temple, "I also found you. We can start a life together, and God even provided for our needs. I'm ashamed I ever doubted."

Camilla kissed him, soft and sweet. "The nature of the human struggle, I'm afraid. What a wonder it is that, no matter how many times we wander astray, our heavenly Father is always waiting with open arms for us to return."

As he held her close, the scent of lavender laced through her tresses enveloped his senses, electrifying every nerve.

"Right you are," he murmured, voice growing husky.

Their gazes locked, and the reflection of a promising future glimmered in her eyes. A shared dream of a life filled with endless adventures and unconditional love. Leaning forward, Daniel found her sweet lips, and electricity surged when she snuggled into him.

His love intertwined with hers, binding them together with the promises of tomorrow. As he deepened the kiss, his heart pulsed with love for this incredible woman who had stolen it with her fierce beauty and generous soul.

And he could hardly wait for their next adventure.

EPILOGUE

M oonlight dripped from heaven and coated the Mississippi in silvery bands of beauty. Camilla breathed deeply, savoring the tranquility and the cool breeze. Moonlight on the Mississippi had to be one of God's most beautiful paintings.

She stood alone in the front yard of Daniel's house, seeking the familiar embrace of the river on such a special night. Running her hands over the smooth white fabric of her gown, she lifted the hem so as not to muddy its perfection and edged closer to the ravine.

Beams shimmered on the calm, dark waters below, their radiant glow a kiss from above. Fireflies twinkled along the riverbank, their flickering lights magical.

She clutched the pendant around her neck—a gift from Daniel in the shape of a miniature steamboat—overwhelmed with the fullness in her heart. Only a few months ago, grief had nearly drowned her. Now, even though the pain of Papa's loss remained, joy seeped around the edges and smoothed away the hurt.

Meandering closer to the cliff's edge, she admired the rippling water.

Life resembled the river in many ways. It rarely took a straight path. There were fast bends and turbulent waters, hidden dangers, and ever-changing unknowns. Yet like a skilled captain, God guided her along the journey and to the place he'd always planned for her. Purpose and contentment welled within her. Although the voyage wasn't always smooth, God remained steadfast.

She tilted her face to the sky and closed her eyes, taking a moment to thank him for his unfailing goodness.

When she opened them, a hundred fireflies danced in the breeze around her. They filled the yard in front of Daniel's house like stars brought down from heaven for her special night.

Grinning, she whispered, "Thank you, Lord. You've already done quite enough, but this special wedding decoration you've added is the perfect touch."

She strolled along the path illuminated by dozens of paper lanterns, guiding the way to Daniel's front porch, which Stella and Mabel had decorated with white roses. Guests would arrive soon, and she'd be chided for standing out here in the front yard in her wedding gown.

But this quiet settled her soul. So much had changed, and many challenges remained. The police still hadn't caught Mr. Durkin, though Detective McCready had assured them he was building a solid case. Policemen had discovered the elder Mr. Gray's wallet among the stash of personal possessions stored in the cave near the Devil's Punchbowl, confirming their fears Daniel's father had been lost to the bottom of the gorge.

There would be continued investigations and legal trials. But after tonight, she and Daniel would face all those challenges together, bound before God and family as a team no one could separate.

The front door cracked open, and Stella poked her head out. "There you are! Come inside before someone sees you."

Camilla smirked. "I'm coming. Just making sure everything is ready."

Hands on her hips, Stella glided onto the porch. "You did that two hours ago." A crease formed between her brows. "Are you all right?"

"I'm doing splendidly, thank you." Camilla dipped into a curtsy and elicited a chuckle.

"Then get on in here. Mabel will have a conniption if her brother sees you in that gown before he's supposed to."

"I'll be right along."

Stella hesitated, then slipped back inside, and closed the door with a soft click. Camilla adjusted a paper lantern on the porch steps, then paused to admire the fairy tale her groom had created.

In the weeks following their discovery of the treasure, Daniel had set to work on the neglected house with gusto, claiming he'd make it a perfect home for his bride. He'd had the floors polished, and the house gleamed with a fresh coat of white paint. She'd told him a life at his side and a home filled with friends and family was already perfect. But he'd enjoyed the project, so who was she to stop him?

Gardeners had tamed the wild foliage around the house, wresting overgrowth and neglect into the lush greenery now alive with fragrance. The breeze waltzed with the roses, teasing delicate scents from their petals. Mabel and Stella had questioned her judgment about a night wedding, but the flickering candles and shimmering lanterns made her feel as though she lived a fairy tale.

As soon as she stepped inside the house, Mabel whisked her away to the dining room, where she'd wait for her time to walk through the roses and to Daniel's side to speak her vows. She didn't complain since Stella had stocked the room with all manner of delicacies from Anna's shop.

Dainty meat pies and fruit tarts, shrimp gumbo, fried frog's legs, and her personal favorite—puff pastries stuffed with jam.

She snagged one and popped it into her mouth. Stella saw her but didn't comment.

The rear door burst open, and Lucas bounced through, dressed in his precious little wedding suit with a smart green cravat. He cradled a wriggling Lula, who had left scores of white hairs all over his black jacket.

"Don't you pick up that dog in that gown!" Mabel's words stopped Camilla from bending her knees to collect her dog.

How had she managed to sneak in without notice? Especially wearing so many strands of beads around her neck?

Camilla and Lucas shared a look, and the boy snuggled the dog closer. He'd been enjoying playing with her since he and his mother had returned, and the pup hadn't seemed to mind how busy Camilla had been with wedding preparations as long as she'd had her young playmate. Soon to be Camilla's nephew. However, now Lula stared at Camilla with big eyes, likely nervous with all the bustle.

Camilla couldn't resist at least giving a soft pat on the pup's head. She shook her ears, jostling the tiny strand of pink beads around her neck.

Mabel let out a long breath, clearly relieved Camilla had not ruined the gown the two of them had spent hours altering. Well, Mabel had sewed while Camilla had learned the nuances of patience required for repeated fittings.

"It's strange enough you're letting that creature attend the ceremony. I don't want her clawing the fabric." Mabel frowned at a stray thread and plucked it from Camilla's sleeve.

Mabel's time with her aunt had done her a great deal of good, if the clear brightness in her eyes was any indication. According to Daniel, Mabel distanced herself from the alcohol she'd begun consuming with far too much frequency and had been spending time with her aunt in Bible study. The time of simple peace and healing had been smoothing the frayed edges of her heart.

Once Detective McCready concluded his investigation and Mr. Durkin and all his men were safely in jail, she and Lucas planned to return. Camilla and Daniel both wanted them to stay here. There'd be plenty of room now that Violet had secured a room at a boardinghouse with other young women and Daisy would be getting married next month.

Camilla caught her soon-to-be sister-in-law and wrapped her in a hug. "Thank you for all you've done getting this wedding ready. I know it's trying on you, being here before...well, you know."

Before all the criminals were safely in jail.

Mabel patted her back. "You've made my brother very happy, you know. I'm sorry I ever doubted you." She stepped back before Camilla could respond. "Now. No more pastries. Can't have jam on the dress. The guests have arrived. We'll gather your bouquet, and then it'll be time."

Mabel pecked a kiss on Camilla's cheek and slipped through the rear door. How had she known Camilla had snuck a pastry?

Their guest list consisted of the members of the household—Stella, Violet, Daisy, and Mabel and Lucas—plus a few dear friends. Hattie and Camilla's old crewmen and Anna and Stella's brothers.

A small gathering, but all Camilla wanted or needed.

The sweet strands of a violin wafted through the open window, and Camilla paused her pacing in front of the food trays. Had Daniel also hired a musician?

Solomon poked his head into the dining room and grinned at her. Then he gave her a low bow, dashing in his pressed suit, and extended his arm. She looped her hand through the crook of his elbow and allowed him to escort her to the receiving hall.

He opened the rear door onto a fairyland.

Dozens of candles topped golden stands placed around the rose garden, and glowing lanterns hung from the oak tree. Her friends gathered underneath the drooping branches, creating a horseshoe with her groom and the minister at the center by the thick trunk.

The young minister from the nearby church they'd started attending together beamed at the diverse gathering, his round face as genuine as the friendly personality they'd come to know.

Her groom wore a fine linen suit, his hair combed back at the temples and tamed with pomade. His cravat matched his nephew's, and he seemed almost as fidgety as the little boy at his side.

Lula yipped, tail swaying as she strained against the rope holding her near Lucas's feet.

Daniel's eyes lit when Camilla stepped down into the rose garden, her long gown rustling down the steps behind her. Behind her short veil, she offered him her best smile—one filled with promise of their life to come.

As fireflies danced around them, she and Daniel professed their love and made their vows before God and those they held dear.

"I now give you Mr. and Mrs. Gray!" The pastor gave a joyous shout and thrust his Bible in the air.

Camilla laughed as Daniel gathered her in his arms, her heart full.

"May God bless my every adventure with you, Mrs. Gray," he whispered in her ear. "And I'm sure there will be many." The private smile gracing his lips had tingles shooting down her spine.

Teasing laced her tone. "Captain Mrs. Gray? Mrs. Captain Gray? Is that a thing?"

He cracked a laugh. "Your title can be whatever you desire, my bride."

"As long as I'm yours, they can call me whatever they want." Camilla kissed him soundly, which brought cheers from their onlookers. And maybe a gasp from Mabel and a round of giggles from Lucas.

As she looked into her husband's deep-green eyes, one thing she knew for certain. She'd been blessed with a partner to weather any storm, rise with any tide, and navigate new waters. She could trust him with her heart, and together they would set out on life's next great voyage.

Stephenia H. McGee is a multi-published author of stories of faith, hope, and healing set in the Deep South. She lives in Mississippi, where she is a mom of two rambunctious boys, writer, dreamer, and husband spoiler. Her novel *The Cedar Key* was a 2021 Faith, Hope, and Love Readers' Choice award winner. A member of the ACFW (American Christian Fiction Writers) and the DAR (Daughters of the American Revolution), she loves all things books and history. Stephenia also loves connecting with readers and can often be found having fun with her Faithful Readers Team on Facebook. For more on books and upcoming events and to connect with Stephenia, visit her at www.StepheniaMcGee.com

Be sure to sign up for my newsletter to get sneak peeks, behind the scenes fun, recipes, and special giveaways!

Sign up using this link and get a free eBook!
https://newsletter.stepheniamcgee.com/u9qdt7amwv

Stephenia H. McGee, Christian Fiction Author

stepheniahmcgee

Stephenia H. McGee

Buy direct from the author's online bookshop!
Support the author and find great deals.

Shop.stepheniamcgee.com

Books by Stephenia H. McGee

Ironwood Family Saga
The Whistle Walk
Heir of Hope
Missing Mercy

The Accidental Spy Series
*Previously published as The Liberator Series
An Accidental Spy
A Dangerous Performance
A Daring Pursuit

Stand Alone Titles
In His Eyes
Eternity Between Us
The Cedar Key
The Secrets of Emberwild
The Swindler's Daughter

Time Travel
Her Place in Time
(Stand alone, but ties to Rosswood from The Accidental Spy Series)
The Hope of Christmas Past
(Stand alone, but ties to Belmont from In His Eyes)
The Back Inn Time Series
(Stand alone books that can be read in any order)

Novellas
The Heart of Home
The Hope of Christmas Past

Buy direct from the author's online bookshop!
Support the author and find great deals.

https://shop.stepheniamcgee.com

"Be warned. You won't be able to put this book down."
-Patricia Bradley, USA today bestselling author of the
Natchez Trace Park Ranger Series

She pretends to be a widow to save a child.
Until he comes home to a wife he didn't marry.

When Ella Whitaker rescues a newborn baby, they take refuge at Belmont — but will Union Major Westley Remington take kindly to discovering his home is being run by a fiery and independent woman—one many believe to be his wife?

Available in most major bookstores.
Support the author and order from Shop.StepheniaMcGee.com where you can find special discounts and deals.

Sign up for my author's newsletter for behind the scenes, early sneak peeks, writing fun, giveaways, deals and more. As my thank you, you'll receive a free eBook (digital book) copy of *The Heart of Home*.
https://newsletter.stepheniamcgee.com/u9qdt7amwv

He asked if he could die on her porch...but instead he brought hope for new life.

Once a wistful romantic, Opal Martin now simply aspires to scrub the remnants of the War Between the States from her tattered life. But when a nearly drowned soldier appears and asks if he can die on her porch, she must guard against the sudden revival of her heart's hope for love.

Fans of *In His Eyes* will also enjoy seeing Ella and Westley again in Opal's story.

"A whirlwind adventure full of action, secrets, plots, romance, family drama and more!"
- InD'Tale Magazine

Captured and mistaken as a spy, can she unravel a conspiracy before her secrets cost a man his life?

Once a privileged heiress, Annabelle Ross is now struggling to hold her home and her life together through the devastation of the War Between the States. But with a forced marriage and a desolate future on the horizon, her hopes are beginning to dwindle. When she discovers an encrypted note on a dying soldier, she seizes the opportunity to use it to deliver a message of her own. Instead, she's mistaken for a spy and captured. Now her only chance to escape is the handsome soldier in charge of discovering her secrets.

★ The Accidental Spy series is a 2020 rewrite of the previously published Liberator Series (Leveraging Lincoln, Losing Lincoln, Labeling Lincoln)

★ Please note these books must be read in order and that while each book has a complete storyline, the overall plot is completed throughout the trilogy.

It was just one night at a B&B. Until she woke up in 1857.

Have you ever wondered what it would be like to visit the eras you love to read about?

The Back Inn Time series books are fun, faith-filled stories of what it might be like to suddenly experience life in a different time. These clean historical romances are packed with humor and adventure, and answer the question every historical fiction fan wonders—what would it be like if I went back to that time? Come visit a seaside Victorian inn where you can "step back inn time and leave your troubles behind!"

Shop.StepheniaMcGee.com